Potluck and Pistols

Veronica Paulina

ISBN 978-0-9794553-2-2

The characters and events in this book are fictitious. Any similarity to real persons, living or dead, is coincidental and not intended by the author.

Printed in the United States of America on acid-free paper.

Published by Hague Clinton, Inc.

HagueClinton.com
2012

First Edition

Potluck and Pistols

Veronica Paulina

Dedicated to

Steven McAuliff

Chapter 1

"Ceasefire! Unload. Cylinders open."

We stop shooting. It's time to check our targets.

"Magazines out, guns on the bench," Jim shouts into the hollowness of the indoor range. As range officer, he makes all the calls.

I push the magazine release button on my semi-automatic Ruger, pull back the slide and place a yellow plastic flag in the barrel.

"Stand back from the bench," Jim calls down the line of shooters.

Madison and Caroline step back behind the safety line. Caroline's .44 Magnum is open on the bench in front of them, a yellow plastic flag propped in one of the empty chambers. Jean flips open the cylinder of her Smith & Wesson revolver and lays it open on the bench.

"I need help!" calls Christine. "I don't know if there's a cartridge in the barrel."

Pete walks over to her, carefully takes the Beretta Neos out of her hands and releases the magazine. He pulls back the slide and peers into the barrel. A cartridge is in place ready to fire. He slowly turns the gun over and removes it.

"Everyone clear?" asks Jim.

Caroline, Madison, Jean and I call out that we're clear. Christine looks anxiously at Pete.

"We're clear," calls Pete.

"You may go down range and check your targets," Jim says, switching on the light to indicate the range is cold and we can now move around. As soon as the light starts to swirl, the heavy metal door leading from the clubhouse bursts open.

"Hi guys!" calls Shelby. "I've been waiting outside for you to take a break. I've been here fifteen minutes already."

"We only started shooting ten minutes ago," says Caroline, brushing past Shelby as she heads down range to retrieve her target.

"Good evening, Caroline, how are you?" asks Shelby, looking Caroline up and down, her eyes resting on a thick black belt studded with turquoise stones. "That's a beautiful belt."

"Arizona. Ten years ago," Caroline says brusquely.

"Come and take position five next to me, Shelby," I say, watching as Shelby's eyes flicker back and forth along the bench. I notice she is traveling light this evening, carrying only one small gun case and the big lavender bag in which she keeps her ammo and shooting gear. Shelby usually comes to the range completely overloaded, bringing two or three handguns, a couple of bricks of ammunition and her standard potluck contribution of a Caesar salad. As usual, Shelby's clothing is unsuitable for a sport which involves playing with gunpowder. Tonight she is sporting a white padded jacket, pink Capri pants and her signature pale blue Stetson. Since the hat's first outing to the range last year, it has been permanently flecked with black marks.

"My Stetson's got everything but bullet holes in it," she often proudly remarks.

Shelby is not known for following instructions and, instead of accepting my suggestion that she take the vacant spot next to me, she stands and watches as Caroline and Madison, their heads close together, study the holes in their targets. She then looks across at Jean and Christine and sighs. Jean is on the far left of the range, a position she took after checking that Caroline was to the far right.

"I'm staying as far away as possible from that Magnum," she'd mumbled as she unpacked her old revolver, opened up the cylinder, placed it on an old dishtowel, put a yellow flag in the chamber, and lined up five .22 cartridges.

"I don't want to lose what little hearing I have left," she'd continued, looking pointedly at Caroline.

"Let me shoot next to you," Christine had said, rushing to take the place next to Jean. "That puts a gap between us and them." This is not the spirit I have strived so hard to engender among the Pistol Belles. But as Christine is chronically nervous around Caroline and Madison—even without the powerful Magnum—I hadn't suggested she move closer to them.

"Come and take number five, Shelby," I say again, anxious for her to get settled. She is always late, a weekly irritant to the punctual Belles.

"She's got a rich husband, a housekeeper and scads of babysitters," Jean had said when I'd first tried to excuse Shelby's tardiness on the basis of her obligations at home. "It's more than I had. It's more than any of my kids had, and more than my grandkids will have."

"I save my sympathy for single moms," said Christine, nodding her head with an authority earned from personal experience. "That's what's hard."

"We all have choices," Madison had said levelly. "Shelby has had many advantages and presumably she has made for herself the life she wants."

"Any woman who gets herself knocked-up four times before she's thirty-years old is just asking for it," said Caroline. "If I have any sympathy at all it's for those kids being born to such an airhead."

These sentiments have not changed in the two years Shelby has been with the Belles.

"I guess number five will work," Shelby says, heading towards me. "It's good to be next to you, Mona. At least you help me. Not like, you know—"

"Good," I say quickly. "We're all here to become better shooters."

"I brought my new gun!" she says suddenly, tossing her bag and gun case on the bench. "It's my new baby!"

I look down at the small gray gun case.

"It really is a baby!" she squeals, pushing her face up close to mine and prodding the front of my sheepskin vest with a French-tipped nail. It seems she always has time for a manicure.

The case has Glock written across it. I know exactly what's inside.

"It's a Baby Glock!" she yells before I can demonstrate the breadth of my firearms knowledge and, with a flourish, she opens the case.

Several pairs of eyes turn towards us from both sides of the range.

"A Glock 26," says Pete, coming up behind us. "A semi-automatic sub-compact designed for concealed carry. A great choice for personal protection but with a three and a half inch barrel, I doubt you'll hit the target from this distance."

"I know that," she says, wiggling her nose and poking Pete's solid chest with the same polished nail. "I brought it to break it in. You can't just buy a gun and hope you'll be able to handle it when you need it."

"No, you can't Shelby, I'm glad you know that," he says, taking the small gun out of its case and turning it over in his hands. "This is a good gun, a 9mm you can hide practically anywhere on your person. And the magazine holds ten rounds which is double the amount of most sub-compacts."

Let's hope Shelby never has to pull a gun out of her pocket and use all ten rounds.

Christine, Jean, Madison and Caroline have gathered around Shelby to look at the Baby Glock. No matter how a shooter may feel about a gun's owner, no-one misses the chance to look over a new weapon. The Baby Glock is discussed, its features noted and Shelby's face beams with the same smile I've seen when she shows off her children. Now, as if flush from the warmth of her fellow Belles, she wriggles out of her thick white jacket and reveals a flimsy, low-necked blouse.

"Shelby, your shirt is too low for the range," I say.

"It was so warm this afternoon," she says, keeping her eyes fixed on her gun as it is passed around the group. "Izzy and Tony are off school this week and we had a blast playing outside today."

Isabella and Anthony are the oldest of Shelby's children.

"That's great," I say. "But we have to be covered up so we don't get burned by flying shells. I thought we all knew that."

Madison stares at me. A junior at an Ivy League university about an hour's drive from the range, Madison Fernandez is an All-American member of the university rifle team. The daughter of a police officer, she joined Junior Rifle when she was barely out of elementary school and, as a marksman with skills far beyond most of the Pistol Belles, Madison tolerates our group for two reasons. The first reason is that she joined our group in order to write her senior thesis about women and firearms. The second, which she alludes to but does not openly admit, is that Wednesday evenings with the Pistol Belles and our mixed shooting abilities are a welcome diversion from the pressures of life as a competitive collegiate shooter.

"Shelby," I say, with an apologetic nod to Madison. "You know what constitutes suitable clothing for the range. Please cover up."

Shelby puts her arms back into the sleeves of her jacket and, with an exaggerated gesture, fastens it up to her neck and then turns and looks me in the eye. Shelby may say she welcomes my help, but she never shirks from challenging my enforcement of range rules.

I hold her stare and, after a couple of seconds, she turns away. Once again, I question my ability to tolerate her presence in our group. Shelby's shooting skills have improved little since she joined the Pistol Belles and she clearly feels no obligation to try to fit in with the other women. Her mood changes several times during each session, ranging from tough to sugary, the latter more of a match for her girly appearance. It had taken Jean, however, no more than a first glance to see through Shelby's flashy appearance.

"She's built like a breeder," she'd said when Shelby had announced early last year that she was again pregnant. "Wide hips and hefty thighs are made for childbirth."

Baby Paolo was born in the summer and with black hair, thick legs and big hands, is a perfect copy of his father, Carmine. Shelby's hair is a mass of blonde curls which fall beneath her shoulders, flicking up in a variety of directions and creating a wild, sexy effect.

"It's a pity she's so dumb," Pete said one evening soon after Shelby had joined the Pistol Belles and he'd patiently shown her how to load and fire her husband's semi-automatic handgun. Carmine had deposited his wife at the range that evening and then rushed off to a business meeting.

"And it's even more of a pity she's close to twenty years younger than you," I'd told Pete. Pete Dexter likes to pretend he's a lady's man but since his long-ago divorce he's rarely been seen with a girlfriend. Along with Jim Mackenzie, Pete is an invaluable presence on Wednesday evenings.

"The Glock is pretty similar to Carmine's Walther PK380," I say to Shelby, bringing the discussion away from her clothing and back to the gun.

"Really?" she asks, as if she isn't familiar with a gun belonging to her husband. "The Baby Glock seems so much better for me."

Baby Glock, Lavender Lady, Pink Lady, LadySmith. Firearms manufacturers seem to believe that for women to be interested in purchasing multiple handguns, they must create models with feminine colors and names.

We return to our positions and wait for Jim to declare that the range is hot. I notice that in spite of Shelby's flaunting of her new gun and her predictably boisterous arrival, her face is pale and she is quieter than usual. I watch as she lays her new gun on a bright pink towel and takes out a box of ammo. She places two magazines on the bench and pulls back the Glock's slide. She puts on ear protectors and a pair of yellow sports glasses. Shelby usually darts up and down the line looking at our guns and asking dozens of questions, although rarely waiting to hear the answers. But tonight her excitement about the Baby Glock seems to have already evaporated and she is standing still, staring silently in front of her.

"Range is hot!" calls Jim. "You may fire whenever you are ready."

I load five cartridges into one of the Ruger's magazines. Five is the standard number of cartridges used by many shooters, a tradition born when the revolver of the Old West was a six shooter. The top chamber was left empty so that if the gun accidentally went off, there would be no cartridge to fire. I figure a practice that began when a gun was a man's or woman's constant companion is a good one for me to follow. I put the magazine into the grip and push up hard to lodge it in place. I pull back the slide and the first cartridge moves into the barrel. I wrap both hands around the grip, resting my right thumb on top of the left. I stand up straight, my left leg slightly behind my right and squarely face the target. My head is up and my arms extended, and in one smooth move I bring the pistol up to eye level and line up the sights so the front is centered in the rear. I put my finger on the trigger, hold my breath and begin to squeeze.

The gun fires. One.

I line up my sights again, straighten my arms, squeeze on the trigger. Two.

I squeeze on the trigger. Three.

I squeeze. Four, five.

The slide locks back in the open position. I press the release button and the magazine drops out. I pick up my binoculars and look down range. The bullet holes are grouped in a neat circle just to the left of the bullseye. I load five more cartridges into the magazine and slowly fire, taking care to aim slightly to the right of the center. After the fifth shot, the slide locks open and I release the magazine, put down my gun and look at my target through the binoculars. I am happy to see that the second group of bullet holes is placed neatly around the bullseye.

I put my gun down and turn to Shelby. Though I've been concentrating on shooting, I've noticed she hasn't fired a single shot. Instead, she is pointing the Baby Glock down range, slowly waving it up and down and staring blankly at the distant target.

"Are you going to fire that thing, Shelby?" Pete asks, striding over to her. I'm happy to leave it to Pete to get her started.

I load more cartridges into the Ruger's magazine, place it in the grip and push hard on the bottom. I line up the sights and squeeze gently on the trigger. One. I squeeze. Two, three, four. I adjust the position of my feet and squeeze. Five.

I release the magazine, put the gun down and place the yellow safety flag in the barrel. I again turn to Shelby. Pete is now helping Christine who, as usual, has emptied a box of cartridges onto the bench and is holding a magazine awkwardly in her right hand while fumbling with the pile of cartridges with her left. Pete makes his usual suggestion that she should switch hands and use her left hand to pull down the lever of the clip and her dominant right hand to push in the cartridges. Christine routinely ignores his advice and comes to the range each week as if it is the first time she has loaded her gun.

"Come on, Shelby," I say, turning my attention back to her. "Don't wave your new gun around like it's a toy. Are you loaded?"

"I'm loaded," she says.

"Hold your gun up, Shelby," Pete says, heading back to us. "Put your arms up and reach forward."

She lifts up her arms and wraps her hands around the grip.

"Put your right thumb on top of your left," I say. "Make sure your hand is out of the way of the slide."

She doesn't move her hands, but keeps staring down range.

"Be ready for the recoil," says Pete. "Sub-compacts pack a big punch."

"Are the sights adjustable?" I ask.

"I don't think so," says Pete.

"You guys are making me nervous," says Shelby, her eyes darting from me to Pete.

"We're here to help," I say.

The words are barely out of my mouth when Shelby suddenly lifts the gun up above her head and slams it down hard on the bench. Miraculously, though the gun is cocked it doesn't fire.

"Leave me alone!" she cries. "Why don't you just leave me alone?"

I grab hold of her arm and pull her back behind the safety line. Pete picks up the gun, removes the magazine, looks inside the barrel and flips out a cartridge. Jim hurries over to Shelby. She tries to wrestle out of my grasp but I maintain my grip on her.

"Shelby," Jim says, sternly. "You must never smash a loaded gun, or an unloaded gun for that matter, onto the bench. Or the floor, or anywhere else."

Shelby stands still, her eyes looking down at the ground.

"You could have caused the gun to fire," Jim continues. "It could have discharged."

"That was a dangerous move, Shelby," says Pete.

Tears are pouring down from beneath Shelby's sports glasses. Tonight's behavior is far beyond her usual impatient response to our instructions.

"Shelby, is something wrong?" I ask.

She buries her head in her hands and her shoulders begin to shake.

"I didn't bring my Caesar salad," she sobs, as if that could be the reason for such distress. "I made it but then I forgot to bring it, and I was even later than usual."

Jim and Pete stand and watch. Shelby's attention-getting antics don't usually result in tears. One of us will have to order her to leave. Her mishandling of the gun constitutes reckless behavior and requires ejection from the range and a temporary suspension from the club.

"It's Daddy," she mumbles, her voice muffled by the wad of pink tissues she has pulled from her pocket.

"Your father," I say. Everyone knows John Williams.

She nods and tears fall from her cheeks onto her jacket. I take her hands gently in mine.

"My father is sick," she cries, her voice echoing around the range. Fortunately, her words are barely intelligible over the rapid firing of guns and the other Pistol Belles are so engrossed in shooting they haven't noticed the drama being played out on our side of the range.

"My Daddy is going to die!"

Chapter Two

As the head of the Pistol Belles, it was my responsibility to remove Shelby from the range and inform her that she was banned from the Skyline Sportsmen's Club for a minimum of seven days.

"Does that include next Wednesday?" she'd asked, her sobbing turning to sniffles.

"Yes, you will have to skip next week, most likely longer. You need a break. You're always in such a hurry."

Shelby had started to cry again.

"I don't want to lose you guys too. I love being a Pistol Belle."

I can't imagine that losing membership in our fragile sisterhood could match the loss she is facing if her father is dying. Jean told me years ago that Shelby's mother died of breast cancer just days after Shelby graduated from high school. She is an only child and very close to her father.

"Don't worry, we're not going to let you go for good," I'd said, wondering if this was, in fact, the opportunity to do exactly that. I'd picked up her gun case and led her to her car. Later I'd told the Belles that Shelby had suddenly felt unwell and gone home. This announcement elicited a curious look from Caroline and raised eyebrows from Jean, but no-one questioned me further.

It is now a week since Shelby's outburst and, as usual, I've arrived at Skyline a good half hour early. I've deposited my tray of fried chicken in the clubhouse kitchen and am pleased to find I have time to fire a few rounds before anyone else arrives. But as I pull open the door to the indoor range, I find Caroline and Madison stapling targets onto cardboard at the far end of the range.

"You're early tonight," I call to them.

"I brought my Magnum in again," says Caroline. "I figured we'd get in some early shots."

"Yes, so we can shoot without everyone complaining about the noise," says Madison. She and Caroline look at each other and laugh.

"Good idea," I say, ignoring their laughter. There are at least two Belles who don't want to spend an evening standing next to a Magnum.

Fifty rounds and ten minutes later, I feel markedly better than when I arrived. I step back from the bench and let my heart rate slow down before loading another five cartridges. I like to shoot the Ruger when I'm tense as it's highly accurate and always makes me feel like a great shot. The therapeutic benefit of putting a tight circle of bullet holes in the center of a target cannot be overstated. I fire off another couple of rounds, smiling as each bullet joins the cluster around the bullseye. Maybe tonight is a good time to challenge Caroline and Madison to a little competition. But I see them taking turns to fire the Magnum, checking the results through their scopes and talking back and forth about the gun and their shots. It's best to leave them be.

"Jim and Pete didn't have time to check out my gun last week," says Caroline, suddenly turning to me. "There was too much going on it seems."

I have no intention of getting drawn into a discussion of Shelby's suspension.

"The guys will be impressed," she adds.

"If you want to impress a man at Skyline, a Magnum is a good way to do it," I say.

Madison laughs and Caroline stares pointedly down at her gun as she smoothly loads cartridges into the revolver's cylinder.

"Do I see some color on that queenly face?" I ask.

"There are a number of things wrong with what you're implying," Caroline says, putting the gun down and looking at me with a stern expression. "First, I'm not here to impress anyone, second, I don't blush, and, third, I don't have a queenly face."

She is wrong on two counts. We all hope to impress our fellow shooters with our guns and skills, and she is possessed of a truly beautiful face. In her early forties, Caroline is tall, slender and graceful and, with her standard shooting garb of figure-molding black pants and a sleek, stretch black turtleneck, she has not gone unnoticed by any man at Skyline. The majority of them, however, stop fantasizing about her after she has sneered at them once or twice.

"Someone needs to tell that woman," Pete said to me soon after I became a member of Skyline, "that being a first-class bitch is not becoming."

"Well, Caroline," I say to her now. "I disagree. Your face could launch a thousand ships and, whether or not you want to impress anyone, I know Pete will be happy to look at both you and your Magnum."

Madison again laughs, but Caroline is silent.

"But, you're right," I add. "You don't blush."

We shoot a few more rounds and the three of us go in to the clubhouse. Jean arrives carrying the ingredients for a large batch of Sloppy Joes. Her great-grandson, Matthew, follows her with her pistol case stopping to look furtively around the room, his head jerking to a sudden stop when he sees Madison. He waves his hand tentatively in her direction and Madison wiggles her fingers in a barely noticeable response and then promptly turns her back on him. In an instant, Matthew buries his head down into his chest and barrels out the door.

"Hmm," says Jean. "I'm starting to think the reason Matthew's so eager to help me get to the range on Wednesday evenings is so he can look at a certain little lady."

"Oh, I'm sure it's because he likes being around his great-grandmother," I say, looking curiously at Madison. Madison may be writing her senior thesis on women shooters, but I could write a paper all of my own. Why do attractive women take up a sport in which men are in the majority and then do their best to ignore them? Do they not realize that you *can* get a man with a gun?

"These brownies smell delicious," says Jim, holding a foil-wrapped baking tray in his hands while wedging the door open with his foot. Christine scurries in carrying a pistol case, a bag containing her ammunition and shooting gear, and a carton of ice cream.

"I'm going to warm them up," she says. "I know how you all like to have melted ice cream on your brownies."

"It was a fine day Skyline started the Pistol Belles," says Jim, patting his protruding stomach.

"No," I say, "It was a fine day Mona Milton started the Pistol Belles. Before that Skyline was a bunch of guys doing nothing more than looking down a barrel."

"Which is the reason we're here," says Caroline coldly, heading into the kitchen.

"Yes, that is why we're here, Caroline," says Jim. "Thank you for reminding us. But shooting on a full stomach is just as much fun as firing on an empty one."

"There've always been women up here shooting," says Jean, making sure I don't take too much credit for forming the club's women's group.

"I'm sorry I'm late," says Christine, almost dropping the carton of ice cream as she rushes across the kitchen to the freezer. Caroline is slicing a loaf of Italian bread with a long, serrated knife and deftly sidesteps out of Christine's way.

"I was late getting home from work," Christine says. "And Sophie was all upset because I couldn't drive her to her friend's house and then she asked me for my credit card so she could order concert tickets. She threw a fit when I told her it was locked in the safe and I didn't have time to get it out."

"I have work for her," says Jean. "Tell her to call me tomorrow and she can help me with my spring cleaning. Then she can buy her own tickets."

"Well, the concert is on Saturday and she had to get the tickets tonight so I don't think that will help," says Christine.

"Tell her to call me anyway. She can work for me all day Saturday and I'll pay her cash. Then she won't be chasing you for money."

"Well, she likes to sleep in on Saturdays," says Christine. "But I'll tell her to call you."

"I won't hold my breath," says Jean, frowning and shaking her head. "I don't understand parents today. All my kids worked! If they didn't have an outside job they worked in the house. I worked, they worked and we all worked."

Jean raised five children almost single-handedly. Her husband died of a heart attack in his thirties and she has been a widow for well over forty years.

"You were widowed and I'm sure your kids wanted to help you," says Christine. "I'm not even divorced."

"You're alone with a child is my point," says Jean, forcefully. "A girl of fourteen or fifteen has no right to expect her mother to be her personal slave. She's not a baby any more."

"I know, I know, I know," says Christine, throwing up her hands in a gesture of defeat. "It's because of everything that's happened with her father. I try to make things as easy for her as I can."

"It's none of my business, but that's a mistake," says Jean, swiftly bringing the discussion to a close by turning to look around the room. "Is everyone here?"

"Everyone but Shelby," I say. "As I told you all last week, Shelby has been temporarily suspended from Skyline. Jim, Pete and I will let her know when she can come back, but I don't anticipate that being for at least a couple of weeks."

Everyone stares at me but no-one makes a comment or asks about Shelby's suspension. Over the weekend I'd emailed the Belles to let them know that Shelby had mishandled her gun and had been suspended. I'd been surprised that no-one called me to learn more details or to vent their dislike of Shelby. I guess they're just happy to be free of her for a while.

"Now let's get started," I say, before anyone can break the silence.

"Don't start without me," says Pete, striding in, as the door slams behind him. "I smell fried chicken and hamburger and…is that burnt toast?"

Caroline jumps down from the stool on which she has been elegantly perching, rushes to the oven and pulls open the door. The small rounds of Italian bread are black and smoking.

"They look like they just got fired through a muzzle," says Pete, laughing.

"I forgot," she says, stiffly, brushing the toast into the garbage can. "It's lucky I brought more bread."

She picks up the knife and starts slicing another loaf.

"Don't do that for me," says Pete, grabbing a paper plate and piling *bruschetta* onto it. "I'll take it as it comes."

"It's meant to be served—"

Pete ignores her, forks the mixture into his mouth and surveys the spread of food on the kitchen counter.

"Looks like the Pistol Belles have outdone themselves," he says. "What have we got tonight? Fried chicken, Sloppy Joe's, everything a man needs."

"And brownies and vanilla ice cream for dessert," says Jim, once again rubbing his stomach in pleasant anticipation.

"Oh, I'm so glad you like it," says Christine. "It's good to know it was worth the trouble."

"And tonight Caroline brought her beautiful .44 Magnum again," says Madison.

Caroline smiles at her. If her *bruschetta* isn't going to be eaten properly, at least her gun will be appreciated.

"I didn't get chance to look it over last week," says Pete, walking over to where Caroline has placed the gun on a table at the back of the clubhouse.

"May I?" he asks, turning to her as he opens the case.

"Of course," she says, quietly.

"It's the real Dirty Harry," says Pete. "A Smith & Wesson Model 329. Make my day, Caroline."

We all laugh except for Caroline who, with a final flourish, cuts the last slice from the loaf. She looks across at Pete, holding the knife upright in her hand. He takes his eyes off the gun and looks at her and, once again, silence hangs in the clubhouse air.

"OK guys," I call out. "We have forty-five minutes to eat. We must be in the range, ready to shoot, at seven o'clock."

I am always anxious to get through our potluck dinner and into the range, but tonight I'm determined to get in more shooting than usual. It will calm me down from a difficult meeting with Dr. Mark Sandersen, the principal of our local elementary school. This morning's meeting had been arranged last Wednesday, the very same day which ended with Shelby's outburst and suspension. The day had started, as usual, with breakfast with my husband, Carl, but had quickly gone downhill. Soon after Carl left for his eight o'clock English literature class, I'd received a call from Dr. Sandersen, a man I'd not yet met but who has since placed me under his command. Carl likes to eat a large breakfast and I spend a portion of each morning scraping bacon fat into the garbage disposal and rinsing stubborn egg yolk off our plates. I'd been wrestling with a greasy iron skillet when the telephone rang and, carefully placing the heavy pan in the sink, I'd picked up the handset on the kitchen wall.

"I am looking for someone to coordinate a gun safety program," Sandersen said, after introducing himself and asking me to confirm that he was, indeed, speaking to Mona Milton.

"I am shocked that we have to do this," he'd continued. "But a requirement has been issued by the Department of Education that we provide a safety program on firearms. I have no choice but to comply."

Though I hadn't been shocked, I'd been surprised that our state has decided that children should learn about guns. We are all painfully aware of the tragic incidents of gun violence in schools and colleges, and that those events have resulted in public demand for stricter gun control. To my knowledge, there has not been a corresponding demand for increased firearms education.

"Dr. Sandersen," I'd said, my curiosity piqued by this unexpected call and its surprising request. "Do you want something along the lines of the bike safety program I've read about in the local newspaper?"

"Yes, that's a good program. Children need to know how to ride a bike safely."

"I agree. It's pretty scary driving around town with all these oversized—"

"Of course, we use real bikes and helmets in that program. We obviously won't be using actual firearms in the gun safety program. Quite honestly, it galls me that we have to teach our students what to do with a gun."

"If you don't believe in a gun safety program, why don't you tell the Department of Education that you'll offer one on preventing children from drowning in unfenced swimming pools or from being poisoned by their parent's pills or cleaning fluids?"

Guns are dangerous weapons, but they are not the only hazard children face.

"Danger is everywhere, Ms. Milton, I agree," he'd said. "My professional colleagues seem to believe that gun safety is important, so we'll go ahead. But I don't think guns should be in the home at all and certainly not where children are present. The Second Amendment is grossly misinterpreted."

I take a couple of deep breaths. The Second Amendment to the United States Constitution states "...the right of the people to keep and bear arms, shall not be infringed." Its meaning and intent is much debated by both scholars and the general public, with some believing it prescribes only for the arming of members of a militia.

"But I understand some of our families are hunters," Sandersen had continued. "And the Chief of Police tells me that the number of people in town applying for handgun permits is increasing."

I'd scribbled a hasty note to report this piece of information at the next Skyline meeting. We could get more people in our Basic Pistol class. Sandersen would no doubt be surprised to learn that most shooters believe gun owners should first learn how to use their weapons safely.

"Dr. Sandersen," I'd said. "I fully believe that children should be taught about gun safety. And adults too, of course. Most firearms accidents involving children are the result of carelessness or stupidity on the part of an adult."

"Well, I don't want to argue with you, Ms. Milton. You are, no doubt, pro-gun or you wouldn't belong to that Skyline place. I'm told that you run a women's handgun league. I got your name from the police department."

I've obtained several handgun permits from our local police department and have shot with many of the town's police officers up at Skyline, so I'm not surprised my name came up when an elementary school principal made inquiries about gun safety education.

"The National Rifle Association has a gun safety program for children," I'd said. "I will contact them for details."

"I don't want NRA propaganda in my school. I can't have my students going home with backpacks stuffed full of flyers telling them how to protect their Second Amendment rights. I would spend the next month dealing with irate parents."

"I'm an NRA member, Dr. Sandersen," I'd said, realizing just how much gun education is going to have to take place. "We focus on gun safety first. A youngster's possible interest in learning to shoot comes second. We're not here to arm the nation."

This last statement isn't exactly true, and Sandersen didn't buy it.

"As I said, Ms. Milton, I don't want any pro-gun propaganda handed out to my students. I'm charged with providing a safety program and I need a volunteer to take it on. You come highly recommended. Well, at least the Police Chief told me to call Skyline and Skyline's president told me to contact you."

Thank you, Bob Finch.

"Is there a budget?" I'd asked, although in the few minutes in which I'd spoken with Sanderson I'd already decided to pay for the materials myself. I'd recently vowed to be more generous with both my time and money, and teaching gun safety to school children would definitely qualify as a charitable endeavor.

"None," he'd said, and then quickly continued. "Ms. Milton, are you interested in coordinating this program?"

"Yes, it just so happens I want to start some volunteer work, and teaching young children about gun safety is right on target."

Either he hadn't noticed, or chose not to comment on, my poor word choice. I was sorry Carl hadn't been around to catch it.

"Good," he'd said. "I assured the County Education Commission that the program would be taught to all grades in every elementary school in our county."

"That must be dozens of schools!"

"Actually, it's thirty-four."

"Thirty-four elementary schools! How many grades?"

"Six, including kindergarten. The program will run between now and the third week in June."

"That's less than three months! How many times would the program have to be given in each school?"

"The students will be divided into two groups. Kindergarten through second grade, and third through fifth. I'd like everything to be covered in one session to each of the two groups."

"Thirty-four schools, with two sessions at each school makes sixty-eight sessions," I'd said, snatching my calendar from the kitchen wall and flicking through April, May and June.

"Correct."

"Sixty-eight sessions in a little over two months! If we start right away we have about ten weeks. That's almost seven programs a week."

Sandersen had been silent.

"Right?" I'd asked after a long pause.

"Correct," he'd said so slowly I'd wondered if basic arithmetic wasn't his strong suit.

"I'll need to find someone to help me."

"I only ask that it's a woman. I don't want the boys imitating those trigger-happy John Wayne types."

Sandersen must be older than I'd thought. Could today's elementary school children have possibly heard of John Wayne?

I'd agreed to put together a basic program and meet Sandersen the following week in his office at Lincoln Elementary. I was to bring an outline and sample materials. He would provide a list of the schools and I would schedule the sessions and be responsible for the program's implementation.

"Ms. Milton, please be officially advised that you cannot bring firearms into the schools. No guns. No ammunition."

"Of course, I wouldn't dream of it."

"Absolutely no guns in the schools," he'd continued, his voice rising as if I hadn't acknowledged his warning. "No guns of any kind, including rifles, shotguns, handguns, air guns, toy guns and cap guns. And no water pistols!"

I'd made a pistol out of my fist and finger and held it up to my head.

"No, sir," I'd said, and we'd bade each other farewell.

And so this morning, arriving five minutes early for our nine-thirty appointment, I'd been told by Dr. Sandersen's secretary—a dowdy looking woman named Sue—that her boss was behind closed doors in an emergency parent's meeting. I'd taken the seat Sue offered me, telling myself that if the relationship with Sandersen starts poorly, it won't be because of a bad attitude on my part. I'd taken extra care with my wardrobe, rejecting my first choice of jeans and boots in case I gave the impression of living out a Wild West fantasy. I'd also chosen not to wear my black leather jacket and black pants in case I fit Sandersen's notion of an international assassin. And so I'd sat outside his office looking every bit the suburban lady in khaki pants, brown flats, a long sleeved brown shirt and a pink quilted jacket; I was neither cowgirl nor special agent.

Emerging from his office a good half hour after my arrival and accompanied by a scowling couple, the principal of Lincoln Elementary had glanced at me and walked out of the outer office. The couple followed him and then scurried out of the school's main door. Left sitting silently by Sue's desk, the two of us watched as her boss ambled down the long, straight corridor so peculiar to suburban grade schools. Sandersen's girth is wide and it had been like watching a grossly oversized boy carrying a blancmange, desperately hoping to reach the table before his creamy, sugary treat wobbled onto the floor.

Ten more minutes had passed before the big man returned. I'd remained seated as he'd stood in front of me and thus had a child's view of the full span of his belly. Dr. Sandersen may be anti-guns, but he obviously had no objection to carrying around a deadly weapon of about one hundred excess pounds.

"Ms. Milton," he'd said, without extending his hand to me, a lack of manners for which I'd been grateful given that it seemed most likely his absence had been due to an extended bathroom visit. "I've been dealing with some emergencies this morning."

"I can see you're a busy man," I'd said, standing up and following him into his office.

Sitting on the desk was a framed photograph of his wife and two broad-faced young girls. I'd settled myself into the visitor's chair facing his desk.

"I've done quite a lot of work since we spoke last week," I'd said hurriedly, anxious to demonstrate my organizational skills. "I'm happy to confirm that we will be able to use the NRA—"

"That name is not to be used," he'd pronounced, looking up from studying some papers on his desk.

"As I mentioned on the phone last week, the NRA has a great program for children and will supply workbooks, instructor guides, DVDs and brochures."

He'd looked up at me through bulbous, pudgy eyes.

"That name cannot—"

"The name is not on the materials," I'd jumped in, letting him know he wasn't the only one who could interrupt. "In fact, they make a point of leaving their name off so the program can't be misinterpreted as a means of promoting the organization or the use of guns. The gun safety program gives no opinions about firearms, good or bad, and focuses only on the protection and safety of children."

"Goodness, you sound as if you work for them," he'd said, leaning back and looking at me intently.

I hadn't responded. My years at Abaco had taught me when to remain silent.

"Alright, get the workbooks and be ready to start," he'd said, after a long minute had passed by in which neither of us had spoken.

"Great! I am really thrilled to be able to run this program—"

"I am running the program. You will coordinate and teach it."

"Right," I'd replied, sinking down in the chair. Maybe the difference between a volunteer and an employee isn't as great as I'd thought. "I've ordered the materials and will have them later this week."

Sandersen had pushed a folder across his desk.

"This is the list of schools, along with the name of the principal, phone number and email address. I'd like you to hold the first sessions here on Friday."

"I hope the workbooks arrive by—"

His pudgy fingers hovered over a desk calendar.

"Friday morning at ten o'clock for the younger children. That's kindergarten, first and second grades. Friday afternoon at one o'clock for grades three, four and five."

"I can't guarantee I'll have everything by—"

"Then call that organization of yours and tell them to expedite the shipment."

"It's already on its way. I just don't know if—"

"Go over the details with Sue. Let her know if you need pens, paper, DVD player and such. Come and see me before the first session with a sample of your materials for my review."

"Well, as I keep trying to say, I hope everything arrives in time. That only leaves two more mail deliveries and—"

"We'll meet again next week so you can bring me up-to-date on your appointments at the other schools. Try to get them all arranged prior to our meeting. Wednesday at nine-thirty is the best time for me."

"Yes, like this morning," I'd said.

"Yes, Ms. Milton, like this morning."

Sandersen had slowly got up from behind his desk and I'd dutifully followed him to the outer office. With barely a goodbye, he'd once again headed off down the long corridor. I'd wanted to tell Sue that her boss was rude and obnoxious but, instead, said I would need pencils and a DVD player on Friday and that I hoped to be back tomorrow with sample materials. She'd looked at me with a mixture of sympathy and concern on her plain face.

"I'm doing this as a volunteer," I'd said, looking for some acknowledgement that, while she may have no choice but to deal with him, I was a free agent. "This is the first time I've done this and Sanders...Doctor Sandersen is rather demanding."

"He likes things a certain way."

"Then we'll do things a certain way," I'd said, and smiled and left before I could say anything I might regret.

Now, several hours later, I'm at Skyline feeling better with each shot. The beauty of target shooting is that you have something at which to aim. Though it's against club rules to use targets bearing images of people, whether real or imagined, it doesn't mean a certain face, or other bodily part, cannot be pictured there by the imaginative eye of the shooter. And what I'm picturing right now is large enough for a complete beginner to nail in one shot.

I take a break and watch Jean as she steadily loads cartridges into her revolver. She fires five rounds and then stops before loading up again. Jean doesn't bother to check her shots for accuracy.

"My eyesight is so bad I can barely see the target back here at fifty feet," she says. "But I've been shooting so long I'm usually on the paper."

She is right. Jean's shots are always well placed. It pays to learn when young and my one regret is not taking up shooting until I was in my mid-forties when my eyesight was already deteriorating.

Christine is loading her Beretta, with Jim at her side. It is hard to believe that Christine has been shooting for four years. Caroline constantly pushes me to cut Christine from the Pistol Belles, and even Shelby has questioned Christine's place in our group. Madison occasionally suggests there are other women who would like to join, but I tell her I don't want our group to be larger than six shooters. I'd met Christine years ago at my first Basic Pistol class and, the truth is, I don't have the heart to let her go.

But I see what is happening to the Pistol Belles. Caroline and Madison work exclusively together. Christine requires Jim's full attention and yet fails to make any progress. Jean is happy to have a bunch of girls to hang out with and fire off a few rounds. Shelby is unreliable and inconsistent and her behavior has now resulted in a suspension. I shoot well, but spend most of my time organizing the group and managing the almost constant conflicts. We are not the team or sisterhood I'd imagined when I formed the Pistol Belles. I thought we'd all become sharpshooters. I thought we'd be a tight bunch of gals who'd watch out for each other. But we are no more than six women who come to Skyline once a week to eat and shoot. We spend more time eating than shooting. We discuss recipes instead of calibers. We have a name, but no identity.

Now I've taken on the task of teaching gun safety to every elementary school student in the county. Has this new commitment made me see how badly the Pistol Belles need my attention? Can I expect to do both within the next three months? If so, I will have to take a leaf out of Sandersen's book.

I'm in charge. Do as I say.

Chapter Three

"Jean called," says Carl as I push open the front door and step into the living room. Carl is lying on the couch, a book in his hands and a glass of his favorite Merlot on the coffee table beside him. Music plays softly in the background and the television screen flashes soundlessly. Our small house has an open floor plan and the living room, dining room and kitchen flow into each other. With one swift scan I can take in the full scope of my husband's evening at home.

"Jean called?" I ask, surprised. "I left Skyline only fifteen minutes ago. I've been with her all evening."

I walk into the kitchen and study the clean, empty surfaces. There are no signs that our young neighbor, Michaela, has been here. The phone call from Jean was probably Carl's only disturbance.

"She said she couldn't say anything to you at the club as Caroline was there and she was going to wait around to talk to you when the others had left, but Matthew was coming for her and she didn't want him to come in and start drooling all over Madison, so she decided she would leave and then call you when she got home."

I stare at Carl as he looks up at me from his prone position.

"Caroline? Matthew? Madison? Carl, honey, I'm sorry but I don't know what you're talking about."

My husband is a professor of literature at our local state university and can find order in the most complex stories. But tonight he is deliberately relaying a rambling message word for word.

"Apparently Caroline is upset," he says, sitting up and smiling at me. Carl enjoys the conflicts and rivalries of the Pistol Belles and always anticipates a juicy tale or two when I get home on Wednesday evenings.

"Caroline doesn't usually wear her emotions on her sleeve," I say, taking the Ruger out of its case and placing it carefully on an old towel I'd laid on the dining room table before I'd left. "If Jean called to tell me Caroline is upset, did she say why?"

Carl watches as I take out cleaning fluid and brushes from the cleaning kit. He picks up his glass and sips slowly.

"Because you haven't asked her to help you with the gun safety program," he says.

"I've barely had chance to ask anyone! Jean only knows about it because I called her this afternoon to vent about Sandersen. And, for the record, I asked her if she would help me and she said no."

In fact, she'd turned me down flat.

"I know guns," she'd said. "But I'm tired of kids. I had five of my own and they had fifteen and the fifteen have had ten more. That's to date. At least, that I know about."

Jean had guffawed down the phone, enjoying counting her descendants even if she'd grown weary of children.

"You'll find somebody," she'd said. "But, to be honest, I don't know who. You may just have to get your butt around thirty-four schools on your own."

"But, Jean, you'd be great," I'd persisted, hoping that with a little buttering she might relent. It hadn't worked.

"Mona, I'm not good with kids anymore. I don't have the patience, I don't have the energy and I definitely don't have the hearing. Kids don't listen to eighty-year olds. I could be Annie Oakley herself and they wouldn't take me seriously. You need to find someone a lot younger than me."

"Well, I'm not exactly young either!"

"No, but you act youthful. You're full of energy and enthusiasm. Most folks wouldn't guess you've got half a century on you."

Jean knows how to bring a compliment down to size.

"How about Madison?" she'd asked.

I'd told her Madison would be ideal but she is already under pressure with classes and her rifle team. Jean had not made any further suggestions.

"Carl, honey," I say as he watches me push the bore brush through the barrel to dislodge lead left there from firing cartridges. "The reason I didn't ask Caroline is because she has a full-time job. I doubt she'd be able to take time off work to visit every elementary school in the county."

"I hear there are thirty-four of them," says Carl, laughing.

"There'll be one less when I blow Lincoln Elementary to smithereens."

"Mona," says Carl, his laughter gone in a flash. "People with guns must not make threats."

"Don't worry," I say, pulling out the brush and peering into the barrel. "I'll make sure Dr. Sandersen is the only person in school."

"That's not funny, Mona. You cannot joke about guns and schools. It is not funny and it never will be."

Carl is right. Careless comments and tasteless jokes paint a picture of gun owners as reckless, violent or ignorant. And as the new coordinator of a public school gun safety program, my words and attitude will be under scrutiny.

"You're right," I say. "I'm sorry."

Carl smiles at me and I blow him a kiss.

Carl is not a shooting man but is a staunch supporter of my right to own a gun. More than once he has sprung to my defense when a friend or acquaintance has made negative comments about firearms or has challenged my right to participate in the shooting sports. There are a couple of reasons Carl doesn't like being told his wife shouldn't own guns. First of all, no-one tells my husband what to do and actually achieves the desired result. Many of his students have fallen afoul of this fundamental rule. "Professor Milton, you should start with Chaucer and skip *Beowulf* and then it will be…", "Professor Milton, you should give the test before Spring Break and not after and then it will be…"

It will be a 'D'.

Carl tells me that the last sentence his former wife uttered to him prior to him starting divorce proceedings began, "Carl! You should have called to…" Apparently, he should have called to tell her that his presentation at the Mid-Atlantic States Higher Education Forum had been moved from late to early afternoon, thus giving him the unexpected chance to catch an evening flight home instead of staying overnight and returning the following day. And it seems he should have called to tell her he would be home by midnight so she would have had time to get her lover out of the bedroom before her husband tiptoed quietly—so as not to disturb his sleeping beauty—up the carpeted stairs of their comfortable town home. I am eternally grateful to Carl's first wife for her faithless heart and her willingness to engage in risky sexual escapades, and I am forever thankful that she did not know what her husband would and would not tolerate.

The second reason Carl doesn't want people to say his wife should not own guns is because he believes in our right to make our own choices, as long as we take full responsibility for them.

"If Mona had taken up golf," he says to the few people who still feel compelled to express an opinion about my hobby, "she would own several golf clubs and lots of golf balls and accessories. She'd belong to a club and she would go to it often. But she didn't choose to chase a ball, she chose firearms. She, therefore, owns several guns and lots of ammunition and accessories. She belongs to a club and she goes to it often."

Carl's willingness to defend me makes me love him more than ever. Slightly built, he stands only a couple of inches above me and, though fifty-five years old, stays slim in spite of mountains of steak, spaghetti, bread, cheese, hamburgers and potatoes. My darling professor does not have sophisticated tastes when it comes to the gustatory delights, although he claims that the bottle of red wine he consumes every evening adds whatever class may be missing from his plate. But deep inside Carl's unimposing physique is an able pugilist who enjoys standing up to my detractors.

"You look worn out, Mona," Carl now says, getting up from the couch and walking over to me.

"It was a rough day," I say, putting my gun down and reaching up to him.

He wraps his arms around me and pulls up hard on my back. I'm locked in a bear hug. It's exactly where I need to be.

"I feel a story," he says, kissing the top of my head.

I rest my head on his chest. He strokes my back.

"I feel a story about gun safety right here on your spine," he says.

"What are you?" I ask, laughing. "A spine reader?"

"No, I'm the husband of a woman I can read more easily than the book I just tossed on the couch."

"Oh, yeah?"

"Yes, and the couch is exactly where you need to be tossed."

He picks me up, carries me across the room and slowly eases me down onto the soft cushions. He climbs on top of me and kisses my face. We lay still for a minute or two.

"Did you find out any more about John Williams?" he asks.

I push Carl off me and jump up and go back to the dining room table.

"Abandoned already," he says, picking up his glass and settling back on the couch. "Someone at Skyline must have said something about Shelby or her father."

"No, everyone is amazingly quiet and I haven't spoken to Shelby since I threw the rule book at her last week."

"Do you have to clean your gun right now," he asks, changing the subject.

"Yes, honey, I do," I say in the mock-tired tone I use each week when he asks me this question. "I prefer to clean it right away so I don't have to lock it in the safe and then get it out again tomorrow. And I don't want to forget to clean it."

"You would never forget to clean your gun. You're obsessive-compulsive when it comes to gun care."

"And Carl care."

Carl raises his glass and smiles at me. His complaint about the smell of cleaning fluid is a Wednesday evening ritual. I continue pushing the rod through the barrel.

"I love to see a woman work a rod," he says.

I smile at him and pull the brush out of the barrel. I then slowly push it in and out several times. He watches me for a minute and then comes and sits with me at the table. He knows I'll stay on task until I'm satisfied my gun is clean.

"I wonder what's wrong with John Williams," he says.

"I'm surprised you're so interested in Shelby's father. You've never had much of a soft spot for his daughter."

"I teach all my classes in Williams Hall, don't forget."

I had forgotten. The university is built on land donated years ago by the wealthy and prominent Williams family. The family has been in our town for generations and is the closest thing we have to royalty. It's not surprising that Shelby behaves like a little princess.

"Have you ever met him?" I ask.

"Last fall," says Carl. "On Founder's day the school invited past supporters. John Williams came and said a few words and I remember him remarking that he's the last Williams alive."

"Shelby's a Williams, born and bred."

"He mentioned her, of course, and his son-in-law and their children. I think the youngest had recently been born. He seemed very proud of them all, but he did mention that they don't carry the Williams name."

"No, but they carry his blood," I say, for some reason defending the ability of a woman to carry on a family line though I have not done so myself.

"True, but the point he was making was that he is the last Williams to carry the name and that there'll be no-one in town with that name after he is gone."

"Sounds like he was already thinking about dying," I say, wiping oil around the trigger and the slide. Good shooting demands a well-oiled gun.

"He looked to be in his sixties, so I guess it's not surprising that he has a sense of his own mortality."

"So it's good to have your name on a building."

"Or a litter of grandchildren," says Carl.

I turn to look at him and a silence hangs between us.

"Maybe Michaela will give us grandchildren," he says, laughing.

I laugh with him. Neither Carl nor I can blame each other for our childlessness. We made our own histories.

"You must have met John Williams up at Skyline," says Carl. "I'm sure he's been to watch his darling daughter shoot."

"He came to see the Pistol Belles once," I say, recalling the tall, fair man with his patrician airs and confident manner. "He was with Carmine and I remember thinking how different they were. Williams is so pale and lean and Carmine is short and very dark."

At the time I'd remarked on the difference to Jean and she'd laughed and said that the stock has run out on the Williams family and that John should be forever grateful to Carmine for marrying his spoiled daughter.

"I don't think his son-in-law's swarthy looks are a concern," says Carl. "He spoke very highly of him and said that Carmine is the kind of guy who keeps our country strong. He said he is proud his daughter and grandchildren are named Lombardi. Carmine works hard, is a dedicated husband and father and apparently develops real estate all over the country."

"And he hunts with his father-in-law."

"He didn't mention hunting, which was smart considering his audience. But I thought it was pretty classy how much he praised Carmine."

"Jean says the one good thing she can say about Shelby is that the girl had powerfully good instincts when it came to choosing a husband. She needed a man with money and when she met Lombardi she snapped him up before anyone else could grab him."

"Yes," says Carl. "Carmine Lombardi will already have worked a lot harder than John Williams ever did. Williams will have gone to the best schools, inherited property, the works."

"Well, I'm sure whatever is left will go to Shelby. I hope she appreciates it."

"She won't appreciate her inheritance the way you do. She's grown up expecting it. It's the original entitlement program."

I pack away the cleaning kit, put the Ruger in its case and take everything down to the basement. Using the combination lock, I open the safe, put the gun inside, close the door and spin the dial. I leave the cleaning bag on the floor beside the safe and trudge back up the stairs.

"I still don't understand why Caroline is upset with me," I say, bringing the conversation back to Jean's phone call. "Even if Jean told her about the safety program, why would she expect me to ask her?"

"Forget that she's upset. That's not the part of the message you need to hear."

"I don't need to know that she's upset?"

"Not as much as you need to know that she's unemployed and has indicated that she'd like to help you with the program."

"I'm very surprised to hear she's out of work. That's bad news."

For as long as I've known Caroline she's worked at Smith Pharma.

"Yes, but it is good news that she's available and willing to help you."

I sit down next to Carl and he puts his arm around me and strokes my hair.

"Mona, this isn't something else for you to feel guilty about. If Caroline has lost her job you will be doing her a favor by asking for her help."

"Am I destined to always gain from somebody else's loss?" I ask, wrapping my arms around his waist and trying in vain to keep my oily hands away from his shirt. I should have washed them before sitting down.

"You've had misfortunes of your own. You've paid your dues. Bad things come to everyone, including you. But the gun safety program is a good thing. You wanted a volunteer project and you found one. You need help with it and it sounds as if Caroline is available."

I nod and rub my nose on his flat belly. How does he stay so lean?

"Call her now," he says, pushing my phone toward me.

"It's late. I'll call her tomorrow."

"She's lost her job and is no doubt feeling rejected. Don't make her wait another night."

"I wonder what happened to her job," I say, picking up the phone and scrolling for her name.

"Don't ask. She'll tell you but probably not tonight."

Carl props his feet on the coffee table, cupping his wine glass between two fingers.

"Caroline, I'm so sorry to call you at this hour," I say, surprised when she picks up on the first ring. "I'm sure you have to get up early tomorrow morning."

Carl raises his eyes up to the ceiling and shakes his head.

"I didn't get the chance to talk to you at the range," I continue, thumping my head with my fist. "I don't know if you heard about the gun safety program I'm going to be giving in the schools. I have a real problem on my hands. I have to start the program on Friday. Yes, the day after tomorrow! I have to do the program twice at each elementary school in the county and there are…"

Carl twirls his right hand in a gesture which tells me to get to the point.

"Gosh, I can't believe you know that! Yes, there are thirty-four schools. That means sixty-eight sessions."

Carl smiles, picks up the wine bottle and fills his glass.

"No, you're right, I can't do it alone. Oh, Jean told you I needed help?"

Carl laughs out loud and I grimace at him.

"Right, the principal of Lincoln Elementary is in charge and he wants the program completed by the end of the school year. That's about ten weeks."

Caroline tells me that she's looked at the calendar and that allowing for Easter break and Memorial Day there are about forty-seven school days left. In the interest of time-management she recommends we do both programs in a particular school on the same day and that, where possible, we do them at the same time. I could take the younger group and she would take the older group. Alternatively, we could split the schools up and each teach both age groups. I could be at one school while she's at another.

I don't know anything about Caroline's work, but I'm guessing it's something to do with logistics. I can't believe Smith Pharma let her go.

"You have no idea what a relief this is to me," I say, smiling into the phone. We talk for a few more minutes and I ask her to come to the house tomorrow morning so we can start making appointments. I mention that I must have the sample materials to Sandersen tomorrow. I don't tell her that he will want to meet her and has the power to either accept or reject her participation. I don't want to lose her before we've even begun. I thank her again and put down the phone.

"She didn't sound in the least bit upset," I say. "Did Jean really say Caroline was upset with me?"

Carl looks at me without smiling. Suggesting Carl might have misinterpreted a message gets the same result as telling him what he should do.

"Of course she did," I continue, answering my own question. "Because Jean knew that if I heard Caroline was upset I would call her. She must have found out that our fellow Pistol Belle was unemployed and knew Caroline would be too proud to ask me to include her."

"Jean got you both the help you need. You need an articulate, reliable woman who is knowledgeable about guns and she needs an outlet for her energy and organizational talents. And, anyway, who else can you ask?"

No-one, Caroline's availability is a godsend.

"I have to get her through Sandersen. I'll have to prep her so she doesn't alienate him with her women's supremacy stuff."

"Maybe he'll like her. Caroline sounds like a no-nonsense, get-it-done type. They'll be kindred spirits."

"That's nice of you to say, but I doubt it. You can afford to be optimistic because you won't be at Lincoln Elementary tomorrow, or on Friday."

I picture Sandersen's fat, wobbling belly and Caroline's lithe, taut body. No-one would imagine this pair would find mutual respect. The shared characteristic of impatient, get-it-done command will probably spark nothing more than competition. Once again, I'll be the referee.

"However, from what you've told me about her, you'll have to make sure Caroline pays as much attention to the boys as to the girls," says Carl, swallowing the contents of his glass and turning off the radio. "You don't want her to direct her talk solely to the little sisters."

"Right and she can't give her usual speech about how girls and women need to be able to protect themselves," I say. "Caroline tells everyone that women need to learn to shoot so they can take responsibility for protecting themselves and not assume a man or the police will be around to defend them."

"She makes an excellent point," says Carl. "But it's not the right message for children in grade school. That can come later. But if you're following an approved curriculum there won't be room for personal opinions on the pros and cons of owning a gun."

"That's right, we're following a program and we'll go through it together as soon as it arrives," I say, knowing that I'll be pacing around the house until the mailman arrives tomorrow. "But if we split up to teach in different schools or age groups, how am I going to know she doesn't go off message?"

"Training and trust. First you train her in the curriculum and then you trust her to stick to the program."

"And if she doesn't?"

"You fire her."

"She's a volunteer!"

"You're both volunteers, but you have to stick to the program. You'll learn the material and do the first session together so you can keep each other on track. After the first session is over, you'll hold a post mortem."

"That's not a good word to use when discussing a gun safety program," I say, enjoying catching Carl in a rare instance of poor word choice.

"OK, so after the Friday sessions you'll review how they went. I'm sure Sandersen will monitor the whole thing and won't be shy in telling you where you went off…off target?"

I laugh, but then groan at the thought of Sandersen. A man I didn't know existed until my phone rang last week is now consuming my thoughts and emotional energy.

The wrong man.

"Carl," I say. "Let's go to bed."

Chapter Four

It takes sharp eyes to find the Skyline Sportsmen's Club. Sandwiched between two wooded lots, the stone post at the entrance holds a weathered sign that does little to signify its identity to passing drivers. The general feeling among club members is that if you can't find the entrance, you probably won't be able to hit a target. Had I not been a passenger in Jean Muirhouse's truck on my first visit, I would have flown right by it. Although I'd driven along Skyline Heights Road many times, I'd not noticed the sign nor had I paid attention to the occasional shot I might have heard from the outdoor range. I'd known nothing about guns or shooting, although I'd been aware that hunters were occasionally allowed to shoot deer in a nearby state park and I'd sometimes seen a neighbor load up his rifle on a cold winter morning. But I hadn't thought about where he and his gun were headed and hadn't the slightest interest in hunting, preferring to believe that meat magically appeared under plastic wrap in the local supermarket. Unlike a number of our neighbors, I didn't have strong opinions as to whether hunting was an ethical way to cull the substantial deer population in our county. Wooded parks butting up against suburban dwellings make for many hungry deer in driveways and properties, and my concern was not whether or not they should be shot, but that they wouldn't eat our shrubs.

But four years ago on a gloomy St. Valentine's Day I'd wandered around the grocery store selecting ingredients for a special dinner, not knowing that my passion for guns was about to be born. Carl and I were newlyweds, having married just the year before, and the evening's dinner was the focus of my day. Tragically, our whirlwind romance and marriage had been followed, just five months later, by the equally sudden loss of my mother and father in a car accident. A year after their passing I'd taken possession of an amount of money far greater than could be believed had come from my plain-living, frugal parents. The realization that their untimely deaths would make me financially independent came slowly over several months as my brother and I discovered bank accounts, stock certificates, brokerage accounts and commodities, each one a bigger surprise than the last.

We sold the house my parents had owned for thirty-five years at what later proved to be the peak of an outlandish real estate bubble. My mother and father would have been appalled had they lived to witness the amount of debt a young couple was willing to take on in order to purchase a modest suburban home. After the estate was settled, the proceeds were split between my brother and me, and my share provided me with an amount of money enough to last not only my lifetime, but Carl's too.

For the first time in my adult life I did not have to work. I'd had a patchwork career, not being inclined to a particular profession, and had changed jobs numerous times. But I'd found sales and marketing to be a relatively pleasant way of making a living and had spent the past twenty years at Abaco managing marketing programs for the firm's industrial clients. But I'd known that if the day ever came that I could afford to quit, I would have no hesitation in doing so, and it hadn't taken long for my inheritance windfall to blow me out of Abaco's sleek front doors. Thus, finding myself in the unusual position of having little to do to fill my time, what tasks I had expanded accordingly, and my trips to the supermarket became complicated projects which could last anywhere from half an hour to two hours depending on who I ran into and how long I spent examining the produce. These errands were always filled with a mixture of guilt and pleasure: pleasure that I could spend as much as I wanted, and guilt that the money had been saved, one dollar at a time, to get my parents through a lengthy retirement.

Leaving the supermarket on this particular Valentine's Day, I'd discovered that my keys were locked in my car. After pulling hard on all four doors, I'd peered inside, seen the keys dangling from the ignition and then looked around helplessly.

"Locked out, huh?" a raspy voice had said behind me. Turning, I'd found an elderly woman watching me from the driver's seat of an idling, battered, grey pick-up.

"My keys are inside!" I'd wailed. "I can't believe I did this!"

"Throw your grocery bags in the back and I'll give you a ride. I'm guessing you live in town."

"I'm just a mile or so from here. So near, but so far, when you're locked out of your car with a mountain of groceries!"

"It's no trouble," the reedy voice said. "Hop on in."

"Really, thank you, but I'll walk home with the cart and return it later. I'm sure FoodMark won't mind."

"I'm sure they will," the woman had said wryly. "If you ask to borrow it they'll say no, and if you don't ask they'll say you stole it."

I'd stood for a minute beside my car feeling frustrated and helpless. I hadn't wanted to start a feud with the grocery store I spent hours at every week. Better to take this stranger's offer.

"Well, if you're sure you don't mind giving me a ride, I live just a couple of blocks from the elementary school," I'd said slowly, my eyes taking in the dilapidated truck.

"Don't worry, she's roadworthy," said my rescuer, slapping the panel of the truck's door. "She's got a few more miles on her before she croaks. Ha, like me!"

"Thank you so much, I really hope it's not too much trouble."

"I have to head out in the other direction first but it's just one stop and won't take me long. From there I can take you home without having to double back here."

With some difficulty, I'd stretched up to put the grocery bags in the back of the truck which had been empty except for a large metal utility box. There hadn't been any means of securing the bags in place.

The woman had stared at me through the tiny rear window.

"I drive real slow so don't worry about your groceries. They won't fly out the back."

I'd pictured *filet mignon*, Portobello mushrooms, green peppercorns, candles, butter and heavy cream catapulting out onto the road, but had decided I'd better get in the truck before she changed her mind.

"Jean Muirhouse," she'd said, thrusting her hand toward me.

"Mona Milton. It's very nice to meet you, and thank you for taking so much trouble for such a dimwit."

"No trouble at all. It's easy to separate yourself from your possessions. We all have too many keys these days. I'd drive you straight home but I have a gun with me and I have to take it right on up to the club."

I'd stared at her and an expression of alarm must have crossed my face. She'd chuckled and pointed down at a small blue case nestled at my feet.

"You have a gun?" I'd asked, so softly she'd turned and peered at me. The case didn't look anything like my neighbor's camouflaged rifle case.

"It's a handgun. And a handgun comes with a bunch of damn fool laws attached to it, at least in this state," Jean had said, gunning the truck out of the parking lot. "Gun owners are treated like criminals here and it causes a whole load of unnecessary back and forth and confusion."

I'd had no idea what this woman was talking about and, before I could ask any questions, she'd continued.

"Here's the stupidity of it. A friend of mine is teaching his girlfriend how to shoot, which is smart. It's good for young women to know how to protect themselves and a handgun is good, although a shotgun works better because you don't have to be that precise. But a shotgun's pretty tough to carry around. At least you can put a pistol in your purse or hide it on your person. Not that we can carry here, either concealed or open."

I'd grown more confused. Shotguns, pistols, concealed carry?

"Anyway, I told my friend he could borrow my revolver as it's an easy way for a young gal to get familiar with guns without being too intimidated. So far, so good, you might say."

Jean had turned to look at me and I'd nodded in agreement. It had seemed I was at the mercy of a gun-toting senior citizen and I'd thought it prudent to agree with whatever she said. I'd squinted through the window into the bed of the truck. My grocery bags were still lodged in the front corner.

"But every time my friend borrows my gun, I have to drive it up to Skyline because if he were to pick it up from me and then get stopped by the cops, he'd be charged with possession of an illegal handgun even though the owner of the gun agreed to lend it to him."

"Really," I'd said, trying to pretend I'd known what she was talking about.

"Now, in my case, I have the time to drive the gun up to the range for him because what else am I doing?" she'd asked without pausing for an answer. "I've been retired for years and I'm pretty well useless, so I don't mind driving around and waiting while his girlfriend shoots. Even so, sometimes I drop my revolver off and then go back later."

"And that's allowed?" I'd started to follow her thread.

"Yes, as long as it stays at Skyline. But the reason we're going straight there now before dropping you at your house is because of another fool law which says you're only supposed to drive your handgun straight from your home to the range. You can't make any detours if you want to be on the right side of the law."

Jean had been parked at the grocery store.

"Yes, I know I made a stop to pick up milk," Jean had said, nodding. "I figure that's alright because it's on the way from my house to Skyline. But I don't want to start heading back on myself to drop you at your house, and I definitely don't want to drive by the elementary school at quitting time."

The clock on the dashboard had said three o'clock. You don't have to be a parent in this town to know when school gets out as the endless line of super-sized vehicles snarls traffic for more than half-an-hour every school day.

"Here's an example of the inconvenience of all these rules," Jean had continued. "There's a couple I know who live in another town but are members of Skyline and like to shoot early in the evening. The wife works at a school not too far from the range but can't leave the gun in her car all day on school property. That would be a real problem. Neither can the husband meet his wife at Skyline and bring her handgun with him. He'd have the same problem as my friend if he was stopped—illegal possession of a handgun. It belongs to his wife! But that doesn't mean anything anymore. I got my husband's guns when he died, but that was decades ago and a lot of things made a lot more sense then. So this woman I'm talking about has to drive all the way home to pick up her pistols and then turn around and go back the way she came. All this driving around burning up fuel and creating pollution and everyone's preaching about the environment! No-one means it. They just think it sounds good, but it sounds idiotic to me! Here we have two law-abiding, tax-paying citizens who follow the rules because of the trouble they'd be in if the wife had the gun on school grounds or the husband drove around with her gun and was stopped."

Without slowing down, Jean had suddenly made a hard right into what turned out to be the entrance to Skyline Sportsmen's Club and we'd headed up the narrow lane. I'd heard my bags slide and had stolen a glance behind me.

"Your bags are there," she'd said, tapping my leg and smiling at me. "They've just shifted to the other side."

I'd smiled and looked down at the blue case.

"You ever shot a gun?" she'd asked, following my gaze.

"No, never."

"This one here is a beauty," Jean had reached down for the case, simultaneously taking her eyes off the road and her hands off the wheel. She'd tossed the gun case into my lap. "It's a Smith & Wesson 17, a classic revolver. It's not heavy and it shoots easy. Come inside and I'll show it to you."

We'd pulled up with a screeching halt on the gravel lot.

"I really don't know anything about guns. I've never even held one in my hands."

"Well, this is your lucky day," she'd said, chuckling. "I'm eighty-years old and have lived long enough to know that when you get the chance to try something new you'd better take it."

Carl would say the same thing. I'd already been imagining what he would say when he learned of my afternoon adventure with an octogenarian sharpshooter.

Jean had hopped out of the truck's cab, with the ease and agility of someone long used to a high vehicle, and had taken long strides across the parking lot toward what I guessed to be the clubhouse. I'd followed after her.

"This is Bill," she'd said as I'd tentatively walked through the door Jean held open for me. "And this here is Tracy his girlfriend. Bill, Tracy, this is—"

"Mona," I'd said quickly, sure she would have forgotten my name.

"Mona Milton, right. Mona has never shot a gun so before you start today's practice I'd like to borrow a couple of rounds of ammo from you so she can give it a try before I take her home."

"I really—"

"Great," Tracy had said, thrusting glasses and earmuffs into my hands. "You can borrow my eyes and ears."

"Take my ammo, Jean," Bill added, handing her a small cardboard carton. "We'll shoot when you're done."

One minute later I'd stood behind a wooden table in the indoor range while Jean told me to put on the ear and eye protectors and had then turned off a flashing light.

"Eyes and ears on always. It's a range rule. I switched off that light so people know we're shooting. No-one's allowed in until that light goes back on. I'm going to show you how to hold the gun and how to shoot it. I'll fire the first two shots and then you can fire off the rest."

"But first," she'd continued. "I have to cover the three basic safety rules. Number one, always keep the gun pointed in a safe direction."

She'd moved the gun up and down to draw my attention to the fact that it was pointing down range.

"Two, always keep your finger off the trigger," Jean had wiggled her finger to show it was outside the trigger guard.

"Three, always keep the gun unloaded until ready to use. We're ready to use it, so now we can load."

Jean rolled out the revolver's chamber, holding it open with one hand and deftly loading five cartridges with the other.

"Pay attention, Mona, because you're going to copy me."

I'd watched as Jean stood up straight, held the gun with both hands, pulled back the hammer with her left hand and then fired. She'd fired again and then motioned for me to take her place.

"Don't be nervous, keep it pointed at the target," she'd said, firmly wrapping both my hands around the gun.

"Now look through the sights and make sure the front sight is centered in the middle of the rear sights."

I'd stood up straight, pointed the gun at the target and moved it around a few times until I could see the front sight was lined up in the notch of the rear sights.

"Now cock the gun."

I'd pulled back the hammer, taking care not to move the gun. I'd then looked sideways at her.

"Very good, you turned to me but didn't move your gun. The biggest problem with people new to firearms is sweeping."

I'd guessed that sweeping means moving the weapon in the direction you are turning.

"Now place your index finger on the trigger, and squeeze. Gently."

I'd placed my finger on the trigger.

"Very good, remember not to move. Make sure your sights are still lined up."

"It looks good."

"Squeeze slowly until it fires."

I'd pulled on the trigger and suddenly the gun had gone off.

"Oh boy, that kind of took me by surprise," I'd said, feeling the recoil.

"Good, that's exactly how it's supposed to be. Every shot should come as a surprise."

"Did I hit the target?" I'd asked, squinting down range.

"We'll find out when you're done. You've got two more."

I'd pointed the gun down range, cocked the hammer, put my finger on the trigger, gently squeezed and fired. I'd then done it again.

"How did that feel?"

"Wow, I can hardly describe it. It's so exhilarating. I'm dying to know if I hit the target."

Jean had switched on the swirling light, saying it was safe to go down range. She'd motioned me to go with her and we'd both headed for the target.

"The two shots closest to the bullseye are mine," Jean had said, ripping the target from the cardboard back. "There are three other shots in a circle at the bottom left which must be yours. That's just the kind of grouping you need."

"But I was aiming for the bullseye. Why do you say this is good?"

"You're using someone else's gun for the first time. All guns are different and you have to make accommodations depending on how they shoot. With your own gun, you adjust the sights according to your eye. Buy a gun and get in plenty of practice and you'll soon have a group of holes in the center."

She'd chuckled and handed me the target.

"Take that home and show it to your Valentine! And let me know when you want to come back."

Chapter Five

The ingredients for our romantic dinner had been secure in the back of Jean's truck when we'd left Skyline and, fortunately, the chilly temperature had kept the food cold enough that the detour had not cost me our steak *au poivre.* I'd already rehearsed the conversation I would have with Carl and my mind had spun furiously as I'd imagined his response to learning that I'd found the hobby I'd been searching for. One thing I'd known for sure is that Carl would ask plenty of questions.

"Mona, are you willing to take on the responsibility of owning a gun?" he'd asked, as I'd blurted out the tale of my afternoon adventure and described the thrill I'd felt on firing a gun for the first time. Carl is a worldly kind of guy and he'd seemed unsurprised that an eighty-year old woman was driving around town with a Smith & Wesson on the floor of her truck.

During this time period, I'd still been adjusting to the fact that, at the age of forty-five, I had a new husband, plenty of money and a lot of free time. I'd begun to accept that my parents would want me to enjoy my inheritance, but I had difficulty dealing with the empty hours I faced every day. A working girl finally got the man and the money she'd dreamed about—and didn't know what to do with herself.

For the first few months of our marriage I'd been fully occupied moving us out of our two apartments and into a new house. Carl had been busy teaching classes and, as always, volunteered for committees or took on additional office hours where he would meet with an endless stream of adoring undergraduates. My husband's days were full. I'd tried to persuade him to take up a shared hobby but after he'd rejected ballroom dancing, golf, yoga and oil painting, I'd admitted that I too had no interest in such pastimes, but was struggling to fill the blank spaces on my calendar. I'd then moved on to household projects and driven him mad with plans to put in a pond or a rock garden. Carl had suggested I plant a vegetable garden, but made it clear that he'd be happy to eat the produce as long as he didn't have to do the work. Carl is not a lazy man and always pitches in when there is a productive task to be completed, but he had no intention of getting drawn into schemes and activities whose sole purpose was to consume otherwise idle time. My new husband was perfectly happy to come home after a day on campus, open a bottle of wine, eat a hearty meal, and retire to the couch where he would work his way through a mountain of magazines, books, newspapers, student essays and movies.

I'd known that Carl's dismissals of my hobby ideas were not a rejection of me, and I'd understood he would have been happy for me to spend my evenings lying alongside him. But I don't read much and rarely watch television. I listen to the radio when I'm driving or cooking or cleaning. On the odd occasion I watch a movie, I get up and down from the couch so many times that Carl says there are fewer bobbing heads at the local multiplex cinema. I'm not even much of a drinker. It's amazing that Carl and I get along so well when we seem to have so little in common. Even Professor Carl Milton grows thoughtful when I ask him to describe what makes us work so well. I know he'd like to answer with several densely-written pages, but he usually says just one word: love.

But even true love and great sex can only take up so much time, and by the time we'd been married a few months it was clear I was turning into Carl's worst nightmare—a needy wife clamoring for his undivided attention.

"Just because we're married," he'd said one wet day when I was huffing, puffing and pacing around the house. "Just because we live together doesn't mean you can rely upon me to be your sole companion. You're far too active and gregarious to be stuck every evening with someone as old and dull as me."

I am only five years younger than Carl and he is far from dull, but I'd known he was right. My husband loved me but did not want me glued to his side. And after circling him for far too many evenings, Carl had gently pulled me down on the couch next to him and told me I needed a hobby, or a cause, or some new friends.

It was ironic that I would chafe at having to occupy my free time. Long ago, I'd wept with relief when my first husband, Bob, moved out of the apartment we'd shared for seven long years. Finally, I'd been able to come home to a quiet space, free of Bob's rock music, hockey sticks, baseball bats, fast food wrappers, empty beer cans and a shifting cast of slackers. I'd filed for divorce not because Bob was messy or because his primary allegiance was to his old high school pals with their impenetrable shared histories, but because he didn't want to work. Bob was undisciplined and lazy, although he was always ready to take cash from busy neighbors. So he mowed lawns, raked leaves, walked dogs, cleaned gutters and painted fences. Bob was at least man enough to accept that he must earn his own beer money.

While Bob stayed locked in a teenager's life, I'd started working at Abaco where punctuality, a professional appearance and the ability to meet tight deadlines were a daily expectation. I'd return home after a ten hour day to cook, clean, pay bills, and accompany Bob to crowded bars and concerts, driving us home late at night and rising early to go to work while Bob slept until noon. In short, I was a full-time employee and wife—and a full-time fool. But, although it took seven long years to accept what my parents and friends had known all along, when I'd finally recognized Bob for the user he was, he'd been gone in a matter of days. He'd complained, and even begged, but he'd known his gig was up.

Many years later I am married to a man who is also locked into some old, treasured habits. But Carl did not marry me in order to satisfy his practical needs, and all he'd asked in that first year of our marriage was that I find a way to satisfy my own restlessness. Carl is a deeply perceptive man and I'd correctly anticipated that his first question on learning about my interest in shooting wouldn't be about the elderly lady, or the club, or the gun I'd fired. Nor would he ask about the couple I'd met or our state's handgun laws. Carl's first question that night was whether I could take on the responsibilities that come with owning a weapon.

"This is a gift to us both, Carl," I'd answered earnestly, taking the peppercorn sauce off the heat and slowly stirring in the cream. "I need something to do and you need me to find something to do!"

With an exaggerated flourish he'd twisted the cork out of a bottle of Moet & Chandon and looked coolly at me across the granite counter. I'd smiled at him and quickly gone back to stirring the sauce. Carl had poured Champagne into two fluted glasses and sipped from one, holding it up between us.

"Mona, I purchased this Champagne as a treat for us both. However, I know from many special occasions together that you'll drink barely one glass and the rest of it will be mine. I knew when I chose such an expensive bottle that, though it may parade as a treat for us both, it is in essence a gift to me."

Carl's mastery of peaceful co-existence is due to his willingness to admit to self-interest. My suggestion that shooting would serve as a gift to us both wasn't going to pass muster.

"But I know how frustrated you are with me," I'd said, picking up the tall, smooth glass. "I pace around you like a caged lioness."

"Mona, we agree that you need a new interest, but there are consequences to taking up a sport which involves dangerous weapons."

I'd taken a small sip, felt the Champagne's kick and placed the glass down on the counter.

"The rest of the bottle is almost mine," he'd said, laughing.

"Mona, are you ready?" he'd continued, looking into my eyes as I'd busily tossed the steak into a hot pan.

"It's as if you're asking me if I'm ready to take on a dangerous assignment," I'd said, feeling cornered. "This is going to be a hobby, not an international mission."

"You are taking on a dangerous assignment! You'll buy a gun, perhaps two. You'll store them in our home and drive with them in your car. You'll be in possession of a weapon that may be used against you, or me. It could be stolen and used in a crime. You may use it to defend yourself and actually kill someone."

This latter is one of the many reasons I practice at least twice a week. Should I find myself in threatening circumstances, I will be familiar with the gun and will be able to focus on the situation at hand. I will thus be in a position to make a sound decision and to know whether I should use my gun—or not.

"And if you kill or maim someone, you will be held responsible," Carl had added, tipping his bubbling flute towards me.

"You seem to know a lot about this," I'd said, flipping the sizzling steaks from the boiling hot pan and onto our plates.

"I don't know a lot about gun laws, but I'm sure there are plenty of rules. You'll have to become an expert, or get to know one. You'll have to deal with the police and firearms dealers. You'll need a safe."

"Carl, you know I wouldn't leave a gun lying around the living room!"

"I don't know that, Mona," he'd said, shaking his head. "I believe I can trust you, but I have an obligation to share my concerns."

I'd cut into my steak and realized it was rare. Carl likes his meat well-done and the blood-oozing, lukewarm offering would not help convince him that I could be relied upon to practice responsible gun ownership. I couldn't even cook our steaks to order.

"Mona, you admit you don't like a lot of responsibility. You were miserable when you were married to Bob because you were the only adult in the relationship. You say you would have liked to have children, but admit to being relieved that you didn't take on the heavy task of raising a child. You are thrilled not to have to go to Abaco because you hated the pressure. Even your inheritance is a guilty burden because you feel you must honor your parents by treating the money responsibly. And you love me because you know I don't need you."

I'd started to exclaim, but he'd continued.

"You are a rare woman, Mona. A woman who doesn't like be needed, not by a man, not by a child, and not by a boss. You don't like burdens."

"I took on the responsibility of a second marriage," I'd said, knowing Carl's description of me was accurate, but feeling obligated to put up a defense.

"To me," he'd said, thumping his chest. "You took on marriage to me. You didn't choose a man whose demands would drain you. You chose me, the genuine no-maintenance guy."

"Don't flatter yourself that you're no work or responsibility," I'd said loudly, thinking the discussion had gone much too far off course and that it was a poor dinner conversation for Valentine's Day. "I do a lot for you. I take charge of this home and our food. I pay our bills and take care of your clothes."

This latter is not exactly time consuming. Carl's wardrobe consists of a pair of black slacks, a pair of khakis and several pairs of jeans. His shirts are white, brown or black. He has one winter coat and one sports jacket.

"And I love everything you do you for me, and for us," he'd said, smiling at me. "But you know you don't have to do it and that if you stopped tomorrow I'd take care of us."

I'd looked at him and raised my eyebrows.

"Except for the cleaning," he'd added.

"And please don't bring Bob into this. Of course I hated being married to such a selfish, childish slob. Who wouldn't? And, yes, I was uncomfortable with my responsibilities at work because my clients were often unreasonable. I am sometimes sad that I—no, that we—don't have children, but I like to believe I would have risen to the task of raising one. Look at how much time I spend with Michaela!"

"You're wonderful with Michaela. But you know you can send her home when you've had your fill."

This is not entirely true as I've never sent Michaela home to an empty house. But, Carl is right. Michaela is not my daughter and my only responsibility toward her is that of a friend and neighbor.

"Mona, do you believe you are qualified to own a gun?"

"Right now, no. But I'll take the pistol class and learn a lot. I'll study the rules on owning a handgun. I'll get the required permits and deal with legal firearms dealers. I'll join the Skyline Sportsmen's Club so I can practice, practice, practice! I won't just own a gun, Carl; I'll become a real shooter. And, I'll buy a safe."

"You have to clean guns quite often."

"I like cleaning and I'm well organized. My guns will be spic and span."

A rare silence had followed.

"Mona, you know I like my steak charred," Carl had said after taking a couple more swigs of champagne. "But with the peppercorns and cream, the rare steak is excellent. It was a good idea not to cook it my usual way."

"Happy Valentine's Day, Carl," I'd said touching my glass against his. I'd taken one more sip and then pushed the glass across the table.

"No alcohol with guns, Mona. You're not a drinker, but promise me you won't even have a sip of alcohol if you're going to be shooting. Guns, ammunition and alcohol are a deadly combination. You can have two of them, but not three."

"So I can have a gun and ammunition, or I can have a gun and alcohol, or I can have ammo and a drink."

"That's about it," Carl had said, smiling and raising his glass again. "Happy Valentine's Day to my beautiful Belle Starr."

"Who is Belle Starr? Another of your fictional heroines?"

"No, she was a real live woman, although much of what is written about her might be considered fiction. Belle Starr was known as the 'Bandit Queen'. She hung around with the James and Younger gangs and was a notorious outlaw, at least according to Wild West legend. I'll find you a book about her."

I'd assured Carl that a book about Belle Starr was one I'd take the time to read. I did not know then that he'd planted the seed for the name of my own pistol league.

Chapter Six

Sitting between Jim and Pete at my first Skyline membership meeting, I'd not only been approved for membership but had been charged with starting a new group for women shooters.

"It doesn't have to be real serious," the club's president had announced to the packed room. "We're not expecting you to go to other ranges or win trophies. But it must be an active, regular group of women shooters. We agreed some time ago that we would be willing to turn over the range to women only on Wednesday evenings if we could find someone to lead such a group."

My first response had been to say that I was still a newcomer to shooting and was hardly in a position to lead a group of women who would have more experience.

"You won't be in charge of their shooting skills, Mona," Jim had stood up and announced. "A couple of us will volunteer as range officers and will help where necessary. We just need someone to get the group started and we think you're the right person."

I'd looked around at the sea of faces, wanting to say that there must be another woman who could start this group. All eyes in the room had been on me.

"Yes," I'd said, after a protracted silence which I'd known only I would end. "I'll do it."

An enthusiastic applause had rippled around the room with several people turning to me and smiling. Pete had stood up and also offered to serve as a range officer and Jim had leaned in to me, saying it would be easy for me to find women for the group. I'd already had my eye on two women sitting close together on the other side of the clubhouse and decided I would approach them as soon as the meeting was over.

"They're hunters," Pete had said, following my gaze. "They come here to shoot skeet and practice on the rifle range. They're not prospects for your handgun league."

"It's my handgun league already?" I'd asked, nervously.

"Yes, it's yours," Jim had said, clapping me on the shoulder. "We'll help, but you're in charge. I already have a list of all the female members so you can call them."

"Why is it so important to have women shooters that the members are willing to wipe Wednesday evenings off the calendar for everyone else?" I'd asked.

"Because the shooting sports, the Second Amendment and gun ownership are under attack," Jim had replied. "Some of us guys get stereotyped as being trigger-happy and building up arsenals. We're characterized as killers of defenseless animals and that we want to be armed when we take the kids out for a hamburger. Most of it is not true, but a lot of nonsense is put out that is detrimental to responsible gun owners."

I'd still not understood how a handful of women shooting each week at one small range would change such entrenched beliefs.

"We want more women to take up shooting," Pete had explained. "Women hold a lot of power and influence and can help shift public opinion to a more reasonable acceptance of firearms."

"We're afraid, Mona," Jim had continued. "We're afraid we're going to lose our right to own our guns. Handguns are the most vulnerable of all. Many people accept shotguns and rifles because they are used for hunting, but they don't see why anyone needs to own a handgun."

It had been during this discussion that a picture perfect group of women sharpshooters had formed in my mind. Women who could not only defend their person, but their rights! I'd imagined leading a glamorous line-up of female marksmen who could outshoot most men. We'd be fast friends who would learn and grow together. I'd pictured us shooting in unison, with people flocking to the range to watch us shoot.

"We need a name," I'd said. "We need a catchy name that people will remember."

"Try to find six shooters," Pete had said, interrupting my reverie. "Any more than that might be too much to handle."

"Six women will become a nice tight knit group. I'm one. I need five more."

"You've already got me," Jean had said coming up behind me. "I'd better count for something."

"Jean! Of course! You have a place in our group for as long as you want it."

For the past few months, Jean had brought me to the range as her guest and we'd become fast friends. But I'd felt she was growing weary of spending so many hours in Skyline's cold indoor range and I'd known she'd be relieved I was now a member of the club and wouldn't depend upon her to accompany me up here.

"Here's another word of advice, Mona," Jean had added. "Don't say something you might regret later. You don't want to have to wheel me in here and coax me into firing a few shots."

"We may have to wheel you in, Jean," Jim had said. "But I don't see us ever having to persuade you to shoot."

The four of us had laughed as Jim handed me a sheet of paper.

"You have the list with you?" I'd asked, looking down at a short list of names and telephone numbers.

"I've had it for some time. I knew the right person would come along."

"It isn't exactly a long list, is it?"

"You only need four more shooters," Pete had said, looking over my shoulder. "Is Caroline Cargill on the list?"

I'd looked down at the grimy, worn sheet of paper.

"Yes, here she is. Caroline Cargill."

"She joined last month but I didn't see her at tonight's meeting. She's a very good shot."

"Then why didn't you guys ask her to start the women's league? She was a member before me."

"She doesn't have the personality for it," Pete had said. "She's not exactly friendly."

Jim had smiled and rubbed his hand across his face, clearly struggling not to comment on Caroline.

"Well, I bet I can get her to be friendly with me. In fact, she's going to be my first call."

"That's why you're right for this, Mona," Jim had said.

"You can probably forget the others," Jean's eyes had quickly scanned the list. "Betsy Logan is planning to move to Florida. Mary Ellen Moran's husband works second shift and she has to be home with the kids. Ruth Leeberg rarely comes up here anymore, and Cindy DeFabio said she was going to practice shotgun so she could go hunting with her husband in the fall."

"That doesn't leave anyone! If twenty million women own guns in this country, where are they?"

"Change it, Mona," Jim had said. "Change it and we'll love you forever."

A couple of years after I'd joined Skyline I'd been at the monthly meeting and, as always, had presented my report on the Pistol Belles, mentioning that the group was in need of some new shooters. Taking my seat beside Jim, I'd found myself staring at a majestic eight-pointer, the buck's head held high and proud against a backdrop of mountains and sky. The glistening silver belt buckle had not only caught my eye but practically my nose, as its owner had stood so close to me I could have leaned forward and clamped my teeth on it. I learned later that it is not unusual for this man to have a wild effect on women. Although perhaps too heavy-set for his modest height, Carmine Lombardi's broad shoulders, muscular torso, thick black hair, chiseled face and outgoing nature place him firmly at the top of the list of Skyline's hunks.

"I hope I'm not interrupting," Carmine had said, in a voice pitched higher than might be expected.

"Carmine Lombardi," Jim had said, shaking hands enthusiastically. "Good to see you."

I'd put out my hand and Carmine had grabbed it with one twice the size of my own, placing his other hand over it and holding on to me.

"Mona, I need you and you need me," he'd said, looking into my eyes.

I'd paused, taken aback by this unexpected declaration.

"Well, I should say my wife needs you," he'd added.

"You're determined to get Shelby to shoot, aren't you Carmine?" Jim had said, laughing.

"Yes and I've finally realized here is my chance to succeed," Carmine had smiled at me, his deep brown eyes glistening. This man knows how to get what he wants.

"I take it Shelby is your wife," I'd said.

"You've got it, Mona. Shelby is my gorgeous wife and the mother of our four children," Carmine had said, grinning so broadly the only thing he needed to add was to beat his chest in triumph. "She is everything a man could want…"

He'd paused and glanced down at his belt buckle.

"…except for one thing."

I'd looked up at him, curious to know what the one omission from wifely perfection might be.

"She doesn't know the first thing about guns," he'd said, the smile fading from his dark face. I'd wondered how many husbands would consider their wife's lack of firearms knowledge a serious detriment to marital happiness.

"Carmine has brought her up here a couple of times," Jim had explained. "Shelby is a lovely girl, but she can't handle a gun and that's why I've never recommended bringing her into the Pistol Belles. She fumbles her ammo, can't point straight, she just doesn't know the first thing…"

I'd later learned that Shelby also doesn't know the first thing about cooking, but as the potluck component of Wednesday evening is, theoretically, secondary to shooting, we don't make the inability to boil water a disqualifying factor.

"I bet the guns she tried were too big for her," I'd said, jumping to Shelby's defense in an instinctive display of sisterhood I would later regret.

"She's pretty small," Carmine had acknowledged. "But she's shot my .22 Ruger and a little Walther PK380 which isn't heavy at all."

"But the PK380 isn't any good for target practice," I'd said, looking pointedly from Jim to Carmine. They shouldn't need me to tell them that a short barrel doesn't make for accurate distance shooting. "Your wife wouldn't be able to hit a target with it from any kind of distance and the gun's recoil can be very off-putting."

"You're right again, but the Walther is good for personal protection which is why I keep one at home and I would like her to know how to shoot it."

I'd had an image of four small children, two handguns, and a mother who doesn't know one end of the barrel from the other. Carmine had quickly sensed what I was thinking.

"We have a big home set far back from the road. I develop real estate all over the country and I'm constantly away. I would like Shelby to be able to defend herself and our little guys. If nothing else, a woman with a loaded gun will serve as a good deterrent if some creep breaks in."

Skyline members are firmly on the side of the right to self-defense and believe wholeheartedly in gun ownership and the importance of knowing how to load and fire a weapon. Many members encourage their wives, girlfriends, sisters and women friends to learn to shoot. They also teach their children to respect guns and are eager for them to learn as soon as they are old enough. I'd understood that Carmine kept guns at home for protection and wanted his wife to know how to use them because she couldn't depend upon him to be there.

I'd seen Lombardi Realty signs on numerous commercial buildings around the state, but only later learned that the family business operates nationwide. Joining his father's firm while a student at a local college, Carmine had turned a provincial commercial realty firm into a major national developer. Under the Lombardi senior's tutelage and, using the family's relatively meager assets, Carmine had earned the firm and his father, mother and three sisters, millions of dollars developing shopping malls, condominiums, retirement communities and downtown revitalization projects. After meeting Carmine and Shelby, I'd paid more attention to the firm and the family and had come to understand not only the level of their wealth, but their propensity to wear it on their backs. Each member of the family owns a sprawling, ostentatious house, but the flagship property is the palace Carmine and Shelby call home.

"If there are guns in the home, your wife should know how to use them," Jim had said. "It's not a good situation otherwise, particularly with the kids."

"The guns are in a safe in my closet."

"Is it your wife's closet and safe also?" I'd asked.

"She has her own walk-in closet which is twice the size of mine," he'd said, smiling. "But the safe is cemented to the floor in my closet."

"Does your wife know the combination?"

"Yes, we keep cash in it and all her jewelry, so she's always in and out of there."

I'd thought that a good first step in the Lombardi's home security plan might be not to tell strangers where they store their cash and jewelry.

"So you feel because she has access to the guns she should know how to use them?"

"Yes, I hunt but I keep my rifles and shotguns in a gun safe in the basement. My father-in-law and I are the only ones who know the combination. Shelby couldn't get in that safe even if she wanted to. But I keep the handguns in the bedroom where we can get to them at night and I want her to be comfortable with at least one of the guns, if only to know how to load it and point it."

"She'd be a good candidate for a laser," I'd said to Jim. A laser shines a red dot on the actual target.

"Yes, a laser would probably scare the hell out of an intruder and she wouldn't even have to fire," Jim had agreed.

"You guys are thinking right. I want Shelby to know the basics and to be able to fire a gun, but also to learn to treat it with the respect it deserves. She looks at everything as a toy. She thinks the Walther is cute."

"Well it is little," I'd said, laughing. "But no gun is cute. It's a weapon."

"Mona, I can't believe I didn't think of this sooner. Will you please let Shelby join your group?"

"I'm not an instructor and I can't be responsible for someone who doesn't know the first thing about guns. Jim and Pete are our range officers but they can't devote their time to teaching any one person."

"We're there to help everyone," Jim had added.

"But if Shelby takes the NRA Basic Pistol course," I'd continued. "And if she becomes a member of Skyline, I'd be happy for her to join the Pistol Belles."

I'd not known how far from happy I would become.

"Fantastic!" Carmine had cried, grabbing my hand and kissing it. "I'll hire a private instructor to put her through the course and we'll get her Skyline membership. Shelby may be nervous around guns, but she's a joiner. She's in the Junior League, Garden Club, book groups, her father's country club, you name it. She'll be ecstatic when I tell her she's going to be a Pistol Belle!"

Chapter Seven

I rarely check my email early on Thursday's as I don't have to be concerned that one of the Pistol Belles is contacting me to say they won't be shooting that evening, but today I'm concerned that Sandersen may have issued a new directive or there may be an update on the NRA shipment. The only message, however, is from Madison who, as a member of a collegiate shooting team has access to inside news on the shooting sports and often forwards information to me that she thinks I will find of interest. Much of it relates to competition rules and regulations and I generally skim the messages and delete them. But as I don't want to discourage Madison from keeping me informed, I decide to read this morning's message in its entirety and give her the benefit of a response.

I haven't been reading for long when I see a word which I know will forever change the Pistol Belles.

Competition.

Madison tells me that she has learned of a competitive women's handgun league which seeks to add teams from our area. The teams will compete in a formal schedule of matches, including a regular season, play-offs and a championship.

My first reaction is to thank Madison for forwarding the information and explain that this is not a good time for the Pistol Belle's to consider competing as we are all busy and, in fact, Caroline and I are now launching a gun safety program which will be extremely time consuming. Fortunately, after crafting such a response, I read it, delete it and, instead, send a message saying, "Madison, the Pistol Belles will be proud to compete. I will contact the organizers. Thank you!"

I shut down my computer and pace around the kitchen. I have no desire to sit at a machine, and my concern about missing an email from Sandersen has now gone. If the NRA package arrives on time, I will go and meet with him. If not, I will call and tell him we will begin our program tomorrow morning as planned. It's time for some proactive assertive leadership.

Glancing at the kitchen clock, I realize Caroline will not arrive for another hour and I cannot spend the time pacing up and down the sparkling tile floor or polishing counters in which I can already see my reflection. The kitchen, like the rest of the house, is clean. I can't burn up time fixing my make-up or changing my clothes. My appearance has never been a high priority and whatever clothing I put on first thing in the morning generally stays on until bedtime, unless Carl comes home for lunch and rips it off me. The only place for me to be is outside. I can start sprucing up the front lawn and flower beds so they'll be ready for the spring flowers which will soon bloom. Caroline will be on time and the mailman is usually here by noon. I vow to push all thoughts of a competitive team out of my head until I can contact the league tonight. Right now, my focus must be the gun safety program and not the daunting prospect of managing a competitive team. But I can't avoid a quick mental assessment of the Pistol Belles and our individual ability to compete. Madison and Caroline will excel. Jean will show-up and shoot her best. I can train myself to shoot under pressure. But what about Shelby? And what about Christine?

It feels good to be outside in the warm sun. I love to work in our small garden and enjoy the change of seasons. I'm always happy to spruce up our patch of land and take a few minutes to chat with our neighbors. I open the garage door and drag out the cedar bench which we keep out on the lawn in all but the winter months. It will now stay out until November and each day I'll spend a few minutes sitting on this old grey bench peacefully examining the flower beds and watching our neighborhood go by. This tiny piece of the world belongs to Carl and me, and that makes it the most beautiful place on earth.

I wipe down the bench with an old rag and sit down with a sigh. I feel as if I've gone from being pleasantly busy to now being under pressure. I laugh. I haven't been under pressure or had a deadline to meet since I left Abaco. Each day is mine to fill. I report to no-one but myself.

I lift my face to the sky and let my head fall back. The sun warms my skin and I close my eyes. I think about Carl. I think about my mother and father and my brother Jimmy. I must call him. We see so little of each other. I think about Carl's suggestion at breakfast that we plan a trip somewhere. We have time, even with the gun safety program being dropped on me.

Hearing the sound of someone tapping on a window, I lift up my head and look across the street. Seeing nothing, I let my head fall back and close my eyes once more. I hear tapping again and I turn around and look up. Michaela is at her bedroom window, looking down at me with a solemn expression on her pale, pretty face. She pushes up her bedroom window and presses her face against the screen.

"I'm not at school," she says, solemnly.

"I can see that."

"I have a fever."

I wonder if the reason she didn't come over to hang out with Carl last night is because she wasn't well.

"What time is your Mom coming home?" I ask, though I know the answer.

"She says she's coming home early this afternoon."

This is not the response I expected. Early in the afternoon is a very unusual time for Michaela's mother to be home.

"When did you get sick?"

"Yesterday, at school. I came home early and my Mom came home early too."

Now I'm really surprised. Maybe Susan LaVecca is finally putting her daughter ahead of her career.

"That's good," I say, smiling up at her. With her small face flattened on the screen, she looks like a caged animal.

"I'll make you some lunch. I have a friend coming over and I'm going to make sandwiches. I'll bring one to you."

"If I can eat it," she says, plaintively.

I smile. Michaela rarely turns down food.

"I'm sure you can try. You can nibble on it all afternoon. Are you drinking plenty of water?"

"I have iced tea."

"I guess that's fine."

"My Mom is going to make me macaroni and cheese when she gets home."

I smile up at her again. It seems Susan is trying harder than usual to be a mother.

"She's going away tomorrow. She'll be gone the whole weekend. It's for her job."

A defensive tone has crept into the young girl's voice. Michaela knows only too well where she stands in her mother's priorities, yet she never fails to defend her. I could have guessed that Susan's maternal excesses would be of short duration. If she is being solicitous of her daughter now, it is because she'll be gone tomorrow.

"What are you going to do all weekend?" I ask. I know nothing of Michaela's father or of grandparents or family members in the area. Michaela has friends at school but to my knowledge she doesn't stay with them other than for the occasional sleepover.

"I think my Mom's going to talk to you when she gets home," says the thin voice.

It is at moments like this that I have to remind myself that I'm not a mother—and certainly not a single mother—juggling the daily, competing responsibilities of money and a child. It is possible that I just don't understand the hard choices some people have to make every day.

"You can stay with us," I say, looking up and shielding my eyes from the sun. I can barely see Michaela through the grey screen. "Tell your Mom to call me, but it's no problem. We're happy for you to stay."

Michaela's face lights up in a broad grin, as if she's in an orphanage line-up and has finally been chosen for adoption.

I must call Carl. It is only fair to let him know that we are going to have a house guest for the weekend. Michaela is used to spending a couple of evenings a week with us, but this will be the first time she has stayed overnight.

"Make sure your Mom calls school and gets your homework assignments. Carl will want to check where you are with your school work."

"I'll probably be able to go to school tomorrow," she says. "That way I can bring everything home with me."

I wonder how much of Michaela's fever has been caused by the prospect of being home alone. I feel like reporting Susan to Children's Welfare. I don't need to be a parent to know that a thirteen year-old girl should not be left alone for a weekend. Apart from the obvious dangers, she would be lonely and frightened.

I tell Michaela to get back into bed and remind her that I'll bring her lunch. With a little wave, she disappears from the window. I pick up a wide rake and start dragging leaves from under the shrubs. I don't have time to be angry with Susan or question why people so ill-suited to be parents are given the gift of a child. I didn't discover today that life isn't fair or that nature makes its own, often puzzling, choices. Today I must concentrate on gun safety. I must focus on Caroline and Sandersen and not be diverted. Competitions and bad mothers cannot be allowed to weaken my concentration.

I am so intent on staying in the present and completing the satisfying task of clearing debris from the front yard, that I don't notice a car has pulled into the driveway.

"Good morning, Mona," says Caroline through the open window of a low-slung black convertible. "I hope I'm not too early."

I turn with a start and see that not only has Caroline arrived, but the mounds of leaves and twigs I have raked into piles on the lawn indicate that more time has gone by than I realized.

"No, no," I say, tossing down the rake and walking over to her. "I'm just putting my nervous energy to good use."

Caroline steps out of her car, closes the door and leans against the car's shiny exterior. She silently appraises my property and I give her similar scrutiny. I am both approving and fearful of what I see. Caroline's thick black hair is pulled back from her face and held in place by a tortoiseshell headband. Her dark brown eyes are lined in black and her lips are a deep mauve. Sleek black slacks grip her long legs and, in place of her standard black turtleneck, she wears a tight long sleeved shirt of a leopard skin print. Her slender waist is accentuated by a heavy black leather belt. High-heeled, pointed-toe, black leather ankle boots make her look longer and leaner than ever.

Caroline never wears jewelry at the range, but today a long, chunky gold necklace is wrapped around her neck, falling seductively down into the low neckline of her shirt, and enormous gold hoop earrings frame her face. With a black leather jacket slung artfully over her shoulder, Caroline looks every bit the tough, glamorous special agent I could only dream of being. Sadly, my first reaction to seeing this beautiful specimen of female magnificence is to worry about her effect on our principal. Sandersen will not see the sophisticated, serious professional within Caroline's casual, if carefully executed, exterior, but will believe her to be an urban vigilante who will bring guns and anarchy to his idyllic suburban school.

"This is a great neighborhood," says Caroline, still leaning against her gleaming car. "Have you lived here long?"

Caroline and I have been shooting together for several years but have not visited each other's homes. I don't even know where she lives.

"We moved here five years ago right after Carl and I were married."

Caroline looks at me and I see a flash of envy in her dark eyes.

"We love it here," I continue, unable to keep the brightness out of my voice. I feel no inclination to apologize for my good fortune in finding a great guy and a good house. "It's a great location, we're close to the stores and restaurants and the neighbors are friendly."

I don't add that some of them are so friendly they hand over their children. But just as Michaela comes into my mind, I look up and see she has come back to the window and is staring intently at my visitor.

Caroline follows my gaze, looks at Michaela for a moment and then turns to me.

"That's Michaela. We'll be taking lunch to her in a little while."

"This is a friendly neighborhood," she says and waves up at Michaela.

Michaela wiggles her fingers in response and then ducks down out of sight. Caroline turns to me and laughs.

"Did we scare her?"

"I'm sure she's awestruck. You look fabulous, Caroline."

I lead her into the house and switch on the coffee maker which I'd filled earlier. We sit at the counter and I tell her again about the call from Sandersen, my meeting with him yesterday, the number of schools we have to cover, the materials that are expected in the mail by noon today, and our appointment with Sandersen this afternoon. I remind her that our first two sessions are at Lincoln Elementary School tomorrow. Caroline picks up the list of schools and runs her finger down the names.

"Elizabeth Smith. I know Betsy. Dr. James. I worked with him a few years ago. Hank Hollister is a good guy. Carole Lanzetti can be difficult. Smith, Vernon and McDonald are fine."

I look at her in astonishment.

"You know these people?"

"I worked with them on the Junior Science Academy."

"That's fantastic!" I say, feeling my shoulders relax. Gun safety programs, competitions, abandoned children and energetic raking have twisted them into a vice. "But how do you know them all?"

"I don't know them all. I was a bench chemist at Smith Pharma for a long time. A few years ago I helped start a science fair in the elementary schools. We were doing great programs in the middle schools and high schools, but I thought kids needed to be turned on to science when they were younger."

I nod and pour her a cup of coffee, correctly guessing that she drinks it black, no sugar.

"I wrote up a proposal to start the Junior Science Academy right here in this county and our public relations folks got excited about it and we made it happen. I got to know all the principals when I met with them to share ideas for suitable science experiments. You know, the kind of things kids can do without blowing up the school."

Carl is right. I'm finding everything I ask for. Yesterday I fantasized about blowing up Sandersen at Lincoln Elementary and today a woman who knows how to do it is sipping coffee in my kitchen.

"Do you know Dr. Sandersen?" I ask, hopefully.

"No, I knew Mrs. Richards. I guess she must have retired and Sandersen has taken her place. She was terrific, very popular. I'm curious to meet her replacement."

I don't say that I'm nervous about her meeting him.

"It sounds like you started a great project and that you really enjoyed it. Why did you leave the company?"

"They let me go," she says, putting down her cup so forcefully I thought it might break. Carl would give me low marks, as usual, for sensitivity.

"They got rid of a whole bunch us last month. We were working on drugs that weren't profitable or didn't make it through trials. By that time, I was no longer involved in the Junior Science Academy. Because it was such a success, senior management claimed it as their own. The original proposal may still exist showing it was my idea, but just because I thought of it didn't make it mine. I was a grunt on payroll at the time and, when it came time to cut the headcount, it didn't matter that for years I'd done much more than my basic job."

I'm so glad to be out of Abaco.

"So you must be busy job hunting," I say in the most positive tone I can summon. I'm also fishing to find out if Caroline is about to start a new job. She is a perfect partner for the safety program and, selfishly, I don't want to lose her just as soon as we begin.

"In a slow sort of way," she says, pouring another cup of coffee. "I got severance and I have savings. I've never spent what I've earned. I've almost paid off my condo and I paid cash for my car. I have money in retirement and the company added to it as part of the severance."

I've learned more about Caroline in the last five minutes than in the years we've been shooting together.

"That's terrific. You've been smart and now you have some choices."

"I guess I do," she says, hesitatingly, as if she's unsure of her worth. "I would like to find something different, but right now I don't know what that is."

"Gun safety will keep us busy for the next couple of months. I hope that works for you."

"Oh yes," she says, smiling brightly. "I'm really looking forward to getting back into the schools. Kids are so willing to learn."

"Maybe you should be a teacher?"

"I don't have the patience," she says, emphatically. "You know that, Mona, from seeing me on Wednesday nights! I have no patience for one—make that two—of the Pistol Belles."

"You shoot at such a different level than Shelby and Christine. You and Madison are terrific shooters."

I'm tempted to tell her about Madison's email and the chance for the Belles' to compete, but I decide to keep it to myself. I don't want either of us to get diverted from the afternoon's task.

"Thank you for the compliment," she says, with a small smile. "I know if we are a team then I have to accept that Shelby and Christine are doing their best. But you know how frustrated I get and I wish they could either become more proficient or call it a day. Although they at least know how to load and fire a gun and could perhaps protect themselves if needed. Hopefully, they'll never have to find that out and they can just keep bringing their potluck and guns up to Skyline on Wednesday evenings and pretend they're shooters."

I am already indebted to Caroline for helping me with the safety program and I will be obligated to consider her opinion when it comes to the line-up of a competitive team. I decide to shelve this thought and I go over to the refrigerator and take out bread, lettuce, ham and mayonnaise.

"I'll make our sandwiches and then we'll both go over to deliver Michaela's lunch. I have a feeling her fever will soon be gone."

Chapter Eight

Firing a gun is tiring. The effort involved in holding a handgun, keeping your sights steady, your arms straight and standing completely still while holding your breath and firing at a distant target is physically taxing. Muscle control, hand-eye coordination and concentration require real effort and after an hour or two of steady shooting I am always ready to pack up my pistols and head for home.

Today I haven't picked up a gun or fired a single shot, but have simply talked about it. It is three o'clock on Friday afternoon and I am yearning to be home with such intensity that it seems impossible I was eating lunch in my own kitchen just three hours ago. I trudge out of the main entrance of Lincoln Elementary, with an empty tote bag slung over my shoulder, feeling exhausted. Caroline and I taught the first session of the gun safety program this morning and the second this afternoon, and I not only have a new respect for teachers, but for Sandersen himself. Working with young children is as physically and mentally demanding as good shooting.

I struggle to make my way through the throng of children, mothers, strollers, backpacks, babies, fathers, bicycles, dogs, musical instruments and grandparents. The orderly lines of boys and girls which had formed in Sandersen's militarily-controlled corridors prior to the ringing of the bell have been replaced by mayhem just outside the school doors.

"Miss, do you have a gun?" asks a dark haired, wiry boy who whirls around me, stopping in my path so suddenly I almost knock him over.

I'd rehearsed, in advance, the many questions that I thought the children might ask, but I'd failed to consider my answer to the one thing I now realize most of them would want to know.

"No, I don't have a gun," I say, in an instinctive response to not advertise gun ownership. I realize immediately I have presented myself as a fraud and that a child's simple logic would see through such a sham. How could I be qualified to teach about gun safety if I don't own a gun? I should have told this curious little boy that I am the lawful owner of two handguns which are under lock and key in accordance with state law.

"That lady doesn't even have a gun," the boy says, turning and grabbing the arm of a friend who had been bouncing from foot to foot behind him. Bang went my credibility as a knowledgeable and experienced shooter.

I continue to make my way through Lincoln Elementary's teeming humanity, looking in vain for Caroline. It would help if I could fire a couple of shots up in the air to disperse the crowd. Like a schoolgirl, I giggle to myself at the image and quickly resolve not to tell Carl that such a thought ever entered my head.

Suddenly the crowd begins to scatter and the crossing guard blows her whistle, engines reverberate, phones ring, and high pitched voices call out to each other. The adults are making more noise than the children. In a flash almost all of them are gone and, with just a couple of tight cliques of parents remaining, I have a clear view of the front of the school. I see Caroline's dark head resting against the trunk of a massive oak tree close to the school's main entrance. She is sitting on the ground, her back against the trunk and her legs crossed in front of her. Three little girls sit at her feet, gazing up at her in rapt attention. I head across the lawn towards her.

"Mona?" calls a voice behind me. I recognize the high-pitched tone immediately. "Mona, what are you doing here?"

I stop and turn around.

"Shelby," I say, forcing a smile. "It's good to see you."

"What brings you here?" she asks, looking at me quizzically as she bends down to pick up her baby from the stroller. In a pale pink satin jacket, she looks as if she is on her way to cheerleading practice.

"He's beautiful, Shelby," I say, stroking Paolo's cheek. A chubby little girl, with rosy red cheeks and long, curly blonde hair, wraps her arms around Shelby's leg.

"How old is Lulu now?" I ask, bending down to take her hand.

"She's three. And this is Antonio, he's five," says Shelby, now tugging on the hand of small boy.

"You were in my class this morning," I say, turning to the solemn little boy. Antonio stares at me with a blank expression.

Shelby is looking around anxiously, murmuring aloud that she doesn't know where Izzy has got to. I follow her gaze to the oak tree and watch as Caroline says goodbye to the girls and then heads toward us with a look on her face which I could, without too much exaggeration, describe as joy. It was obvious this morning that Caroline enjoyed teaching our younger group, but she was fantastic with the older grades this afternoon. I was little more than an observer as she talked to the class, smiled at both boys and girls, listened patiently to their questions and made sure each student received her attention.

"Is that Caroline?" asks Shelby, the quizzical look she'd given me now turning to bewilderment.

"Mommy, Mommy," cries a girl running toward us. I realize now that Izzy is one of the members of Caroline's little fan club.

"Izzy, baby, I didn't know where you were," says Shelby, reaching down to hug the girl. "Don't let Mommy lose you."

"Hi, Shelby," says Caroline curtly. The fulfilled teacher seems to have vanished.

Shelby adjusts her grip on Paolo and pushes him up onto her shoulder, simultaneously reaching down and unclenching Lulu's hands off her leg.

"Isabella, hold your sister's hand," she says pushing Lulu toward her oldest child. "Tony, where are you? Oh, there you are."

Izzy is staring up at Caroline, ignoring her mother's request to take charge of her baby sister. I grab Lulu's hand and she takes a step closer to me. Isabella moves toward Caroline and tentatively reaches for her hand. Caroline grasps it and beams around at us. The gifted teacher has returned. Shelby again shifts Paolo on her shoulder and, with her spare hand, grabs Antonio. Her head is spinning around looking at each of us in turn.

"What are you guys doing here?" she cries, moving in to us as if Caroline and I might take off with two of her children. It occurs to me that if our intention was to kidnap them, Shelby would be so encumbered with Paolo and Antonio that saving her two daughters would be almost impossible. Keeping four young children safe from harm is an enormous burden. Not yet thirty years old, Shelby has taken on more responsibility than I have done in fifty years.

"We are the proud teachers of the county's new gun safety program," I say, smiling at her. "We began here today. Tony was in this morning's session and Izzy was with us this afternoon."

"Bang, bang!" shouts Tony, suddenly springing to life. He makes a gun out of his fist and forefingers and points it at Lulu. "Bang, bang you're dead!"

"Oh, my goodness, he'll get suspended," I say. The ban on guns on school property extends to make-believe weapons. "I swear he did not learn this today."

"Don't worry," says Shelby, laughing. "He does it all the time. He goes wild when Carmine and Daddy go hunting. He cries because he can't go with them. Carmine's already checked out the minimum age for the hunter education program."

"Bang, bang!" he shouts again, circling our group at great speed and firing with both fists.

"Not now, Tony," I say, grabbing his hand and anxiously scanning the area for Sandersen or a disapproving parent. Our gun safety program will be cancelled if anyone believes this is the result. As I grapple with Antonio, I wonder if Shelby will be annoyed that I have disciplined her son. When I recently told a young bully in our neighborhood that the next time I saw him push a smaller child to the ground I would come and do the same to him, the mother had knocked on my door to tell me she knew I'd threatened her son and, next time, would report me. I'd laughed and closed the door in her face, although Carl says I slammed it so hard he spilled wine on his shirt. Fortunately, Shelby seems to appreciate my interference with her little boy.

"That's right, Antonio, listen to Mrs. Milton. You can play cowboys and Indians at home but not here."

"And you, Isabella," Shelby continues. "You listen to Ms. Cargill."

Isabella is still clutching Caroline's hand and, amazingly, Shelby smiles at them both. Isabella closely resembles her mother and is a bright, outgoing child who was the first to put up her hand to ask questions.

"Ms. Cargill and Mrs. Milton know a lot about guns and whatever they told you today will be correct."

Shelby is being remarkably respectful and generous in her treatment of us.

"I can't believe you guys are teaching this program! I saw the flyer in the kid's backpacks yesterday and thought the police would be teaching it. It's awesome that it's you!"

"Dr. Sandersen called me last week and dropped it in my lap. I barely had time to prepare. Fortunately, Caroline is working with me. We'll be in every elementary school in the county over the next few weeks."

I don't mention that I'd also tried to involve Madison and Jean and that the only two Pistol Belles I hadn't asked were Christine and Shelby.

"Can I come back next week?" Shelby asks, avoiding my eyes as she puts Paolo back in his stroller and motions to the three older children to follow her. Caroline and I hold onto Isabella and Antonio and, with Lulu again clutching her mother's leg, we all walk behind Shelby.

"Are you ready to come back?" I say to her shimmering pink back.

Sandersen suddenly appears outside the school doors and Caroline waves to him and he nods and smiles at her. We'd met with him earlier this morning and he and Caroline had miraculously found an instant rapport.

"I need to come back," says Shelby, stopping at her enormous vehicle and turning to me. "It's the only break I get!"

She starts wrestling Paolo into his car seat. Antonio pulls away from me and climbs into the back as Lulu and Isabella elbow each other to get in. I can understand how much Shelby must enjoy coming to the range alone every Wednesday.

"Yes, you can come next Wednesday," I say. "But don't bring the Baby Glock. It's no good for target shooting. You and Carmine can practice with it at other times."

She smiles at me. "Thank you Mona, I know I was out of line. I don't want to make excuses but I'm so upset about Daddy."

"How is he?"

"He went to another oncologist this week," she says, her eyes immediately filling with tears. "It's the fourth opinion he's had, but they all say the same thing."

I wait while she fumbles for a tissue. Lulu and Antonio are fighting in the back of the van and Caroline steps over to them and starts to straighten their tangled seat belts.

"Daddy has lung cancer. They've given him a few months, maybe six. I only know this because my stepmother, Karen, told me. He's pretending he's going to make a full recovery because he daren't tell me how bad it is. Karen thinks it's wrong that he's trying to keep it from me."

"I'm sorry, Shelby, this must be so hard for you. But, at least it sounds as if you can depend on Karen."

"My stepmother is tough. She's one of those strong types. They've been married a while and she's good to him. He's been very good to her, of course. I don't know what's going to happen when he dies. But I can't think about that right now. I just have to spend as much time with him as I can."

"Let me know if there's anything I can do."

"Keep me in the Pistol Belles! I know I don't always get along with everyone," she says, looking at Caroline who, as if by magic, has all four children quieted and buckled into their seats. "But I really need you guys. Wednesday night is my only release."

I think of the team of skilled, disciplined shooters we must field if we are to hold our own in a competitive league. With four children and a dying father, Shelby does not have the time to put in the amount of practice it would take to improve her shooting. And, like Christine, it remains to be seen if her poor performance is based on fear or lack of discipline or if she does not have the ability to achieve the level of marksmanship we need. But one thing I know for sure is that we are going to have to find out.

Chapter Nine

Of the eight students in the Skyline clubhouse on the first day of Basic Pistol class, only two of us were women. In my yet to be dispelled belief that female solidarity would be necessary for survival in the male-dominated world of guns, I'd grabbed the seat at the table next to the other woman. I'd been unaware of the generally positive attitude male shooters hold toward their female counterparts and that, with few exceptions, men welcome women into the shooting sports with open and fairly uncomplicated arms.

"Marksmanship is a skill at which women can excel," said Jim Mackenzie, our instructor for the first segment of the class, nodding to me and my neighbor.

The six men sitting around the wide table, as well as a second instructor who would be introduced to us as Pete Dexter, had turned to look at us. I'd smiled and tapped my neighbor's arm in sisterly affirmation of our good sense in signing up for something for which we might have the aptitude. The woman was looking down at the table and didn't look up, but her eyes darted sideways and I knew my friendly gesture had not gone unnoticed. Christine Jones would later tell me that right before I burst into the clubhouse and sat down next to her, she'd decided to leave the class. The only thing that had stopped her was her discomfort at being watched by the men as she walked out. She'd thought of escaping in the diversion my arrival created, and the only thing that prevented her from doing so was that I had immediately and loudly walked across the room and seated myself next to her.

Jean may call me a do-gooder, but had I known what hard work Christine would become I would have not only encouraged her departure but held the clubhouse door open for her. I had enrolled in Basic Pistol so that I could learn about handguns, and was expecting to have fun doing it. There was to be no such fun as far as Christine was concerned. She was a frightened woman who was taking the class because she needed to be able to protect herself. Four years later she is still struggling to achieve basic shooting proficiency, and yet my regard for her has grown. Christine may not have the aptitude Jim ascribed to us both that morning, but she has worked hard to learn how to defend herself.

Jim had started our first session with the three fundamental gun safety rules: always keep the gun pointed in a safe direction; always keep your finger off the trigger until ready to shoot; and always keep the gun unloaded until ready to use.

"Treat every gun as if it's loaded," he'd said, adding that most gun accidents are caused by carelessness or ignorance, or a deadly combination of the two.

We learned that a .22 bullet can travel a mile and a shooter must always know what lies beyond their target.

"You can never take a bullet back," cautioned our instructor, a phrase I remember every time I fire a gun.

We were told that guns must be stored so they are not accessible to unauthorized persons and that ammunition must be the correct type for any particular gun and should be stored separately. Using alcohol or drugs before or during shooting is not recommended and, in fact, will result in expulsion from Skyline and most other ranges. Jim reminded us that the Basic Pistol class isn't designed to teach students how to be gangsters, or cowboys, or criminals, or any other imaginary hero, but would educate us about the parts of a pistol, how to operate them, the difference between revolvers and semi-automatics, and single- and double-action. We would learn about cartridges and understand that a bullet is just one component of the cartridge.

"You don't load a bullet in a gun. You load a cartridge and the bullet is fired."

We would learn how to clean a gun, how to determine our dominant eye, and how to stand correctly and control our breathing so that we could become proficient shooters. Becoming good or great would be entirely up to us.

Just as it seemed our entire class time would be spent sitting at a table in the clubhouse, we were told that after lunch we'd go into the indoor range to shoot and that a wide variety of handguns would be available for us to try. The six men in the class, all of whom had announced during our introductions that they knew a lot about guns, let out whoops of joy.

"Finally, I'll get my hands on a 9mm…"

"Can't wait to try a Magnum…"

"I shot in the military, but it's been a while…"

Lunch had been served and Christine got up quietly from the table, bringing a small sandwich on a paper plate back to her seat. I'd grabbed some food and resumed my place beside her.

"Well, guys," I'd said, looking around the table. "My total shooting experience is a few rounds out of a Smith & Wesson revolver, and that's been in the past two weeks. I really have no idea what I'm doing."

I'd looked at Christine, hoping my admission of inexperience would draw her out. She had not asked any questions all morning, but had sat with her head down studiously taking notes in the margins of her workbook.

Between mouthfuls of tuna and ham sandwiches, the guys in the class had all murmured encouraging words reminding me that everyone is a beginner at some time and that I'll soon get the hang of it.

"Women are naturally intimidated by guns," Pete Dexter had said. "But it's this innate fear that makes women excellent students. Women want to learn properly and they never pretend they know more about guns than they really do."

His eyes had traveled slowly around the table looking at the men.

"And they are usually more patient than men and willing to put in the practice," he'd added. "Women can be outstanding shots."

I'd smiled at Pete and touched Christine's arm again.

"Sounds like we're in the right place," I'd said and she'd looked up at me for the first time and then quickly gone back to picking apart her sandwich.

That afternoon we'd spent two hours in the range taking shots. Several club members had come in to serve as volunteer instructors, bringing their own handguns in for us to use. Each student was paired with an experienced shooter who'd watched as we loaded a gun, took up position, pointed down range, lined up our sights, put our finger on the trigger, and fired. It had been both educational and exhilarating. I'd loved it.

After the class was over, we were told to return the following Saturday so we could go over the material, spend two more hours in the range and complete a written test. All the men groaned. I'd laughed and picked up my handbook, thanked Jim and Pete for their time and patience and called a general farewell to the other students. Heading for the door, I'd felt someone behind me.

"Can I walk out with you?" Christine asked, practically stepping on my heels.

"Of course," I'd said, holding the door open for her. "Wasn't that exhausting? But it was wonderful, too! I can't wait to come back next week."

"We have to take a test," she'd said.

"Yes, but if we study the material we'll pass. It's like taking the written driving test."

"You're right, I guess. I can handle the studying and the test. It's the actual shooting I don't think I'll ever manage."

I'd noticed that Christine had fired very few shots and that several club members had taken turns working with her.

"Are you learning to shoot for a hobby?" I'd asked, already guessing that this was not the case.

"No, I'm not here for a hobby. I'm here for one reason only. I need to be able to defend myself."

"And my daughter," she'd added. "But I'm not sure I'm going to go through with it. I don't know if I'll buy a gun, but I promised myself I would learn to shoot."

"Do you live in a bad neighborhood?"

"No, I live in Hillside Garden Apartments. There's no trouble there."

I'd later learned that Christine lived in a one-bedroom apartment, sharing the bedroom with her eleven year-old daughter.

"I have a restraining order against my husband," Christine added. "He moved out last year and I'm afraid of him. I'm scared for me and my daughter."

She'd paused and looked at me.

"You seem like a strong woman and I'm sure you don't have these kinds of problems. I'm embarrassed, to tell you the truth."

She'd stopped by an old Chevrolet with a rear door which did not match the rest of the car. Christine hadn't said a word all day but now it seemed she'd found her voice.

"I keep hearing that restraining orders don't work and that women get them from the courts but their husbands or boyfriends come back and attack them anyway. What's a piece of paper going to do in the middle of the night when a man is out to get you?"

I'd looked at her. I had no answer.

"And it's you he's after, no-one else! It's not some random situation where you got unlucky. If a man's determined to get you, and only you, what's going to stop him?"

"A gun, maybe?"

"Right," she'd said, nodding her head vigorously in agreement. "Which is why I may get one whether I want to or not."

"It's only going to help you if you know how to use it properly and that's why you're taking the class."

I didn't add that for a gun to be of any use, you have to be able to get to it and load it before your attacker gets to you.

"It might scare him. That's really what I'm thinking. If I had a gun I could handle, I could at least scare the heck out of him."

"You've got your daughter to worry about. You'd have to be extremely careful."

"Of course I would!" she'd exclaimed, clearly upset at my suggestion that she might not take adequate precautions in keeping the gun out of her daughter's hands. "I'm used to being careful. I have to be careful right now. That's how we live. I look around corners and jump up in the night when I hear the slightest noise. I often can't sleep because I think he might come and attack me."

Christine had started to cry.

"And I'm deathly afraid he'll take Sophie."

I'd put my arm around her shaking shoulders and pulled this lonely, frightened stranger towards me.

"I don't know if I can do this," she'd continued, pulling away from me and dragging a ragged tissue out of her jacket pocket. "Maybe I'm just pretending I could be the kind of woman who pulls out a gun and points it at her own husband."

"And fires it," I'd added.

Suddenly I'd felt Carl looking over my shoulder, gently reminding me not to be so blunt.

"I can't even think about that," Christine had said. "Except in my dreams. But, even then, I'd be killing Sophie's father. She still thinks he's going to come back and love us again."

"Well, I'm sure you'll never need to shoot him or anyone else. You just need to know that you can protect yourself and your daughter if needed. Scaring him might be all you'll ever need to do."

Christine had opened her car door and flopped into the driver's seat. The upholstery was torn and spongy material was sticking out.

"Would you like me to pick you up next week?" I'd asked her, ignoring the voice in my head which told me I should neither encourage nor discourage this fragile woman.

Her smile had given me her answer. She'd fumbled for a notepad in the glove compartment, written down her address and phone number and, with shaking hands, handed it to me through the open window.

"Thank you, Mona, you're a nice person. If you pick me up, it will stop me from changing my mind. I'll be ready and waiting."

Chapter Ten

My mother's blue and white china plates look crisp against the bright yellow tablecloth. I've put out chunky tumblers for orange juice along with blue and white striped mugs, which miraculously survived the years with Bob, for coffee. The heavy sterling silver cutlery is from a canteen Carl claimed in his divorce, a surprising item for him to own as although he loves his three wholesome meals a day, he cares little about their presentation. I know he will take great care preparing our brunch this morning, but if I wasn't paying similarly close attention to the table, he would be just as happy if we ate off paper plates at the counter.

I take white linen napkins out of a drawer in the kitchen, roll them tightly and push them through silver napkin rings. A clear glass vase, already filled with water, sits in the center of the table and I go outside to clip a few branches of forsythia. The table is bright blue, yellow and white and is a welcome burst of spring. My mother's old china looks comfortably at home in its contemporary setting. Given to my parents as a wedding present over fifty-years ago, I use it a great deal more than my mother did in the forty-five years it sat in her gleaming breakfront. She believed in keeping the good stuff for special occasions as, once broken, they would not be replaced.

The shower door slams shut and a rush of water cascades from the power faucet. Carl has risen. I go to the refrigerator and take out eggs, butter, bacon, mushrooms, milk, Swiss cheese, whole wheat bread and two green peppers. Carl is going to make an omelet and he will come down scrubbed like a surgeon, ready to step into a sluiced kitchen and make the first incision. My husband does not always expect me to provide such high level kitchen help, but I want to ensure that cooking remains a pleasurable experience for him. His willingness to play the role of master chef occasionally gives me a break from cooking. Self-interest lies just below the surface of many loving actions.

"I'm going to wake up Michaela," I say, as Carl and I rush past each other on the stairs. He stops to kiss me and I feel his smooth chin. "Nice shave this morning, honey, you're going to drive us girls wild."

"I've already got one wild woman," he says, pulling me close. "I couldn't handle any more."

"That's good, especially as one is thirteen-years old and the other is a man-hater."

"What time is Caroline coming? Should I get my armor out?"

"In half-an-hour, but you won't need protection," I say, laughing. "You can handle her. But, remember, she's a very good cook, at least if the food she brings on Wednesday evenings is an indicator."

I knock on the door of the spare bedroom and slowly push it open. The shades are drawn and the south facing room is still dark at this time in the morning. Michaela is completely hidden under the quilt but as I gently nudge her, her tousled head slowly comes up from beneath the covers.

"Time to get up, Michaela. My friend is coming for brunch and I'd like you to be up and ready to eat with us."

"Do I have to?" she asks, retreating back under the twisted covers.

"Yes, you do," I say, stroking her head. "Carl is making his special omelet. Be downstairs in half an hour."

"Half an hour! Really?"

"Yes, really," I say, pulling open the drapes. "Take a shower. It will wake you up."

"Ok, five more minutes," her voice is muffled. I pull back the covers and smile. Michaela's flannel teddy bear print pajamas remind me she is still a child.

"The lady you met a few days ago is coming," I say, knowing that the mention of Caroline will get Michaela out of bed.

As if on cue, she sits up.

"What should I wear?"

"Jeans and a clean shirt."

I leave the room, close the door behind me and go back downstairs.

"How is our house guest?" asks Carl, briskly chopping mushrooms.

"She's getting up. As soon as I reminded her that Caroline was coming, she perked up. She's really a lovely girl."

"I agree. Maybe negligent parents make good kids. The children have no choice but to be responsible."

"I'm still amazed at Susan's laxity. Michaela knows us well by now but we could be running a child pornography ring for all her mother knows."

"Or we could keep guns in the house," says Carl, pushing his knife down with both hands on a whole onion, as if he chopped dozens every day.

"I've made no secret of my guns," I say, defensively. "Michaela has seen me come home from the club carrying my pistol cases on numerous occasions.

"But you don't tell her what's in those cases, nor do you open them in front of her."

"No, of course I don't! I wait until she's gone home before I clean them or open up the safe. I don't need to wave a gun under her nose."

"If you played tennis would you show her your racquets?"

I look at Carl and recognize the smile on his face. He is setting up the conversational ping pong at which he excels.

"If she was interested in tennis, I'm sure I would show her my racquets," I say, swatting my right hand in a neat volley.

Carl laughs. "Maybe she's interested in guns."

"When she's a little older, I'll ask her that question. And if she's interested in learning to shoot she can join the Junior Rifle Club."

"If her mother gives permission," Carl reminds us both.

"Right, there is that issue," I say, taking a seat at the kitchen counter. "I honestly don't know if Michaela has figured out that I go shooting on Wednesdays. Even if she has, she wouldn't tell her mother because she wouldn't want to be forbidden from coming here. Perhaps it's better if it's all left unsaid."

"Well, Michaela is going to get a real taste of gun women today. If the reason for this brunch is for you and Caroline to work on the schedule for the safety program, then guns are going to be all over the table."

"No, they're—"

"Conversationally, that is."

"Yes, Caroline and I have to figure out how we can get around all the schools. We'll make calls and send emails to the principals tomorrow and then report back to Sandersen's office on Tuesday."

"I'm impressed, Mona, with how you've taken this on. It's a big responsibility."

"Thank you, honey," I say, flashing a fake smile. "You know how I resist responsibility."

"You don't resist it. When a responsibility is dealt you, you accept it with grace and determination. You just don't seek it out."

"Responsibility seems to be finding me these days," I say, wryly. "I have to talk to Caroline about the competitive league, but I don't want to do that today. I need time to think about it."

"I thought you'd already agreed to do it."

"I emailed Madison to tell her that we would do it, but I haven't contacted the organizers or discussed it with anyone else."

It occurs to me that Caroline may already have heard from Madison about our chance to join the competitive women's league. They are friendly at the range on Wednesday evenings, but I don't know how much they communicate outside the Pistol Belles.

"I really don't want to discuss it with her until I have more information."

"I'm not trying to bug you this morning. I'm sorry, you have a lot going on," says Carl, stroking my back.

"I'm starving. I would normally have eaten breakfast two hours ago."

Michaela is making a lot of noise going between the bedroom and the guest bathroom. I can't imagine why it takes so many trips for one small person to get showered and dressed, and for a slender girl she is remarkably heavy-footed. I look up at the ceiling and roll my eyes in Carl's direction.

"Michaela," he calls loudly. "Try not to come through the ceiling. We'd prefer it if you use the stairs."

I hear her giggle and then walk more quietly between the two rooms. She must be on tip toes. Carl covers the bowls containing the chopped ingredients and we go into the living room and sit on the couch. Within moments, Michaela thumps down the stairs. She is wearing dark blue low-rider jeans, a long, flimsy shirt and beige suede boots.

"Oh, the table is really pretty!" she exclaims, walking around it. "Everything in your house is so nice."

On my brief visits next door, I'd noticed that home décor isn't one of Susan's interests. But maybe she can't afford it, or hasn't heard of paint and garage sales.

"Thank you for letting me sleep over this weekend. My Mom kept hoping she wouldn't have to go away, but then she had no choice."

I don't know if this is true or if it's Michaela's way of dealing with the hard fact that her mother made plans for her care only at the last minute.

"Your Mom works hard and has a demanding job," says Carl. "We're happy to help out whenever we can. You're always welcome here."

"OK," says Michaela, smiling at us both.

"But you'd be more welcome right now if you'd come in the kitchen and beat up some eggs," says Carl, jumping up from the couch. Michaela trudges behind him in the same downtrodden manner she assumes when Carl orders her to do her homework. I can't help but think that she enjoys adopting the manner of a child with a bossy, overly-involved parent.

It is another fine, sunny morning and I open the front door to let the light shine through the glass storm door. Suddenly I see Caroline standing there, her hand raised ready to tap on the glass. She is wearing a thin white cotton shirt which sits just above a pair of dark blue low-rider jeans. On her feet is a pair of high-heeled cream leather boots. The similarity between her outfit and Michaela's is startling. Balanced on one hand is a ceramic pie dish covered with a linen cloth.

"Come in!" I say, hurriedly pushing open the door. "You didn't have to bring a dish, but I guess the potluck habit is a hard one to drop."

"Good morning, Mona," she says, smiling broadly as she steps inside. "Should I put this in the kitchen?"

"All contributions welcome," says Carl, coming out from behind the counter. He takes the dish from her with one hand and shakes her hand with the other.

"Carl Milton," he announces, "Mmm, still warm."

"I just took it out of the oven," says Caroline. "It's a quiche."

"Your own crust too, I bet," says Carl, as if he's a regular on the pastry-making circuit. "I hear you're an excellent cook."

"And this is Michaela," I say. "You'll remember you met her the other day."

"Of course I remember," says Caroline, smiling at Michaela who, once again, is struck dumb by Caroline's presence. "I hope you're feeling better."

"Yes, thank you," says Michaela, her voice a few notches higher than usual.

"Is it too early for Mimosas?" asks Carl, pulling a bottle of Champagne out of the refrigerator and deftly unscrewing the wire from around the cork.

"I think you've just answered your own question," I say. "I'll have orange juice."

"I'll join you," says Caroline, smiling at Carl. "But just one. Mona and I have work to do."

Michaela is staring at her.

"If Mona says it's alright," Caroline says, leaning in to her as one chum to another. "You can have a sip of my Mimosa."

Guns, alcohol and a minor. If Susan hears about this, poor Michaela won't be allowed here ever again. Perhaps Caroline could be her new *de facto* foster parent. Between the students at Lincoln Elementary and her easy rapport with Michaela, I've discovered she is surprisingly good with children.

Carl has worked the cork out of the bottle and he pours orange juice into each of the four glasses and then tops two of them up with Champagne, handing one to Caroline and keeping one for himself. I pass a juice to Michaela and take the other.

"Don't try the Mimosa until after you've eaten something," I say.

I get everyone seated and help Carl bring the food to the table.

"This is a step-up from our potluck at Skyline," says Caroline, surveying the table. "Your colors are just beautiful."

"Thank you. Carl's in charge of food today, and I'm in charge of everything else."

We all laugh and start to eat. Carl suddenly puts down his fork and raises his glass. The three of us follow his lead.

"Here's to a beautiful morning with three lovely ladies at our table."

I wince inwardly, wondering if Caroline will dislike being referred to as a lady, but she is smiling at him.

"Here's to Michaela, our charming neighbor and weekend guest," Carl continues.

"Michaela!" the three of us say.

"Here's to Caroline, a Pistol Belle and a new guest in our home."

"Caroline!" Carl and I say.

"Caroline," whispers Michaela, and then adds even more quietly. "What's a Pistol—?"

"Here's to my beautiful wife, Mona," Carl says quickly. "Without whom my life would be a dull wasteland."

"Mona!" the three of them shout.

"And here's to Carl, our cook today and my love forever," I say, softly.

"Carl!"

I take a sip of orange juice and put the glass down beside my plate. Carl keeps his glass up in the air and I realize he isn't finished with his toasts.

"And here's to the gun safety program and to the Pistol Belles' success in competition," says Carl. He puts down his glass and picks up his fork. Michaela copies him and begins to eat. Caroline takes a long sip of her Mimosa and then turns to me. I look at Carl and laugh out loud.

"Caroline," I say, turning pointedly away from Carl and toward her. "We have an exciting opportunity for the Pistol Belles."

Chapter Eleven

"The property belongs to John Williams," says Phil Johnson, Skyline's most senior member. "It's been in the Williams' family for generations."

"Then how come the Township engineers are over there sniffing around, taking photographs and checking measurements?" asks Bob Finch, the club's ornery, combative president. "If it's private property why are they trespassing?"

"I hate to keep reminding you," says Phil, enjoying his unofficial position as the club's historian. "But it's my understanding that John Williams agreed a long time ago that when he passes the property will go to the town."

It's the monthly membership meeting and we are huddled together in the crowded clubhouse. Of the six hundred members, only about one hundred men and no more than fifteen women regularly attend the meetings. Such low attendance shows a certain lack of interest on the part of most members, but no-one complains as greater attendance would put us in violation of the fire code. When you're a private shooting facility, you strenuously avoid trouble with the local authorities.

The ownership of the five acre lot which lies adjacent to the club's outdoor range is, once again, a topic of discussion.

"If Mr. Williams leaves the property to the town, we'll have a problem," continues Bob Finch. "But fortunately he isn't elderly, at least not by my standards, and will be around for a good while."

"That's not what I hear," says a voice from the back of the room. "I've heard it on good authority that he's very sick with cancer."

Phil Johnson turns to look at the speaker in order to determine the veracity of his information, and then turns back shaking his head. Phil deals with facts and not gossip. As tempted as I am, I decide not to add that I also have it on good authority that John Williams is, indeed, dying of cancer. As the information was given to me by his daughter, I am not going to announce it as a news item at an open membership meeting. Neither do I intend to pass the information on in private to the club's president. Carmine and Shelby are members of Skyline and may decide if they want to discuss John Williams' health—and whether or not the land will be bequeathed to the town—with the club's officers. It seems extremely unlikely that either of them would discuss Williams' estate plans outside the family.

"If it's true that John Williams is sick, we must get him to change his mind," says Bob. "The minute the town gets ownership of that land, they'll try to shut us down."

"There's always stuff in the newspaper about the recreation leagues needing more fields for soccer and baseball," says another member. "They'll take one look at that nice flat five acre field and before you know it they'll be up here installing goal posts and a home plate."

"The property has good drainage," says Phil. "It would be ideal for sports."

"Then it will be us going down the drain," shouts a man, as hollow laughter erupts around the room.

"We need to own as much land around us as we can," says a new member, explaining that he has recently relocated from out of state and believes the club's existing property is not sufficient to stave off challenges to its existence.

"But Skyline has been here for forty years," says Caroline. "The town can't just decide to shut us down."

I cross my arms and legs and hunker down in my chair, reminding myself to keep my mouth firmly closed. I don't want Carmine or Shelby to hear that I was part of a conversation about her father's property. They would assume I'd told the club that John Williams is dying.

"The town can't shut us down without cause," says Bob. "But give them a year and they'd find a reason. If they inherit the property they'll zone it for recreation and then declare that a shooting club—with an outdoor rifle range to boot—is a hazard."

"Then we'll argue that they should have thought about that before they put a ball field up here," says a gruff voice from behind me.

"That would be the reasonable and fair way to do things," our new member adds. "But I've moved around a lot and I've seen more than one town give approval for a new facility to be built next to an existing shooting range and the next thing that happens is they shut down the range on the basis that it creates a danger. What was obvious is that the objective all along was to shut down the firing range."

"Somebody needs to throw the Second Amendment at those morons."

"The Second Amendment doesn't say anything about having a dedicated facility in which to fire your weapon."

"More is the pity."

"Pretty soon there'll be nowhere to shoot."

"There'll be no guns either, at least not for law-abiding citizens!"

"Is playing baseball and soccer more important than knowing how to shoot a gun?"

"Quiet!" Bob calls, and the room goes silent. "Let's not get carried away. We're fine right now and we get along well with the Mayor and most council members. In October a couple of them were here at the outdoor range practicing with their shotguns before the opening of hunting season. We don't need to turn them into enemies."

"The Mayor and Council are not the problem," says Pete. He is standing next to me and I'm happy to hear him speak. Pete always manages to bring a discussion back to reality. "You have to look at things from their point of view. Council has been under pressure for years from parents and new people in town to close down this club. And there is a genuine need for more sports fields as many kids, girls and boys, play ball year-round."

"That's not necessarily a good thing," says Phil Johnson who, like Jean, grew up roaming the fields around town shooting rabbits, squirrels and groundhogs with a .410 shotgun. Phil loves to talk about how he legally took his shotgun to school and would leave it in his locker so he could hunt on the way home. "Kids need to be out roaming, that's how you learn."

Numerous heads bob up and down.

"And the way things are going in this country," he continues, "young folk should learn how to handle a gun. They may need to hunt for food one day."

More heads nod.

"That's right! Parents would do their kids a service if they made them learn to shoot."

"Can you shoot a pizza? That's all my kids ever eat."

"Alright, that's enough," Bob calls out to quiet the laughter.

"We need to expand the Junior Rifle program," says a woman sitting in the front row. "We should encourage kids to choose shooting over kicking a ball around. The more kids we get involved, the more supporters we'll have in town."

"Hear, hear."

"And the Women's League," Caroline shouts out. "We need more women shooters. We can train those who have the aptitude, but we're in serious need of women who can shoot competitively."

Caroline doesn't look at me. This is her way of telling me, in the safety of a public forum, that we must find new shooters if we are going to field a competitive team. Our brunch last weekend had got off to such a convivial start, but had later been spoiled for me by Caroline's insistence that neither Shelby nor Christine could compete. Carl had realized his colossal error in bringing up the subject of the competitive team and had worked extra hard to maintain a festive mood. He'd steered the conversation to food and let Caroline assume the role of expert. She'd relayed the vast numbers of ways to cook eggs, and he'd even acknowledged that his much-loved fried egg was the unhealthiest choice.

Later, Michaela had gone upstairs to do her homework and Caroline and I had concentrated on the safety program. She'd clearly been itching to get to the topic of the competitive league and, as soon as we'd come up with a safety program schedule she'd asked me about it. I'd described how Madison had passed the information to me and I'd, in turn, assured her that the Pistol Belles would compete, but I hadn't done anything more. Caroline had said she would be happy to take the lead and that she could always get the information from Madison. I'd thought that trying to wrestle the leadership of the Pistol Belles away from me while enjoying my hospitality was a bit much. She'd been quick to notice that I was becoming upset and, by the time she left she'd made an effort to get us back to our usual respectful friendliness. As soon as the door had closed behind her, Carl had thrown his hands up in the air.

"Mona, shoot me!"

"Carl, honey, don't ask me to shoot you," I'd said, reaching up and pulling his hands down into mine. "I'll decide when it's time to put you down like a rabid dog."

He'd winced and then smiled at me.

"And I will also be the one who decides when it's the right time to speak up about something that is my business," I'd added.

Now just a few days later, Caroline has hinted to the Skyline members about the Belles becoming a competitive team and I'm still not ready for to discuss it. I need more information on the league's timetable and on the skill level of the other teams. If Caroline makes a formal announcement now, the members will endorse the idea and I'll have no choice but to proceed. I'll be boxed in before I've considered my next steps. I am in no doubt that we'll join the league. My problem is figuring out how to be loyal to all the Pistol Belles.

"Bringing in more women should be a priority of the club," says Pete, with a nod to Caroline. "Women hold the key to our Second Amendment rights."

"Don't forget we have a waiting list," says Steve Smith who handles membership. "There are a few women far down on the list. Do you want me to move them up to the top?"

A number of heads around the room nod in answer.

"Tell them to come to the women's night as guests and get them started," says a member.

It's time for me to jump in.

"You have to be a full member of Skyline in order to join the Pistol Belles," I say, using our name to remind the members that we are a formal group and not just a hodge-podge of women who show up on Wednesday's with a covered dish and a handgun. "First you must complete the Basic Pistol class. Then you must join the club, and then you can sign up for the Wednesday night women's league. There is an order to it. It's not as simple as just showing up."

I am relieved to hear a general murmur of agreement that our present policy should continue. I don't want to be responsible for a group of shooters I don't even know.

"But let's speed up the process by putting women to the top of the list," says one of the club's officers.

"Here we go. Affirmative Action is alive and well."

"It's not an Affirmative Action program," says Pete. "We will all benefit if we bring more women into the shooting sports. As we are a private club, the current members control who gets to join. Let's make a choice that works for us all."

"Thank you, Pete," says Bob, and then announces formally to the room. "Would the members present like to put forth a motion that women on the waiting list be given the opportunity to join first?"

"Yes, it makes sense."

"Aye."

"Do it."

"I need a motion," says Bob.

Pete repeats the statement in a clear, understandable form, emphasizing that all prospective members must have completed the Basic Pistol course.

"All in favor?" asks Bob.

The motion is approved. I must be at next month's meeting so I can meet any new members and explain that the Pistol Belles are going to be shooting competitively. This gives me a month to determine the status of the current Belles.

We continue with the meeting's agenda and I present my regular report. I don't mention that one of the Pistol Belles was suspended due to reckless handling of a gun. I'd sent a confidential report to Bob in accordance with club policy and am not obligated to make an announcement here. It's likely, however, that many club members will have heard about Shelby's outburst and I am relieved no-one asks questions. The Williams name is truly powerful.

The meeting adjourns and Caroline strides over to me.

"Why didn't you tell them about the competitive league?" she asks.

"Two reasons, Caroline," I say, drawing upon my dwindling reserves of patience. "First, you practically made the announcement for me."

She raises her sculptured eyebrows and looks across at Pete.

"And, second, I have to contact the organizers and find out how many shooters we will need."

"You haven't contacted them yet?" she says in a reproachful tone. It seems I now have two bosses. I'm starting to see why Caroline and Sandersen get along so well. At our meeting today to review the schedule, she and Sandersen were falling over themselves to compliment each other. If Sandersen weren't so fat—and married—I would have thought the seeds of a romance were being planted.

"Mona runs the Pistol Belles, Caroline," Pete reminds her. I love being rescued by a forceful man. I think of Carl at home with his book and wine and the flashing, soundless television. I want to be with him. What good is it to have money and a loving man if I'm stressed and tired?

"I know Mona is in charge," answers Caroline, a chill in her tone. "But Madison and I are the best shooters and we want to be on a team where we can learn. We don't want to be stuck forever with the same group of housewives who don't take shooting seriously."

"I don't know anything about the competitive league," says Pete. "But I would encourage you to join. You all need goals to work towards and you need to be tested."

"Right," says Caroline, a look of satisfaction spreading across her face.

"You and Madison are great shots," Pete continues. "And you've got Jean and Mona close behind you. The Pistol Belles is a good group."

Pete isn't going to let Caroline get away with her imperious ice queen stance.

"There are four of us who could hold our own in a competition," she says, her voice is cold but her eyes flash brightly at Pete. "But that won't be enough. We need to field a strong team."

"The Pistol Belles is a group of six," I say, putting some ice between my own teeth. "That is a manageable number. I can't get rid of Shelby and Christine without giving them a reason. The first thing I need to do is find out if the league requires shooters to prove a certain level of skill."

If so, it is unlikely that Shelby and Christine will make the cut. That will take a difficult decision out of my hands and place it firmly on the fair and square shoulders of ability.

"That's right," agrees Pete. "If the league wants proof that each shooter can perform at a certain level, then no-one can argue with that. If you can't shoot well enough, you can't compete. Everyone will understand that."

Everyone, that is, except Christine and Shelby.

Chapter Twelve

If Carl was home, I would practice my speech with him as there is no-one more eager to chew around a set of words and spit them back than a man who makes his living critiquing literature. But Carl is on campus today and I don't want to interrupt him so, instead, I imagine what he would say: "Speak from your heart, Mona. Stand up as if you're announcing it's someone's birthday. You'll be natural and get everyone's attention."

I stare down at the pile of papers on the kitchen table. Every sheet is crisscrossed with scribbles and phrases, including "it's time to move on to the next level", "we need to raise the bar", "we're turning a corner", "it's time to retool" and "the dress rehearsal is over." I feel as if I'm back in a marketing strategy meeting at Abaco. I don't want to speak to the Pistol Belles using jargon I could barely tolerate when I was paid to do so. I cross out the clichés and write three words: cooperative, committed and competitive. These three words describe the characteristics of the new Pistol Belles and are all I need to guide my speech tonight.

I am at once excited and sick at heart. I know where these words will lead. The six of us who will be at the range tonight are unlikely to be the same six putting up their targets next week. If a minimum level of competency has to proved, neither Christine nor Shelby will make the cut.

It's also time to end the time-consuming distraction of our potluck dinners. Serious shooters don't go to tournaments in order to eat, and if we are a competitive team, we'll eat at home before heading out to the range. I open up the refrigerator and check that I have romaine lettuce, arugula and cucumber for the green salad I'll take tonight. This will be my final offering. The days of breading and baking and carrying oversized platters into the clubhouse are over. I would be a better shooter today if I hadn't spent so much time cooking and eating. I've treated the group as if it's a girl's night out when I could have been building a line-up of skilled shooters. The new Pistol Belles will finally be the sisterhood of sharpshooters I'd hoped for in the beginning.

Feeling in a mood for self-flagellation, yet still willing to assign some of the blame elsewhere, I finger Betsy Logan as the reason the Pistol Belles got off on the wrong foot. Jean's quick run-down of the women on the list handed to me at my first Skyline meeting had turned out not to be entirely accurate. Her assessment of Mary Ellen Moran, however, was correct and she'd confirmed that her husband worked an evening shift and she could not join a weekly shooting group. But Cindy DeFabio had jumped at the chance to join the new women's league, saying that she planned to hunt with her husband in the fall but would be happy to come up to Skyline every Wednesday to shoot her pistols. She'd shown up faithfully every week for several months and only when hunting season began had her attendance become erratic. Later, Cindy said she could no longer shoot with us as she was getting up at dawn two or three times a week to climb into a cold deer stand and wait for dinner to pass by. Jean had nodded knowingly upon hearing Cindy was resigning from our group, noting that that was exactly what she'd figured back in the spring. I had been disappointed to lose Cindy, but happy she'd shot with us in those early days of the Pistol Belles as she'd help boost our numbers at the time the club's officers were watching to see who, if anyone, showed up on Wednesday evenings.

Ruth Leeberg had confirmed what Jean had predicted, saying she couldn't get to the club because her husband had fallen off his bulldozer and hurt his back and she was also taking care of her aged parents. She'd said that she'd welcome the diversion of a weekly shooting session, but the only time she could leave her husband alone were the hours she spent taking care of her mother and father. I'd shuddered at the extent of Ruth's burdens and, once again, been reminded about my own carefree existence.

My call to Betsy Logan had proved that Jean's social antenna was sometimes out of kilter. Without hesitation Betsy had signed-up for the Pistol Belles and, when I'd tentatively asked if she was about to move out of the area, she'd said she was not moving to Florida, though her husband spent most of the year there golfing and fishing.

"I don't fish and I don't play golf," Betsy had scoffed. "Nor do I play bridge or shop."

Betsy was a big woman who, it turned out, could shoot one-handed with the same degree of accuracy I could manage with both hands. She owned several handguns but favored a 9mm Glock which she brought to the range every week. With the exception of a month or two when she visited her husband on Marathon Key, Betsy was a faithful Pistol Belle for over two years. Finally, her husband's purchase of waterfront property in Islamorada was too great for her to resist, and she bade us farewell.

"I told you Betsy was moving to Florida," Jean had said, her eyes twinkling. "I just didn't say when."

Betsy was a marksman and had been an enthusiastic champion of the Pistol Belles, standing up to any Skyline member who questioned why women's night wasn't attracting scores of new shooters. Betsy was quick to point out that while we understood the club's objective was to bring in hundreds of new women, it was also important that we bring in good ones. She was a forceful woman and a valuable ally in those early months, but it was Betsy who had insisted that we share a potluck supper each week. I'd quickly become concerned that we were spending more time eating than shooting and had suggested we limit our dinners to once a month. But Betsy liked to eat as much as she liked to shoot and was obviously eating too many dinners alone.

"If we share food and eat together we'll become friends and be unwilling to skip a week," she'd said, bellowing down the telephone in response to my protests that we would be taken more seriously at Skyline if we spent our range time shooting and not exchanging recipes.

"There's less likely to be problems between us all," Betsy had insisted.

On this latter point she'd turned out to be wrong, although few conflicts had arisen with the original group and if Jean, Betsy, Cindy and I had stayed together, we may have become a solid group of gals who could not only shoot well, but get along together. Later, no matter how much bread was broken together, conflicts became as much a constant as Jean's Sloppy Joes.

At my first meeting I'd promised Jim and Pete that I would contact Caroline Cargill. I'd called her the next morning, leaving a message on her answering machine and she'd called me back early that evening. Carl had just walked in the door when the phone rang and I like to talk to him for the first few minutes he is home rather than sit on the telephone with someone I could have been chatting with all day. But, like a robot, I'd picked up the receiver on the kitchen wall phone and announced my name. Old habits from Abaco had not left me and I'd answered the phone in the manner I'd used at work, a habit which had amused Carl greatly when we were first dating.

"Who else would it be?" he'd ask as I'd pronounce "Mona Johnson" from my solitary apartment.

"I love you, Mona Johnson," he'd responded late one evening when I'd picked up the phone in my usual brisk way.

"I love you too, Carl Milton," I'd said. Carl had then hung up, leaving me to wonder and to dream. Somehow I'd resisted the temptation to drive to his apartment and fling myself across his bed. Instead, I'd huddled under my down comforter feeling both elated and fearful that the thousands of nights I'd slept alone were coming to a close. The next morning my doorbell rang and, thinking it was one of the many neighbors who stopped by to chat or ask a favor, I'd grabbed my coat and yanked the door open ready for a quick exchange before heading out to work. I'd walked smack into Carl's arms. He'd steered me back inside, pulled a small box from his pocket, got down on one knee and asked me to marry him. Before I could stammer out a response, he'd placed a two-carat diamond ring on the third finger of my left hand. It was the only day in my entire working life I called in sick without actually running a fever. But I did spend the day in bed, and I still have the fever.

"Mona, this is Caroline Cargill," a haughty voice had said in response to my business-like pronouncement. "You left a message for me."

I'd told her about Skyline's decision to dedicate Wednesday evenings to a women's league and described my hope for a team of six women who would shoot together every week. Caroline had barely given me time to finish my pitch before saying she would join the group and would be there the following week. She'd shown up early in what would become her standard uniform of black slacks and turtleneck, bringing a 9mm Beretta which she'd recently purchased. In accordance with Jim and Pete's first impressions of her, Caroline had been distant and stand-offish with the other women. But within a couple of weeks she'd gained respect for Cindy and Betsy's shooting abilities—and they for hers—and she'd soon come to value Jean's knowledge of firearms and ammunition, not to mention her endless yarns of shooting folklore. I'd been concerned that the potluck suppers and the time we used up eating and chatting would turn Caroline away from our group, but soon learned that this cool feminist was an outstanding cook. No-one had been more surprised than Pete at this pleasant discovery, remarking that as hard as it was to ignore Caroline's perfect body, it was nevertheless easier than resisting the temptations that came out of her kitchen.

And so the Pistol Belles got its start with five shooters. Though I'd contacted numerous other women, no-one else had been interested in joining a group that met every week. I've often wondered if it was not that they were reluctant to take on an obligation to come to the range each week, but to cook.

When Cindy dropped out the following winter I'd been determined to find two more members and bring the group up to my original plan of six regular shooters. Having been turned down by every woman in the club, and with the waiting list at that time being stacked with men, I'd been free to look beyond the confines of Skyline. In the year or so which had passed since we'd met at Basic Pistol, I'd stayed in touch with Christine Jones. Christine had remained timid around guns during the Basic Pistol sessions, but before the course ended she'd had the good sense to ask Jim to recommend the best gun for her if, she'd added quickly, she decided to buy one.

During our phone conversations in the weeks following the course, I'd been hesitant about encouraging Christine to buy a gun which she may not have the ability to use effectively. But, after a lot of soul searching and flip-flopping, she'd finally come to the conclusion that, having taken the course in order to learn to protect herself, she should take the next step and get a gun of her own. I'd offered to help her and together we'd obtained her Firearms I.D. card, as well as the required permit to purchase a pistol. I'd also offered to take her to the gun dealer from whom I'd bought my first gun, a Smith &Wesson Model 617 revolver which I loved.

On the day of our trip to the gun dealer, I'd pulled into Hillside Gardens parking lot and waited for Christine to come out of the two-storey brick building which housed her small apartment. The parking lot was riddled with potholes and broken pieces of black top and was chock full with cars which either were a match for Christine's dilapidated Chevrolet or were late model sports utility vehicles and muscle cars. The complex was rundown and shabby, yet curtains framed many of the windows and planters were placed attractively on the stoops of several units. For some people, Hillside Gardens was home-sweet-home. But as I'd looked at the row of dumpsters in the far back of the lot and the overgrown shrubs around the buildings, I'd thought of Christine's fear of her estranged husband and how hard it must be to live with the constant threat, real or imagined, of being attacked.

In preparation for gun ownership, Christine had bought a small safe which she'd somehow managed to drag into her apartment and wedge in the bottom of her closet. She said Sophie would not be given the combination and that the only place it was written down was on a sheet of paper taped to the inside of her desk drawer at work where the six numbers were of no use to anyone who might read them. I'd thought they'd also be of little use to her if in an emergency she forgot the combination to her safe.

And so that day, Christine had scurried out to my car and with her permit in order and the gun she'd wanted in stock, become the legal owner of a Beretta Neos .22 caliber semi-automatic handgun. She'd taken the gun home and locked it in her safe, along with five hundred rounds of ammunition.

Several months later on one of our occasional phone conversations, Christine told me that she had not taken the gun out, let alone shot it, since that day.

Believing it to be a poor policy for anyone to be in possession of a weapon with which they are not familiar, and particularly a woman as fearful as Christine, I'd insisted she start practicing with her gun on a regular basis. I'd invited her to come and shoot with the Pistol Belles and, being touched that I included her, she'd accepted without hesitation. I'd quickly been sorry that I'd thrown Christine into the middle of an established group of skilled shooters. She was even nervous during our potluck dinners and would take tiny helpings of food from the groaning clubhouse counter, rarely uttering a word. Most troubling of all was that, though she'd been reluctant to fire a gun in the low-expectation atmosphere of Basic Pistol class, she was terrified of shooting alongside Betsy, Caroline and Jean. I might as well have put her in the show ring with Annie Oakley and Buffalo Bill.

Betsy, Caroline and Jean believed the Pistol Belles were on track to become a crack shot team and clearly wondered why I'd brought Christine into the group. But they all rose to the challenge of accommodating a raw and nervous recruit, taking the time to help her and giving her hours of painstaking instruction. Betsy had been the first to show signs that her patience with Christine was fading and had commented numerous times that if the Pistol Belles were to be a group that good shooters would want to join then setting a minimum level of skill would be a good place to start. I'd usually responded by saying that eliminating the potluck dinner in favor of more shooting time might also help. Months later when Betsy announced she was moving to south Florida we all feigned surprise, but it had become clear that she was growing tired of the Pistol Belles.

"Maybe we should all head down to Florida," Jean had said. "There must be some fine shooting gals down there. I'll bet they grew up shooting like I did."

"Yeah," Betsy had replied, grinning at Jean. "I'll find myself a team of real pistol packers. Y'all will be wishing you were down there with me."

But Caroline, giving the first indication that she was not just the cold operator she presented to the world, had sprung to Christine's defense, declaring that all women need to be able to protect themselves and must be allowed to learn at their own pace and according to their abilities. I'd been grateful to Caroline for defending

Christine, but I'd nevertheless questioned my decision to include someone who may never be able to shoot straight.

That decision has now come home to roost. If the new Pistol Belles are to be cooperative, committed and competitive, I know Christine can offer two of these qualities. But she will never be able to give us the third.

Chapter Thirteen

The Ruger is locked in the trunk, my ammo bag and the green salad are secured on the floor of the backseat, and the note card bearing the crucial three words is in the pocket of my jeans. I put the gear stick into reverse, glance in the rear view mirror and am about to press my foot down on the gas pedal when I see a figure dart behind me. I quickly shift my foot from the gas pedal to the brake and thrust the gear back into the park position. A pair of arms is flapping behind the car.

"I just want to have a quick word," calls a shrill voice.

"I almost ran you over," I say, opening the window, surprised to find that the flying figure is Susan. "One more second and I would have backed right over you."

"That was stupid of me," she says, panting and leaning her hand on the roof of my car.

It suddenly occurs to me that if Susan was to die, Michaela would be all alone. Neither Michaela nor Susan ever speaks of her father, and the only relatives they've ever mentioned are an uncle and aunt in California.

"I'm sorry, Mona, I know you're always in a hurry on Wednesday evenings, but I want to thank you for last weekend."

Three days have passed since Susan returned home to find her daughter safe, nourished and happy, although the latter may be an exaggeration as I would not describe a lonely thirteen year old as happy.

"Consider me thanked," I say, looking at the clock on the dashboard. "I have to run, Susan. We'll chat some other time."

Being late makes me feel out of control and this evening I must convey leadership and authority. I cannot do this if I don't feel completely in charge.

"You're very kind, Mona," Susan continues, ignoring my last statement. "I just wanted to say how much I appreciate all you do for Michaela. She loves you."

We live next door to each other and I can describe the physical characteristics of her daughter in intimate detail, but I realize I haven't seen Susan in the flesh for several months. Our brief conversations take place over the telephone and Susan usually thanks me by email for taking care of Michaela. A distance of no more than twenty five feet separates our homes and it irritates me that she doesn't simply knock on my front door in order to say please and thank you. But, in spite of our proximity to each other, I rarely see Susan arriving or leaving her house. She must scurry in and out of the back door, no doubt racing to be either across the threshold of her home or behind her desk at the office. The place she will want to be least of all is in transition. Looking at Susan now, I notice how much older she appears than when I last saw her and that, even in the soft evening light, her face is lined and drawn. I guess maternal guilt doesn't make for a pretty face, and neither will the constant pressure of trying to be in two places at once.

"We love Michaela, too," I say, smiling and putting the car back into reverse. Right now there is just one place I need to be and it isn't sitting in my driveway with the engine idling. "We're happy to help whenever we can."

Once again, I look in the mirror and start to back out.

"There is something I was going to talk to you about," Susan says. I slowly put my foot on the brake and turn to her. "But I know you're in a hurry."

Her face is crunched up as if she is in pain and she is wringing her hands.

Is another weekend out of town coming up? A business trip she can't avoid? Are Susan's constant absences really due to working overtime or does she have a secret lover? Right now that doesn't appear to be the case. A woman run ragged with sexual *assignations* wouldn't look so worn and dispirited.

"Are you alright, Susan?" I ask, accepting that I will be late and putting the gear back into park. "If there is something you need, just ask."

"No, it's nothing in particular. I'm really fine," she says, apparently forgetting that a minute ago she had something to talk to me about which was so urgent she risked getting mown down.

"You must go," she mumbles. "We can talk some other time."

Not wanting to miss my chance to leave, I smile at her and reverse out of the driveway. Susan stands and watches me as I turn the car forward and then wave and head down the street. I am curious to learn what it is she wants to talk about and know I'll be chewing it over with Carl later tonight. He'll hazard a guess which will later turn out to be one hundred percent accurate.

My anxiety about being late turns out to be wasted energy as, in spite of the brief delay, I've left sufficient time to be the first to arrive at Skyline. I put the salad in the clubhouse kitchen and place my Ruger case and ammo bag outside the door to the range. I take my speech out of my pocket and say the three words out loud: cooperative, committed, competitive.

As if on cue, the personification of this message hurtles through the door.

"The ice cream is melting," Madison shouts. "I bought it near school and now it's a dripping mess."

I run into the kitchen and open the freezer door as Madison rips a container of ice cream out of a plastic bag and hurls it in. She throws the bag in the garbage can and goes to the sink to wash her hands.

"I hate sticky things. Ice cream seemed like a good idea but I didn't realize it would melt so fast."

"You'd think the chemicals would keep it rock hard," says Caroline, appearing behind us. "Don't worry, Madison, in another hour your ice cream will have been entirely consumed."

"What was that about rock hard, Caroline?" asks Pete, coming through the door from the range. "Is there something you need?"

Madison and I laugh, but Caroline glares at us as she puts her dish on the counter and sits down on a stool, her legs spread out in front of her.

"There is nothing I need from you," she says, looking directly at Pete, and then jumps up and starts to unwrap her dish.

"What delights do we have tonight?" says Pete, ignoring her rudeness. "I got here early because I didn't want to miss the celebration."

"What celebration?" I ask.

The three of them are silent.

"What do you mean, Pete?" I ask, turning to him. "What would we be celebrating?"

"Mona, Mona," he says, putting his arms around my shoulders. "Don't take everything so seriously. I thought from last night's discussion you'd be making an announcement about the Pistol Belles joining the competitive league."

"Pete, you know that's not decided yet. You also know there are some difficulties attached to that decision."

"Not for us," says Caroline. "The only difficulty for us will be if we don't do it."

"We need to do it, Mona," says Madison. "We're spinning our wheels right now. We need to stretch and grow."

"I don't disagree," I say, reminding myself that the decision to set the future course of the Pistol Belles is not mine alone. "I came here ready to make that announcement tonight. I just don't want it discussed during dinner. You have to give me the chance to handle it properly."

"Ok," says Caroline. "Your chance is immediately after dinner. If you don't talk about it then, I will."

"I don't even have the facts," I say, pathetically. Caroline really can be intimidating. I wonder how many of her former colleagues at Smith Pharma were glad to see her go. "I haven't contacted the league's organizers yet but I'll do it first thing tomorrow."

"You said you came here tonight ready to make the announcement," she says.

"I am and, trust me, it will be done. The Pistol Belles will be different by the time you leave tonight. But you have to let me do it my way."

"I contacted the league," says Caroline, a faintly apologetic tone in her voice. "I told them we wanted to join and that you would call them back."

I should have known that my failure to take immediate action would leave an opening which Caroline would be eager to fill. But at least she had the grace to present me as the leader of our group.

"That's fine," I say, slowly. "Thank you for doing that. I'll speak to them first thing tomorrow."

I must stay calm and assured and not let Caroline rattle me.

"Come on, Caroline," says Pete, watching as she continues to fuss over her dish. "Put me out of my misery."

"What are you?" she asks. "A sick dog?"

Pete laughs dryly. "Some would call it that."

"Chicken *parmigiana*," she announces, removing a heavy lid with a flourish. Caroline covers her food with a glass lid and then wraps foil over it and I have seen her look on in horror as Jean and Christine pick pieces of aluminum foil off the top of their potluck dishes.

"I told you it was a celebration, Mona," says Pete. "This is one of Caroline's finest dishes."

Caroline smiles but looks flustered. Can an attractive woman have such little experience accepting compliments?

"Baked ziti tonight," says Jean, slamming the door behind her. I notice Matthew isn't with her. Maybe Jean has decided he shouldn't come to the range if his only purpose is to moon over Madison. Jim follows behind her.

"Jim, this is your wife's favorite," Jean says. "I made it specially, so everyone else take notice that there better be leftovers for Jim to take home."

Jim smiles and rubs his hands together.

"I am forever indebted to you lovely ladies. You have no idea how much my wife appreciates all the food you send home with me."

"With a bit of luck, she'll have dessert too," says Christine, who seems to have appeared out of nowhere. "I made a peach cobbler."

Could she have come in while we were talking about the announcement?

"I think we should cancel the shooting and just eat," says Pete. "Whether or not the Pistol Belles can shoot may be up for question, but they sure can cook."

Madison picks up the ball of aluminum foil which Jean ripped off the top of her baked ziti and throws it at Pete.

"Nice shot, Madison," says Caroline.

"Maybe if you can't compete at shooting you could take up softball," says Pete, tossing the foil back to Madison.

I have yet to reach for my gun when provoked, but right now I would like to grab my Ruger and fire a shot. Placing a bullet just one inch from Pete's foot would make a point.

"No, we have to stick with shooting!" says Christine, as if Skyline would actually field a softball team. "If it wasn't for Wednesday nights I wouldn't shoot at all."

On the other hand, if I'm going to shoot I might as well put the bullet *in* Pete's foot.

"Me too," says Shelby, who also seems to have been miraculously spirited into the middle of the clubhouse. "Thank goodness I'm back tonight. I really missed you guys!"

Shelby is once again in full spring regalia, sporting pale pink jeans, a bright pink padded vest on top of a white shirt and, of course, her pale blue Stetson. Either she has a laundress at home or does not possess any dark clothing. But I notice the shirt is a turtle neck and I won't have to remind her about the discomfort caused when a hot shell finds a warm cleavage. And, if this is the last night of our merry band of six shooters, I will never again have to concern myself with Shelby's clothing. I feel sadness welling up inside me. In spite of my misgivings about her shooting abilities and the number of times she has exasperated me, I know I will miss her. I also know that if she is ousted from the Belles, I will have to deal with Carmine.

"Caesar salad," she says, putting her huge glass bowl on the counter. "I know it's always the same thing, but next week I'm going to start bringing different dishes. Like you guys do. I know I've not really been trying and I'm going to do better."

If she were talking about her shooting, we'd be able to keep her.

"And I bought a .22 Ruger! It's exactly like Carmine's, only it's mine. I bought it the other day."

Somehow I don't believe this, but it's not my job to stop her from driving around with a gun which she does not own. She knows the rules.

"It's better for target shooting than my Baby Glock," she adds, as if she figured this out all by herself.

"Everyone," I call, clapping my hands. "We have some business to take care of this evening. So let's eat right away and then I have some announcements to make."

This is misleading and I know it. I have made it sound as if I have several things to say that concern everyone. I will start by telling them about our progress with the gun safety program, but then I will tell them we are joining a competitive league and that to ensure we field a good team we will be spending the rest of the evening scoring our shots. Those scores will determine who will be in the new Pistol Belles.

And who will be out.

Chapter Fourteen

Carl heard the news first. Walking across campus to his early class, a secretary from the Math department stopped him and asked if he'd heard about the shooting at the home of John Williams' daughter.

"Someone broke in last night," said the woman. "A man was killed."

"My goodness, I hope it wasn't Shelby's husband," Carl said, trying to match this shocking piece of news with my report to him last night of Shelby's angry response upon hearing of the new Pistol Belles. Just as I'd feared, as soon as I'd made the announcement that we'd be joining a new league and that we each had to prove we could shoot well enough to compete, she had flounced out saying it was all just a big ploy to get rid of her and she might as well quit right away. Shelby believes she is the central character in any drama and will undoubtedly think that our only reason to become a competitive team is so we can permanently oust her from the Belles.

"I don't believe it was the husband who was shot," said a campus security guard who had stopped to join the discussion. "A pal of mine at the police station says the husband was away and a guy broke into the house. Apparently the wife had a gun and shot him dead right in her bedroom."

Carl had quickly excused himself and, walking briskly in the direction of his classroom, called me to find out what I'd heard in the half hour since he'd left home. I'd heard nothing. Last night I'd watched silently as Shelby grabbed her gun case, ammo bag and empty salad bowl and slammed the clubhouse door behind her. I'd been sorry that Shelby's enthusiastic return to the Pistol Belles had ended on such a swift and bad note, and I'd discussed the evening's events at length with Carl when I'd returned home. Rational as ever, his first comment had been to point out that Shelby hadn't given herself the chance to try out for the new team, and that if she'd joined the line-up, she may have made the cut if only by pure dumb luck.

If what we've now heard turns out to be true, Shelby made the cut when it came to protecting herself and her children. I can only imagine her terror when faced with an intruder while alone in a large house with four young children.

Carl asks me to assure him that I will not make any attempt to contact Shelby until we learn more about what happened. I make my promise, hang up and then quickly pull on a jacket, jump in my car and drive over to Jean's house. I need contact with someone who knows Shelby as well as I do. Two vehicles are parked in the gravel driveway outside her cottage; her old pick-up and a large, luxurious sedan.

"This is my granddaughter, Maggie," Jean says as I open the front door and step into her house. Jean grew up in a community which never locked its doors and she believes there is no reason to change this habit now.

"I've got my revolver," she will respond to anyone who suggests that she should increase her home security. "An old lady with a loaded Smith & Wesson will scare off most creeps. I could be nuts for all they know."

"Maggie is my daughter Mary Ellen's eldest girl," Jean now adds, waving a wooden spoon in the direction of a blonde, elegant woman sitting on the edge of a battered kitchen stool.

I nod and smile at Maggie.

"You heard what happened over at the Lombardi house last night?" Jean asks.

"Why didn't you call me? Carl heard on campus and if he hadn't I wouldn't even know about it!"

"I was about to call you and then Maggie stopped in and reminded me I didn't have too many years left to break a lifelong habit of being the early bird bearer of bad news. She said I shouldn't make any calls."

Maggie looks at me and rolls her eyes upwards.

"I'm sure Maggie has a point," I say, smiling again. "But, considering it's only twelve hours since we saw Shelby and we both know how upset she was when she left the club, I don't think it would be considered gossiping for you to call *me*."

"It's possible you saved her life, Mona," Jean says solemnly. "Maybe your plan for the new Pistol Belles got her so riled up that when someone broke in she was mad enough to shoot him."

I'm not sure I want to be the driving force behind a homicide.

"Do we have any idea what happened? Who was shot? Did Shelby really kill someone?"

Maggie picks up a set of car keys from the table and says she must get to work. She kisses her grandmother goodbye and promises to call if she hears any reliable facts on the Lombardi break-in.

"Call me even if the facts are not reliable," says Jean. "Mona and I will be able to separate truth from fiction. We know Shelby and we know how she shoots. And I'm guessing that the only way she nailed this punk is because she shot first."

Maggie stops at the door and turns to face her grandmother. Her beautiful face is stern.

"Do not, under any circumstances, put that idea out there. There may be charges and lawsuits. You must not circulate potentially damaging commentary."

Jean stands at the stove, studiously stirring a thick red sauce.

"I won't, honey, don't worry," she says, after a moment. "I know better than that. Any such discussions will be between me and Mona and no-one else."

Maggie closes the door behind her and her car starts up softly in the driveway.

"Your granddaughter is a beautiful woman. What does she do?"

"She's a lawyer. Not a criminal lawyer like those who handle things like this Lombardi shooting. She does corporate law which sounds boring but she makes bushels of money. She's shrewd. She got her first husband to pay for law school. Then she got divorced and got married again. Then she got divorced again and the second one sued her for alimony. Ha! I said, I guess you're about even now. You took one man's money to get your law degree and now another man is taking your money from your law practice. Consider it even."

I laugh. "I'm sure she didn't see it quite as clearly as that."

"No, but she knew in her heart she'd taken advantage of her first husband, and she is wise enough to accept that the alimony is payback."

"I'm sure the first husband would rather have been paid back himself. It sounds like the second husband is getting what rightfully belongs to the first."

"That's true, but her first husband didn't go after her. He's a good man and still cares about her, poor thing. I talk to him often. They got married right out of college and then she enrolled in law school. She's been making lots of money and been making lots of men miserable ever since."

"Does she shoot?" I ask. Caroline and Madison would undoubtedly consider her the right caliber for the new Belles.

"No, she's never shown an interest in guns, which is a pity. She does just about everything else, skiing, tennis, golf, and she goes off everywhere windsurfing and sailing and who knows what else."

Jean continues stirring her sauce and is quiet for a moment.

"I never did any of those things."

"You were busy raising five children in difficult circumstances. You raised Maggie's mother and helped make Maggie's affluent independence possible. You also gave her a fine face and figure."

"Flattery will get you everywhere," Jean says, smiling and licking sauce off the spoon. "Maggie appreciates her life and that's why she stops in for coffee a couple of mornings a week."

"You're the Muirhouse cement, Jean. Every family should have a woman like you at its head."

"It's come with a price," she says, turning down the gas and putting a lid on top of the pot.

"What are you making? It's barely nine o'clock and you've got dinner on the stove."

"I'm making another tray of baked ziti," she says, looking at me with surprise. "The Lombardi house will be crawling with people. Shelby can't cook on a good day and I doubt that after killing a man stone dead in her bedroom, she's going to rustle up dinner."

"We must find out what happened. It would be ironic if after refusing to try out for the new team, Shelby went home and put her shooting skills to work in real life."

I'm already wondering which gun she used. Could her new Baby Glock have saved her life? Or the Ruger which she claims is hers? Did she get Carmine's Walther out of the safe? Was the gun she used even in the safe? A picture is starting to form in my head of Shelby alone in bed with the Baby Glock under her pillow; a sleeping beauty ready to shoot if roused.

My cell phone whirs in my pocket and I answer it without checking the caller. It will be Carl with more news from campus.

"Is this true?" Caroline bellows into my ear. "Dr. Sandersen just called me and said there's been a fatal shooting at the Lombardi home. He wouldn't say anything more except that Shelby's husband was out of town and that she and the kids are apparently alright. Do you know who got shot?"

"I'm at Jean's house and all we've heard is that Shelby killed an intruder, but we have no idea if it's true."

"My God! Maybe the girl can shoot after all. I can't believe it."

"We don't yet know if we have to believe it," I remind her, suddenly remembering we have to be at a school several miles away at eleven o'clock. "What else did Sandersen say?"

"He says none of the Lombardi children are in school. If some creep broke into their house, I'm glad she killed him."

"Caroline, we don't know what happened," I say, surprised that Caroline is jumping so quickly to Shelby's defense. "Don't forget we have a program this morning."

"I'm dressed and ready to go. But this incident proves that everyone should be armed and able to shoot. Imagine what would have happened if Shelby hadn't been able to defend herself. What about those kids? They could have all been murdered!"

"Caroline, we don't know that and we must not talk about this in our classes today. The gun safety program must stay on message and not react to this news."

"I think it's a little hard not to mention it. Everyone will be talking about it and the kids will ask questions. What are we going to say?"

"It's not our place to comment. And anything we might say would frighten the children."

"I agree it's frightening. A thug breaks into a house when the father is away, but fortunately the mother has a gun and shoots and kills the guy. At least there's a happy ending."

"Somehow I don't think it's a happy ending, but I agree it could have been a great deal worse. But we can't celebrate a man being killed."

Caroline sighs into the phone. "Mona, I know you're right, but this makes me mad as hell. All these anti-gun people need to wake up and smell the…the gunpowder. I can guarantee that the guy who broke in had a gun, and I'm sure he didn't fill in a form and apply for a permit. I'm certain he didn't pay a fee and go for fingerprinting at his local friendly police station. If his fingerprints are on record with the police or the FBI it's because he's already done time and not because he followed the rules and bought a handgun legally."

"You may be right, but we cannot use this incident to encourage gun ownership. That would not only be wrong, it would come back to bite us. People can read about the facts of the case and make their own decisions as to whether or not they should get a gun for their protection."

"Alright, I won't say anything in school. The kids may not even know about it. Their parents wouldn't give them their cereal this morning and tell them that Izzy and Tony's mommy killed a man last night. And I promise I won't say that everyone should get a gun and learn how to use it."

"By the way, why did Sandersen call you? He hasn't called me and I'm supposed to be in charge of the program."

Sandersen obviously seized the opportunity to make a phone call to Caroline.

"Just to let me know about the Lombardi's," she says, coyly. "He probably didn't want to bother you. He knows Shelby is in our pistol group. Or, I guess, she used to be..."

Her voice trails off.

"Of course, he told me we couldn't mention the incident in school and I said I wouldn't dream of it," she adds.

At least Caroline didn't rant to Sandersen about the need for an armed nation. I am not fond of our principal and don't agree with his anti-gun position, but I accept he must maintain control of the information which is imparted to his students.

"Mona," Caroline says softly. "Do you think it's wrong to throw Shelby out of the Pistol Belles if it turns out she can load and fire a gun in an emergency?"

Caroline's hard-nosed professionalism appears to have left her. Mine has not.

"Shooting and killing an attacker has nothing to do with a person's ability to shoot in a competitive pistol league. Shooting in a pistol league means being able to consistently hit a distant target and score points. If it turns out that Shelby got her gun, loaded, fired and killed a man who was going to attack her, then I think we'll all have a new respect for her shooting skills. However, she cannot qualify for the new Pistol Belles on this basis."

"You're right as usual, Mona, but maybe she could join a practical shooting group where they simulate different scenarios where you have to defend yourself."

I laugh. "Yes, she might be glad to leave the Belles and become the star of a practical shooting team. On the other hand, she may not want to be reminded of what must have been a terrifying situation."

"All those kids," says Caroline, breathing hard into the phone. "I hope they were asleep. Can you imagine what was going through Shelby's head when she realized some guy was in her house?"

"No, I can't imagine but let's be happy she and the kids are alright. I guess Carmine is on his way back from his trip. He's crazy about his family. He'll never want to go out of town again."

"We have to run," says Caroline. "Our program begins in an hour. I promise I'll stay on message."

"That woman has more of a heart than she likes to let on," says Jean, who has accurately filled in the other half of my phone conversation.

I look at my cell phone. It beeped several times during Caroline's call. I recognize the numbers. Christine. Madison.

Now feeling pressured to return home for the gun safety materials and get to the elementary school in time, I rush out of Jean's kitchen telling her I will call her later. I hear her phone ring and her brisk, quick answer.

"Hi Jim, honey, did we leave you enough ziti to take home last night?"

Chapter Fifteen

Last night seems so long ago. The anxiety I'd felt about speaking to the Pistol Belles has become more wasted energy. I'd worried for days about Shelby and Christine losing their places in our group, and had anticipated Shelby's predictable reaction to learning she had to try out for a place on the new team. But now, instead of petty concerns about the Belles' feelings and sensitivities, my mind is playing a continuous reel of Shelby under attack. I picture her waking, hearing sounds downstairs, rushing into Carmine's closet, struggling to remember the safe's combination, grabbing a gun, fumbling for the right ammunition, and then facing her attacker.

And firing.

And a man is dead on her bedroom floor.

If Shelby had chosen to try out for the team last night she would have been lucky to hit the outermost ring of the target. She would not have made the cut. After she'd flounced out of the range, Christine had followed her lead by pronouncing that she could not shoot under pressure and there was no point in pretending she could compete. Madison and Caroline had exchanged knowing glances, making it clear what they were thinking: the two weakest shooters were not even going to attempt to earn their places on the team. If our two best shooters needed further convincing that Shelby and Christine were unqualified to compete, this was it. Their refusal to demonstrate their ability, weak or strong, was a disqualification all of its own. Though Shelby and Christine had regularly shot with the group and had not seemed embarrassed by their poor performance, that could not make up for their failure to be tested when required. As Carl had pointed out, Shelby's refusal to try out had eliminated the possibility that dumb luck might have got her a place on the team.

But today it seems fortunate that Shelby held on to her luck and took it home where it may well have saved her life. Like Jean, I too believe that if an intruder was shot and killed in the Lombardi house last night, Shelby must have fired first. I do not believe that after being fired at she was then able to level a deadly shot at her attacker.

After Shelby's dramatic exit from the clubhouse, Christine's departure had been more dignified. Holding back tears, she'd packed up her half empty dish of peach cobbler, mumbling under her breath that she would get out of our way. I'd walked out with her to the parking lot in an almost exact replay of our first Basic Pistol class, and told her I would hold a place open for her if within the next few weeks she could improve her shooting.

"If I can't shoot any better now than I could four years ago, a few weeks isn't going to make a difference," she'd said, wiping her eyes. "I learned to shoot to defend myself not to win a competition. I never dreamed of being as good as Caroline and Madison. I learned to shoot because I was tired of feeling helpless and I believed Frankie was going to get me."

The tears had flowed down her pale face.

"And because you encouraged me and helped me," she'd added quietly.

"You've learned a lot and if you find yourself in a bad situation, you'll be able to use your gun to your advantage."

"Yeah," she'd said, smearing her hand across her face. "I could threaten him even if I couldn't bring myself to shoot him."

At the exact time I'd been talking to Christine in the parking lot, Shelby would have been tucking her children into their beds, not knowing that within a few short hours she would not only have to threaten, but shoot.

"Please don't cause trouble with the Belles by trying to save a place for me. They don't want me and I'm never going to be good enough. And even if I thought I could practice and do better, I don't have the time. I have a job and I have Sophie. I came here every week because of you and Jim. You are both so kind to me."

Christine's tears had turned into sobs.

"People like you and Jim help someone like me do things I otherwise could never do. I can't handle Caroline or Madison. They're so clever and good at everything and I can't imagine being like them. And how could I ever relate to Shelby? A girl like that has always had her way and gets the best of everything. We're not even living on the same planet. I know she's upset right now, but she's only crying because she's angry."

This last statement was true. Shelby's losses are cushioned by money and the many people who surround her. A loss to Christine means that she will be more alone than ever.

"Even Jean intimidates me. She's an old lady but she's so tough. I know she has a good heart but I feel useless when I'm around her."

"She's a tough bird," I'd said, smiling. "But she'll always have time for you if you need her."

"I know. I never pushed Sophie to go over and work for her, but I think I will now."

I'd grabbed hold of the dessert dish as Christine fumbled in her bag for her car keys.

"I meant to give the rest of this peach cobbler to Jim. Please give it to him and tell him I'll get the dish back some time."

I'd realized with a jolt that I hadn't discussed the new team with our senior range officer. Pete may have kept Jim up-to-date, but I should have taken the time to speak with him myself. I hadn't given any thought to his reaction to our new group or to the possibility that he will feel Christine has been treated badly.

"And Pete!" Christine had continued. "He reminds me of my husband, so cool and handsome. He's madly in love with Caroline and she pretends not to care, but Caroline is the right woman for a man like Pete. Frankie and me were a disaster. I could never believe such a good looking guy was interested in me and I did everything to try to keep him. I had many horrible years before I realized he was a just a big bully who needed me to push around. Pete's not like that or he wouldn't be interested in Caroline. I was a sitting target for Frankie, especially once I became his wife."

"You're not a sitting target any longer."

"I don't know. I haven't been put to the test. But being a single mom and taking care of Sophie has made me stronger. I know you all think she rules me and I should get tougher with her. I need to do it before I run out of time."

I'd smiled at her. This was the most Christine had talked in a long time.

"Being a Pistol Belle has been good for me even though I'm not really a shooter. It's good to be part of a group."

Her sobs had started again and I'd wrapped my arms around her.

"I don't want to lose you and Jim," she'd cried, laying her head on my shirt.

"You won't. Let's meet here once a week. That way you'll keep shooting. I'm sure Jim will come as well."

My offer had been honest and sincere and yet as I'd spoken the words I'd known I was taking on one more weekly commitment which I would come to regret. I'd thought of Carl lying on the sofa with the television playing silently in the background, a novel and a glass of Merlot in his hands.

"Well, maybe not every week, but every couple of weeks," I'd said.

Christine had pulled away from me and smiled.

"Mona, whatever you can do is great. Call me when you have time and I promise I'll come and shoot with you. And tell Jim I'll be dropping off some pies at his house."

Christine had climbed into her old car and slowly pulled out of the lot. Her concern about Jim's desserts gave me heart. Christine would be alright.

And now, less than twenty-four hours later, food is being prepared all over town for the Lombardi family. In spite of my promise to Carl, I decide that a platter of lemon chicken will give me a legitimate reason to drive over to Shelby's house and find out what happened last night. Since leaving Jean's house my phone has been whirring constantly and as soon as I pull into our driveway I call Carl and, catching him between classes, tell him what little I know.

"There's gossip all over campus about the shooting," he says. "I've heard that Shelby was sleeping with a handgun under her pillow and that she shot the guy the minute he stepped into her bedroom. I've also heard that she thought it was her husband and she'd been waiting for the chance to get rid of him so she fired knowing she could make up a self defense, I'm-so-scared-when-you're-not-home story."

"That's ridiculous and a lie," I shout into the phone. "Shelby loves Carmine and is dependent upon him. Why would she kill him?"

"Mona, honey, you know I don't believe what I hear in this hotbed of higher learning. With all these students and faculty and staff who know—or know of—the Williams family, there is no chance of getting accurate information. However, I did hear from my friendly security guard that she definitely killed the guy and that he's been identified. The intruder's name is Frank Jones."

The name sounds familiar to me.

"Frank Jones? They have a name?"

"The police recognized him on the scene right away. Apparently he's been a problem for a long time, although he never killed anyone, at least not according to his record. But he had a long list of charges for armed robbery, burglaries, car theft."

"Was Shelby hurt in any way?" I ask, wondering why this man's name is ringing such a bell.

"Not according to my source, which could well be true or all kinds of gruesome stories would be flying around campus."

"Was this Frank Jones ever found guilty of a violent crime?"

I'm thinking of the charges that might be filed against Shelby for killing someone who may have intended to threaten her, but not harm her. She will have to prove she fired in self-defense and, even if she doesn't face criminal charges, may be subject to a civil suit.

"I don't know. I'm repeating what I've heard so I wouldn't put too much credence in it."

"But his name is Frank Jones?"

As I speak it, the name grows even more familiar.

"Apparently that is the dead man's name."

"Do you know anything else about him?"

"White, about forty years old, born and raised around here," answers Carl promptly. He is always on the frontlines of campus intelligence even though he pretends he's above idle gossip.

"And apparently he's married to someone from town," he adds.

"How on earth do you know that?"

"My security guard buddy came by my classroom about ten minutes ago. He said Frank Jones' wife has been taken in for questioning."

"Frank Jones has a wife?"

My stomach starts to churn and my phone whirs again. Christine. Christine Jones.

"Carl! Carl! It's Christine's husband! Frank Jones is Christine's husband."

"Calm down, Mona, if the man wasn't already dead, I'd think he was coming in the front door."

"Christine calls him Frankie. Frank Jones must be the same man. She's deathly afraid of him."

"Isn't she divorced?"

"No, she's been separated from him for years, but they never divorced. She took up shooting because she was afraid he'd come after her. She's calling me right now for about the third time this morning. She must need my help!"

"Mona," says Carl, slowly. "Mona, please be careful. If what we know is correct, Shelby's home was broken into by Christine's husband. Shelby then shot and killed Christine's husband. You must not to get too involved or take sides."

"Carl, you know me better than that," I say, primly. "I'll call Christine and find out why she's calling me. If it's to tell me she's now a widow, I will, of course, be there for her. Other than that I have precisely fifteen minutes to get to today's elementary school. But I'll be back in time to make lemon chicken for the Lombardi—"

"Mona, you promised—"

"And for us," I add, quickly. Carl loves lemon chicken and I can practically feel him smile into the phone.

"I'll make up a small dish for Christine and Sophie too. I doubt they'll have a house full of people but she won't be able to concentrate on cooking. I'm going to need more chicken. I'll stop at the store on the way back from school."

"Mona," says Carl, softly. "You're a good friend, but please be careful."

"Christine and Shelby are my Pistol Belles. At least they were until last night. A lot has happened since then, but they're still mine."

Chapter Sixteen

"Christine sent her husband here to murder me and my children," says Shelby, sitting cross legged on her plush family room couch. "We would have been slaughtered in our beds if I didn't sleep so badly when Carmine is away."

I have no response to this preposterous accusation.

"Thank you for helping Shelby learn to shoot," says Carmine, striding across the cavernous room and then swiftly turning and heading upstairs when Shelby asks him to help Angelika, the Lombardi's German *au pair*, put the children to bed.

John and Karen Williams have just left, looking gaunt and exhausted. They have apparently been here since Shelby's panicked call to them at three o'clock this morning. If John Williams is seriously ill, the last seventeen hours will have done little to assure him a peaceful passing.

It is now eight o'clock and no more than ten minutes have passed since I arrived with my platter of lemon chicken. Having inched my car through the media throng at the end of the Lombardi's sweeping driveway, I'd been stopped and asked my name and the nature of my business by a young patrolman stationed at a police barrier. Having assured him I was a close friend of the family, he'd placed a call to a colleague and, after a few minutes, Shelby had told the police officer that I should be granted entry. I'd parked alongside a collection of luxury cars and headed for the front door when a handsome young man, who turned out to be Carmine's younger brother, Dominic, tapped on a first floor window. He'd motioned for me to go around the back of the house where he'd held open a patio door. I'd stepped into Shelby's ornate dining room and, seeing the platter in my hands, Dominic had nodded his head in the direction of the kitchen. Having found my way there through a long passageway with floor-to-ceiling glass cabinetry, Shelby's stepmother had greeted me, whipped the dish out of my hands and placed it alongside numerous others in a vast stainless steel refrigerator.

Now I'm in the family room listening to Shelby's astonishing accusations. Coming here directly from Christine's apartment, I am still reeling from what I've learned from my two Belles. Christine's husband, Frank, broke into the Lombardi home last night, armed with a handgun. The gun, which was still in Frank's right hand as he lay dead on Shelby's lush bedroom carpeting, is Christine's Beretta Neos, the very same gun she has brought each week, and as recently as last night, to the Pistol Belles.

"Christine's fingerprints are on the gun," says Shelby. "It's her gun and she gave it to him."

I sit silently opposite her. Shelby goes on to explain that she had been so nervous and upset when she got home from Skyline that, as she was putting the Ruger back in the safe, she took out the Baby Glock and placed it under her pillow, along with a magazine which she'd loaded with a full ten rounds. She says she has never done this before, but her intuition told her that she needed some extra security. And, because she was feeling so lonely and rejected, she gathered up all four children and put them in bed with her. She'd woken in the middle of the night to find a man in her bedroom pointing a gun at her, and she'd pulled the Baby Glock from under her pillow, slammed the magazine into the grip and fired at the intruder. If Frank Jones had the chance to fire back, he didn't take it. Perhaps his shock at learning that a suburban sleeping beauty, snuggled in a king-sized bed with two children on either side of her, was armed and willing to shoot had derailed his surprise attack and, in the few seconds it might have taken him to respond, he was dead.

The police have had confirmation from a positive identification made by his wife that the dead man is, indeed, Frank Jones. He is well-known to the police from a long list of assault and domestic violence charges but, according to his record, Frank had never killed anyone and the police believe he planned to force Shelby to open up the safe and hand over cash and jewels. The police also believe that, based on his past behavior, it is unlikely he would have harmed Shelby or her children. We will never know if last night might have been the moment when Frank escalated his criminal history from robbery and assault to rape or murder and I, and many others, are relieved that the only body in the Lombardi home is his.

Christine, as Frank's long-fearful wife, is overcome with feelings of relief.

"I know this means Sophie has lost her father for good," she'd said to me this afternoon. "And I know I am in deep trouble because he had my gun but, may God forgive me, I am glad Frankie is dead. Now I'm his widow and no longer his wife."

If anyone is left to mourn Frank Jones, it isn't Christine and it doesn't appear to be his daughter. This afternoon Sophie clung to her mother, struggling to comprehend the trouble her Mom now finds herself in, but did not appear to be grieving over her father. It seems, however, that both mother and daughter are responsible for the fact that Frank got hold of Christine's gun. Sophie confessed that she had been secretly communicating with her father through text-messaging for the past several months. Frank apparently convinced his fourteen-year old daughter that he wanted to make them a family again, and asked Sophie to hide her door key under a shrub as she left for school one morning so that he could make a copy and then return it to the same hiding place. He'd told the gullible girl that one day soon he would be able to surprise Sophie and her Mom with a special celebration, telling Sophie that he would have Champagne for Christine and Sophie's favorite cookies-and-cream ice cream. It is clear that Frank had no intention of using the key to their apartment in order to prepare a reconciliation feast, and that getting his hands on Christine's gun was his sole intent.

Christine believes Frank knew she owned a gun, most likely from watching her on Wednesday evenings as she hurried from her apartment to the parking lot with her pistol case. I'd asked her why she did not put the gun case inside a larger bag and thereby disguise what she was carrying. Blatantly advertising gun ownership, especially when living in the midst of so many strangers, is foolish. No doubt many of Christine's neighbors know she keeps a gun in her apartment and there is no knowing if that fact might encourage, or discourage, a robbery, or worse. Christine, who is timid around guns at the range, appears to have been carrying her pistol case around the apartment complex as if it were no more than a pocket book.

"I don't know why I never tried to conceal it," she'd said. "I was only going from the front door to the parking lot and I always put it straight in the trunk of my car. I didn't think about anyone watching me."

Such blithe ignorance of being observed seems strange from a woman who owned a gun because she wanted to be able to protect herself from her own husband. We will never know what Frank's true intentions were last night, but we do know that he let himself into his wife's apartment sometime between seven-thirty and nine o'clock in the evening. Christine had left for Skyline at her regular time of a quarter to six. The events of the evening had resulted in her returning home about two hours earlier than usual and, feeling upset about no longer being a Pistol Belle, she'd placed her gun in the safe and decided to go to the supermarket.

"I didn't want to sit home feeling sorry for myself, and I couldn't pick Sophie up early because she'd gone out with her friend Grace and her family. I realized I had time to go food shopping and I left about five minutes after I came in. I didn't come home until after picking up Sophie at our usual time."

"How did Frank get into the safe?" I'd asked.

Christine had buried her head in her hands.

"I didn't lock it. I put the gun inside and then took out an envelope of cash I keep in there. I grabbed a bundle of bills and knew I'd taken too much money but I was feeling flustered and I was in a rush to get to the store. I pushed the safe door closed but didn't lock the handle. That way I wouldn't have to bother with the combination when I returned some of the money to the safe."

She'd slapped her hand on her forehead.

"Stupid! Stupid!"

"And how fortunate for Frank that the one day he came into your apartment the safe wasn't locked," I'd said.

"Frank's always been lucky. He's always got away with everything."

I'd listened to Christine's story and made a conscious decision to believe what she told me. Frank Jones' wife will have to face many doubters and detractors and I don't plan to be one of them. But I had also wondered about the odds of Frank entering his wife's apartment—with the sole objective of stealing her gun—on the one and only occasion that the safe was left unlocked.

"His luck ran out today," I'd said. "Getting his hands on your gun turned out to be not so fortunate after all."

"I'm in big trouble, aren't I? My gun was used in a crime."

I'd assured Christine that, while she owns a gun which has now been used in a crime, she has explained to the police how Frank got hold of it and has acknowledged her own carelessness. We must hope that they won't hold her responsible for how Frank then used it. We'd talked for a few more minutes and I'd been getting ready to leave when Jean called to say she was on her way over with yet another platter of baked ziti. This would be her third donation in twenty-four hours. The anticipation of Jean's arrival had reassured Christine that she and her daughter would not be alone, and she'd calmly accepted my departure.

"I'll see you tomorrow," I'd said. "Try to go to work and school tomorrow. I'll come over in the afternoon to stay with Sophie and I'll help you take care of the funeral arrangements. You're his widow, but you'll have to speak to the police about burying your husband's body."

And now Shelby is telling me that she is convinced that she and her children were about to be murdered, and that Christine not only provided Frank with a gun but incited him to make them his victims.

"Shelby," I say. "Christine had no reason to wish you or your children harm. She was afraid of her husband and they hadn't lived together for years. I don't believe she's behind this."

"She's jealous of me. She's poor and plain. I've had this problem before."

"It's understandable that many women would be envious of you. You have a terrific husband and four beautiful, healthy children. And you have money and a wonderful father. Many women can only hope for some of this."

Shelby smiles at me, a smug little sneer on her face.

"But they don't plot to have you murdered," I add.

"It was her husband and her gun," she says, jumping up from the couch and pointing her finger at me. "Mona, he was in my bedroom with a gun—her gun!—staring at me. One more minute and I would have been dead. And my children!"

Shelby flings herself onto the couch and starts to sob.

"Thank goodness I woke up!" she wails. "Thank goodness I had my Baby Glock under my pillow."

I walk over to her and kneel down in front of the couch and stroke her hair. I don't say that sleeping with a gun, a loaded magazine and four young children in the same bed is putting everyone at grave risk.

"The safety was on," she says, answering my unspoken thought, and suddenly sitting up and wiping her tears. "And Izzy and Tony have taken your gun safety class and know not to touch it."

The gun safety class teaches children what to do if they find a gun, but is not designed to give adults permission to leave a weapon within a child's reach.

"Daddy and Carmine say I must never do it again and I won't. I don't want my babies in bed with a gun! But I was so upset when I got home, and Carmine was away. He's always away!"

"Carmine loves you very much. He must have been terrified when he heard the news."

"It's because I got so upset about the Belles that I told Angelika to help carry the kids into my bed. She started arguing with me that we shouldn't disturb them, but I wanted to have them with me. I don't know why she argues with me. She's the *au pair* and I'm the mother! And she's no help in the middle of the night. She didn't wake up even after I fired three shots."

I stare at her.

"Yes, three shots, Mona," says Shelby, pride in her voice. "And I got him with each one. One in his neck, one in his leg and one in his heart. How's that for a bullseye?"

That's a bullseye alright. Caroline and Madison will be amazed.

"Angelika only woke up when the police arrived with their lights flashing and sirens wailing. We would all have been murdered in our beds if we had to depend on her."

From my seat in the family room I watch as Carmine walks into the kitchen and goes over to the sink. He turns on the faucet, rinses out three juice cups and places them on the counter. He pulls open one of the doors of the gigantic steel icebox, takes out a gallon container of milk and goes back to the counter. Angelika suddenly appears behind him, reaching over and grabbing the container of milk out of his hand. In a flash, Carmine turns and lunges at her, grabbing her arm with one hand and her neck with the other. The gallon container of milk flies across the kitchen and hits a cabinet door with a bang.

"What the hell are you doing?" he shouts as Angelika disappears from view. I hear a loud thud on the tiled floor. Shelby jumps up from the couch and rushes into the kitchen.

"Get off him! Get away from him!"

I follow Shelby into the kitchen and see Angelika lying on the floor. Carmine is leaning against the counter punching one hand into the other.

"Keep her away from me," he says, now tossing his arms up in the air. "Keep her away!"

Shelby clings to his chest and starts sobbing again. I lean down and take Angelika's hands as she pulls herself up from the floor.

"I was trying to help with the milk," she says, also weeping. "I didn't think it would scare you."

Carmine looks at her and rubs his hands across his eyes.

"How did you think I would react to someone coming up behind me and grabbing something out of my hands? Less than twenty four hours ago my wife had to kill a man to save her own life. And to save my children! And now you sneak up on me in my own house!"

"Daddy! Daddy!"

The children's cries reverberate around the vast stairwell. Carmine looks up and down Angelika's big, muscular body and disgust spreads across his face. I suspect his distaste for her is compounded by his embarrassment at over-reacting to what was an innocent attempt to help him, as clumsy and thoughtless as it might have been. Angelika has accurately read the expression on Carmine's face and her tears suddenly dry up and turn to anger.

"I'm here nine months and no-one wants me here! I help you and care for your kids but you always know a better way. I'm here but you still hire a babysitter. I cook but you don't eat my food."

Carmine looks at her. "I don't eat—"

Angelika is not to be interrupted. This is probably the first time she has had their combined attention.

"And now Mrs. Lombardi is angry because I not wake up when she shoots and kills!"

What a story this will make for the folks back home in Germany.

"You want me to leave, I leave!" she shouts, starting to walk out of the kitchen. "I not stay where I'm not wanted! I not stay where I get thrown on floor!"

As a businessman and property owner, Carmine is fast to detect the suggestion of blame; blame begets lawsuits.

"Angelika, if you ended up on the floor it is because I thought you were going to attack me. Under the present circumstances that's understandable. Please go to your room and calm down and we'll talk tomorrow."

The children's cries have turned into wails. Carmine rushes to the bottom of the stairs and calls that he'll be up in a minute and then comes back into the kitchen and puts his arms around Shelby.

"I not want to stay here anymore," says Angelika. "Too many rooms, too many doors to the outside. And now guns. I not know about guns."

"If you want to leave, Angelika, I, for one, won't stop you," says Shelby, a mean tone in her voice. "But we can talk tomorrow."

"Tomorrow, no. Maybe dead tomorrow! Too many guns. Too many doors!"

A silence hangs in the kitchen as the four of us look down at the floor. Suddenly I feel Carmine's and Shelby's eyes on me.

"Mona?" they say in unison.

"I need to get home to Carl."

"Would you…?" asks Carmine.

"Oh Mona," cries Shelby. "It would be such a help tonight."

"I go with this Mona lady? I go now, yes?"

"Well, I guess until tomorrow," I say, slowly. "I have a spare bed made up. I don't think Carl will..."

Izzy and Lulu suddenly run into the kitchen and throw themselves against their parents' legs.

"Get your things, Angelika," says Shelby, stroking Izzy's hair. "Just for an overnight. Mona will bring you back tomorrow. At least this nightmare of a day will be over then."

Shelby picks up both children and buries her face in the top of their heads. Angelika strides out of the kitchen and I go back into the family room to pick up my bag. I pull out my phone and call Carl.

Chapter Seventeen

"I'm here on an Exchange Visitor Visa," Angelika says, answering my question about her legal status. "I got it through the *au pair* agency."

"Does that mean you can only work for the Lombardi's?" I ask, hoping that's not the case. Angelika may have come home with me for just one night but, judging from the expressions on Carmine and Shelby's faces, I'm guessing they'd be just as happy if they never saw her again. I doubt the problems between them began in their kitchen this evening, and it is clear the Lombardi's haven't bonded with their children's European caretaker.

We'd arrived home to find Michaela watching television with Carl, each of them lying horizontally on our twin couches. A plan had immediately become clear to me. If Susan had an unasked question for me last night, I now have one for her. Will she take Angelika as her *au pair*? If Angelika's employment can be transferred to a new family, the pressure on Susan to be constantly trying to be in two places at once will be greatly alleviated. I know Susan will say she cannot afford an *au pair* and I plan to present her with an offer she would be crazy to refuse – I will pay Angelika's wages and expenses.

Carl and Michaela had stared in genuine surprise at seeing a tall, blonde girl follow me into the living room.

"This is Angelika," I'd said. "She's staying with the Lombardi's."

"No more," Angelika had pronounced in her deep, husky voice, immediately striding across the room and dropping down on the couch next to Michaela.

Never at a loss for words, Carl had jumped up and leaned across the coffee table with his hand outstretched.

"Carl Milton," he'd said, smiling and reaching down to her.

Angelika had thrust out her hand.

"I hope I'm not disturbing you. Mona is very kind."

"Yes," he'd said, glancing at me with a rare expression of confusion on his face. "My wife is a very kind woman."

No-one had spoken for a moment.

"Mona, why don't we get some drinks for our guests?"

"Wine is good," Angelika had said quickly, visibly brightening at the prospect.

Following Carl into the kitchen and making use of what little privacy it afforded, I'd whispered to Carl that Angelika was Shelby's *au pair* and that she and Carmine had asked me to bring her home with me. I'd assured him she was staying for one night only. He'd laughed.

"One night, Mona? I thought we were the home for lost girls."

I'd given him a forceful kiss, grabbed a couple of cans of iced tea out of the refrigerator and followed him back into the living room. Carl had put a bottle of red wine on the coffee table and started to open it.

"I prefer white," Angelika had said, with a quick glance at the bottle. "In Germany, the best wine is white."

I'd tossed a can of iced tea to Michaela and pulled the ring on the other can and taken a sip. Without saying a word, Carl had gone back into the kitchen and returned with a chilled bottle of white wine.

"A light German Riesling," he'd said, pouring the wine into a glass as Angelika beamed at him. Carl rarely drinks white wine and I couldn't imagine how he could not only conjure up a bottle which was already chilled, but one from the right country. My husband truly is a remarkable man. I'd then decided to get straight to the point and asked Angelika about her legal status and whether or not she could transfer to another family.

"Yes, my friend moved twice before she left. She did not like any of her families. But I have to talk to the agency. My host family is Lombardi."

"Call the agency tomorrow and ask if you can move. Then they'll find you a new family."

The purpose of this last comment is to hide my plan.

"Why not stay with you?" she asks, cutting through my subterfuge. Her glass is already empty and she slowly tips it from side to side. Carl gets up and goes back into the kitchen.

"Because we don't have children for you to take care of," I say. "There's nothing for you to do here."

Carl brings in the bottle of white wine—now placed in a terracotta wine cooler—and puts it on the coffee table. Angelika is quick to realize she is to serve herself and she fills her glass and then turns to look at Michaela.

"Where do you live?"

"Next door," Michaela says, with a little squeak, once again intimidated by a fine specimen of womanhood.

"My Mom wouldn't—"

"We don't need to discuss this tonight," I say. I must have this conversation with Susan tomorrow, not with her daughter tonight.

"How much time do you have left on your visa?" asks Carl, as usual getting to the most important question.

"Three months only. I've been with Lombardi nine months. This year is the worst of my life."

The Lombardi children are no doubt a handful and Shelby will be a demanding boss, but it's hard to imagine that nine months in her home could be so terrible.

"I can get an extension," Angelika continues. "My friend stayed two years."

"The same friend who didn't like any of her host families?" asks Carl.

"Yes, but she loves America."

"She just hates the people," says Carl, taking a slow sip of wine.

"Not all," says Angelika, smiling, Carl's humor not lost on her. "She has a boyfriend and doesn't want to go home."

"But she ran out of time," says Carl.

"She'll come back. American men want to get married. He'll marry her."

"If he loves her, he will," says Carl, turning to me and blowing me a kiss.

Michaela giggles, but Angelika's face turns solemn.

"Mr. Lombardi always hugging and kissing his wife. Mrs. Lombardi always wanting this, needing that, Carmine this, Carmine that, never leaves him alone."

"Maybe that's why he goes away on business so much," says Carl.

"I don't think so," I say, frowning at Carl.

"No, not like that," agrees Angelika. "His job makes him travel. Runs inside when he gets home and grabs her. What she's got, I don't know."

"She's got the same thing Mona's got," says Carl, brightly. "She's got a husband who loves her."

Michaela giggles again and grins at me. Angelika looks even more downcast.

"This is what I want," she says. "I come here to find it and all I find is husbands crazy about their wives."

"There must be lots of men who are crazy about you, Angelika," I say, hoping she doesn't have designs on Carl. My compliment to her is not idle flattery. Angelika is a big girl but she has a handsome face and thick, glossy hair. Her legs are long and muscular and are perfectly built for the tight leggings she is wearing. It occurs to me that she would make a fine shooter; strong legs to hold her steady and big hands to hold a big pistol. Angelika has the makings of a fine new Pistol Belle. Caroline and Madison would love her.

"You must have been terribly frightened during the break in last night," says Carl, changing the subject.

"Mrs. Lombardi upset because I not wake up. I not hear anything until she runs into my room and police are in the house and children crying."

I'm impressed that she doesn't try to dramatize her role.

"But I saw the body," she adds. "I saw the dead body carried downstairs. Mrs. Lombardi screams at me not to look and to go to the children. Now all I see in my head is the dead body."

"Well, fortunately, Shelby and the children are fine and Carmine is home," I say.

"Mrs. Lombardi never stops saying that I told her not to put the kids in her room last night," says Angelika, her head down as she rummages in her bag and pulls out a worn tissue. "She says that kids would be dead if she'd listened to me."

"That is cruel and unjust!" Carl exclaims.

"No-one knows what might have happened if the children had been sleeping in their own beds," I say. "It's likely the intruder would have gone straight into the master bedroom because, from what we've heard, it was a robbery attempt which went wrong."

Michaela is staring at me, an expression of fear on her face. I realize I have no idea what she knows about the fatal shooting.

"Michaela, I'm sorry. We shouldn't be talking about this."

"Everyone talked about it in school today," her voice is little more than a whisper. "They say the lady killed the man because he was going to attack her children."

"He didn't have chance," scoffs Angelika, leaning toward Michaela and clutching her arm. "Mrs. Lombardi had gun under her pillow and sat up and shot him."

Michaela's eyes grow wide.

"Shot him dead," Angelika adds, squeezing Michaela's arm as the girl simultaneously winces and giggles.

"We don't really know what happened," I say. "Let's leave it to the police to establish the truth."

"Mr. and Mrs. Lombardi have a lot of guns in their bedroom. She goes out every Wednesday night to shoot. She always left with a gun and a salad. I ask myself, what woman goes out with a gun and a salad?"

"Mona goes out with a gun and lemon chicken," says Carl.

I turn to him and scowl.

Angelika and Michaela look at me.

"OK," I say, deciding its time to explain. "The reason I know Mrs. Lombardi is because she's in the women's group I run at the shooting range. We get together on Wednesday evenings to eat a potluck dinner and shoot pistols."

Angelika and Michaela continue to stare at me.

"That's why she always brings a salad with her," I add, as if to provide some needed clarity.

Carl laughs and fills his glass.

"So that's where you go every Wednesday?" asks Michaela.

"Yes, every Wednesday evening I take a gun and a dish to the Skyline Sportsmen's Club. For the past few years I've run the women's league."

"Why is it a secret?" our young neighbor asks.

"It's not a secret. I haven't mentioned it before because I thought it was better if you, and your Mom, didn't know that I have guns in the house or that my hobby is shooting. I'm not sure your Mom would approve."

"Does everybody have guns in this country?" asks Angelika. "I thought just on TV?"

"Not everyone has guns, Angelika," says Carl. "But there are as many guns in America as there are people, although some people have a lot of guns and some have none. Mona's guns, like the Lombardi's, are legal and are stored properly. There's no reason for Mona to tell anyone she owns guns unless she chooses to do so."

"If I stay in this country, I'd better learn to shoot!" says Angelika. "Shelby shoots, Mona shoots!"

"If you stay in this country," says Carl, thoughtfully, "you should perhaps learn to shoot."

"That means I have to learn to shoot as well," says Michaela.

"Before you could do that," I say, feeling the discussion has gone far enough, "your Mom would have to give permission. You're old enough to come to the range with me, but I'm not sure your Mom would let you."

"You don't have to tell her," says Michaela.

"Yes, we do!" Carl and I shout.

"We would have to talk to her, Michaela," adds Carl. "You're only thirteen."

"Ask her tomorrow. Then I can come with you next week."

"No, no, not next week. Things are a little complicated right now, but I promise I'll ask her sometime and, if she agrees, I'll take you to the range."

Michaela seems content with this response. Angelika refills her glass and takes a long gulp of wine.

"It's like I'm in a movie," she says, twirling the glass in front of her. "Big mansion, screaming blonde wife, dead man carried downstairs, kids screaming, police all over, lights flashing."

She takes another swig of wine.

"Phones ringing, Mr. and Mrs. Williams arrive, everybody crying, kissing and hugging."

Carl and I look at her and nod. Last night must have been quite an experience for this young woman.

"But no-one kissing me, no-one hugging me, only saying "Angelika, how could you sleep through it?", "Angelika is no help" and now "Angelika, be gone."

I agree it is wrong that a deep-sleeping *au pair* should be made to feel guilty for not coming to her employer's aid during a robbery and, fortunately, Shelby managed the situation without assistance. If Angelika had suddenly burst into the bedroom, the outcome might have been tragically different.

There is a knock at the door and Carl gets up.

"Susan," he says brightly, as if opening the door to an expected guest. "How nice to see you."

Susan walks into the room and Michaela stares at her as if she another complete stranger has suddenly arrived at our home.

"Hello, Carl, Mona," says Susan in the same squeaky voice her daughter used a little while ago. "I'm sorry to disturb you, but Michaela needs to come home now."

Susan usually calls Michaela on her cell phone to tell her it's time to come home.

"Michaela, honey," she continues. "Please go and get ready for bed. I need to speak with Mrs. Milton for a minute."

At our insistence, Michaela stopped calling us Mr. and Mrs. Milton several months ago. As always, Susan is behind on information about her own daughter.

"Do I have to?" asks Michaela, edging toward Angelika. "This is Angelika, she's from Germany."

"Angelika," I say, seizing the opportunity to break up our little party. "Let me show you upstairs and you can get settled in. It's been a very long day for you."

"Better end than beginning," says Angelika, emptying her glass of its contents. She gets up from the couch and I lead her upstairs.

"I'll see you tomorrow, Michaela" I say, turning to her as she shuffles towards the front door.

Carl motions Susan over to the now empty couch and asks if she would like a glass of wine, which she refuses. I quickly show

Angelika the bedroom and bathroom, grab some towels out of the linen closet and hurry back downstairs. Carl is talking about Michaela's Algebra grades, but Susan is looking down at the floor as if she is somewhere far away. She does not give the appearance of a mother listening to an intelligent, caring man who takes a great interest in her daughter's scholastic achievements.

"Mona," she says, as I sit next to Carl and take his hand. "Mona, I need to talk to you about something important."

"Perhaps I should leave the two of you alone?" Carl asks politely, although I hear the reluctance in his voice. Carl spends a lot of time with Michaela and shouldn't be excluded from hearing what her mother has to say.

"No, no," Susan adds, hurriedly. "It's best if I speak with you both."

Is Susan going to be traveling even more? Working longer hours? Or is it about her house? Is there some problem with our shared property line?

"I have a brain tumor," she says, as quickly and calmly as if she was telling us about her plans for a new patio. "My doctor has given me six months to live."

Carl and I are silent. Guilt is already beginning to well up in me. I've long thought of Susan as a neglectful mother and haven't given much consideration to the possibility that something other than her job might be occupying her time. A brain tumor doesn't materialize in a matter of a few days. She must have been dealing with this for months.

"Michaela's father has never been a part of our little family," she continues. "Our relationship was already over when I discovered I was pregnant. After Michaela was born I asked him to relinquish his parental rights, which he did."

She takes a long breath and then looks at us, her eyes moving from me to Carl and back again.

"I'd like to ask you to be Michaela's guardians," she says, smiling weakly.

I squeeze Carl's hand.

"But, unfortunately, I can't."

Have we won a prize, or not?

"I have a brother in California. I appointed him Michaela's guardian years ago and I don't see how I can change it now."

"Does your brother know about your health condition?" asks Carl.

"Does Michaela know?" I interrupt, surprised that Michaela hasn't spoken to us about her mother being sick.

"I wasn't on a business trip last weekend," says Susan, looking at Carl. "I flew out to California to tell my brother. I didn't want to talk about it over the phone."

"Does he know that a guardianship agreement made years ago is now going to be put into effect?"

I scratch the inside of his palm. This last question is excessively blunt.

"At least, it might…" he adds.

"I told him last weekend," says Susan, in a brisk manner I've never heard her use when she tells me she's going away on a business trip. "He says he will be happy to take Michaela. He's going to talk to their local high school about enrolling her next year."

"Have you told Michaela?" I ask again. Why didn't Susan take her daughter with her to California if that is soon to be her home?

"No, I haven't plucked up the courage yet. But I'm less worried about telling her I'm dying than I am about telling her she's going to have to move to California. I know I should have taken her with me so she could see my brother's house and get to know her cousins, but I couldn't deal with seeing her in what is going to be her new life."

She is silent for a moment, rubbing her hands across her face.

"And, anyway, I know she'd rather stay with you."

Carl and I exchange a sideways glance.

"My brother has three boys, all teenagers. They're pretty rowdy. Michaela is so quiet. I don't know how she's going to fit into such a crazy house."

"They'll love her," I say. "Why wouldn't they?"

"My sister-in-law says she always wanted a daughter."

Susan starts to cry.

"Now she'll have mine."

I walk over to the couch, sit down beside her and put my arms around her shoulders. She leans into me just as Michaela does when I hug her; two lonely little girls.

"Susan, for as long as you and Michaela are here," says Carl. "We will do everything we can to help you."

"You can depend on us," I say. "You already know that."

"You've been so good to us, already," says Susan, now sobbing. "I think Michaela would be able to deal with me being sick if she thought she could move in with you when I'm gone."

I want desperately to ask Susan to make us Michaela's guardians, but know I must speak with Carl first. And Carl will be against us meddling in plans that have already been put in place.

"We can help you in many ways, not only with Michaela, but the house and paperwork," I say, knowing I'm now even more determined that Susan take Angelika as her *au pair*.

We sit for a few more minutes and Susan describes her symptoms, the diagnosis, the medical tests and opinions she's obtained. There is no mistake, she will live just a few more months and will be gone before Christmas, possibly Thanksgiving. Michaela will have to move to California in the middle of the school year.

I hear Angelika moving around upstairs, her feet thumping on the corridor between the bedroom and bathroom. Either our floorboards are in need of repair or all young women stomp around like elephants.

Susan says she must get home and I walk her to the door and step outside.

"Let me know when you tell Michaela and we'll make sure we're around for her."

She nods in silent thanks and I watch as she hurries in the side door of her home.

I walk back into the living room and sit down beside Carl. We clasp each other's hands and he leans his head against mine.

"I'm sure you can feel my mind spinning," I say.

"I can, Mona, and whatever you're thinking and whatever we're going to do, we're going to do it together."

Chapter Eighteen

As soon as the appropriate authorities gave approval for Frank's body to be buried, Christine asked her minister at the First Presbyterian Church to conduct a funeral service. She wanted Frank to be laid to rest in a respectful manner and for Sophie to attend the service and see people gather to mourn her father. But the church was almost empty on Tuesday morning and the few people scattered around the pews turned out to be curiosity seekers or, as Christine noted, those who were there to make sure Frank was truly dead. She recognized few faces in the crowd and had been unable to locate any of Frank's family members prior to the service.

I'd told Christine that I would pay for Frank's burial and she'd reluctantly accepted, insisting that if Frank turned out to be worth more dead than alive, she would repay me. Given Frank's apparently sketchy employment history, it seems unlikely he would have a retirement fund or a fat bank account. According to Christine, he'd taken out an insurance policy years ago but she doubted he'd kept up the premiums. Jean's granddaughter, Maggie, had called Christine—on her grandmother's insistence—and advised her that, although her husband was guilty of a break-in, he'd been killed without firing a single shot himself and Christine may have grounds to sue. Shelby's killing of Frank could be deemed self defense, but the man's death left a widow and a dependent child. Given the Lombardi and William's wealth, the possibility of Christine suing for damages could not be overlooked.

"I'm not going to sue Shelby," Christine said when Carl and I arrived to drive them to church. As she buttoned up a black wool coat, I commented on the unusually warm weather, but Christine said she only had one black coat and wanted to play the part of a widow if only for a few hours. Sophie wore a short black skirt and long sleeved black shirt and clung to Christine's arm as if she thought her mother was about to run away.

"I'm not going to sue Shelby because that's exactly what she's expecting me to do, and I'm not going to fall into her trap."

"I'm not sure it's a trap," Carl said. "Even if criminal charges are not made against Shelby, you have a legitimate claim. Your husband was killed and you were dependent on his support."

Christine snorted.

"I'm sorry, Carl, I don't mean to be rude, but Frankie hadn't paid child support for months. He was always behind. Why do you think we live in a one bedroom apartment?"

"Why would suing Shelby be a trap?" I asked.

"Shelby looks down on me because I have no money. And now I have a worthless husband who broke into her house and was supposedly going to kill her and her kids. Frank was a stupid, brainless thug, but he wasn't a killer. He was looking for money, nothing more. But Shelby will tell everyone that if she hadn't got him first, he would have killed them all."

There is no doubt that Shelby will dine out on this story for decades.

"Shelby did me a favor," Christine continued. "I don't have to be afraid of my own husband anymore. And now I'm supposed to go chasing after her money as if I have a winning lottery ticket?"

She looked at us both intently.

"I did win the lottery. I won because today we're putting Frank in the ground. If it turns out he had any money, I'll go after it as back child support or to keep for Sophie. I don't need Shelby's money."

It could be argued that given Christine's lean financial situation, she very well needs Shelby's money.

"I admire you, Christine," Carl said. "A lot of people would see it as an opportunity to get a payout, or simply to get even."

"I'll be less even with the Shelby's of this world if I go after her money," Christine had an authority in her voice I'd not heard before. "That would make me seem even more pathetic. It would be proof to Shelby that she has something I want, and she would look down on me even more. That's why it's a trap. She did something for me. She got rid of Frankie and I didn't have to do it. Imagine what that would have done to Sophie?"

Sophie moved in even closer to her mother and Christine pulled her tight.

"It's alright that Sophie's listening to this. Sophie knows her Dad was trouble and that we were afraid of him. We'll try to remember his good parts. Maybe now we can relax and something good will happen. We'll start over, but we don't want to do it with someone else's money."

Carl and I smiled at her. Her pride and dignity were impressive.

"But the thing I'm most worried about is being in trouble because Frank had my gun."

Christine has not yet heard from the police about her Beretta and, even if she does not face criminal charges, it is possible Shelby could sue her in a civil suit because the gun used to threaten her in her bedroom that night belonged to Christine. Fortunately, Shelby seems to have dropped her preposterous notion that Christine put Frank up to the break-in, telling me on the phone yesterday that she doubts Christine would have the spunk to even think of it. But even though it seems Christine is choosing to take the high road, there is no telling whether Shelby will join her on that route. A rich woman may go after a poor one if only to prove a point.

"Sometimes people sue because they are going to be sued themselves," I said. "It's sort of a pre-emptive strike."

"Let her sue me!" she scoffed. "Let her show her true, spiteful colors. I have nothing!"

The hearse pulled up in the Hillside Gardens parking lot and Sophie tugged on her mother's arm.

"I'm sorry, Christine," I said. "We shouldn't be talking about this now. Things are upsetting enough without bringing up money."

"Bring it up whenever you like! Money is a pretty simple subject with me. I don't have any! But I don't want Shelby's money, and if she wants to go after me, she can. You can't get blood out of a stone."

Christine was less stone-like than in all the years I'd known her. Frank's death seems to have energized her and given her a confidence and spirit she'd not shown before. Yet I remind myself that a woman who takes up shooting in order to protect herself is demonstrating that she doesn't intend to be a victim. Christine had spunk all along and Shelby better be careful if she thinks Christine is an easy target.

After the service and burial were over, we drove Christine and Sophie home and sat with them in their apartment. Jean and Caroline had been in church and came back with us, bringing cheese, crackers, brownies and ice cream. Carl opened a couple of bottles of red wine he'd brought, believing a drink would help lift the gloom of the funeral. Caroline set out the cheese and crackers on the coffee table in the living room, while Jean laid the brownies out on a platter on the kitchen counter.

"We'll have dessert in a while," Jean said, sitting down beside Sophie and stroking her arm.

"My Mom said you might be able to use my help," Sophie said tentatively. "I could come over after school if I could get a ride."

"I can pick you up if you don't mind climbing into an old lady's beaten-up truck in front of your school friends."

Sophie smiled, not seeming at all like the sullen, indulged girl we'd all heard about.

"That's OK, let me know when you want me to start. "Tomorrow is good. I'm always cooking for the Pistol Belles on Wednesday's so you can help me with the dishes and then we'll set up a schedule for cleaning and gardening."

At the mention of the Pistol Belles, Christine glowered at Jean. I also looked at my favorite senior citizen, wondering what age a person had to achieve before they could be relied upon to be possessed of even a modicum of tact. Jean flashed me a quick smile and, grabbing Sophie's hand, announced that on such an upsetting day it made sense to eat dessert first. The two went off into the kitchen, returning a few minutes later with warm brownies and two cartons of ice cream. Sophie passed around the plates and by the time we left, Christine and Sophie appeared to be in good spirits.

Now it's the following evening, the Pistol Belles are at Skyline and Jean is telling me that Sophie is already working out well.

"I told her she's now like my kids. With a widowed mother she'll have to grow up a lot faster."

Not surprisingly, none of us have been able to avoid talking about our two former Belles, with Madison expressing dismay at Christine's negligence in leaving her gun unsecured and outright amazement at Shelby's three hits.

"We all know how hard it is to hit a moving target."

"I've shot plenty of ducks and deer," says Jean. "Not to mention skeet. You're right, Madison, hitting something that's moving is a lot different than firing at a fixed target."

We all nod in agreement, though our shooting is generally confined to firing at paper targets stapled on cardboard.

"But *we* don't think Frank Jones was moving," adds Jean.

"Jean, remember what Maggie said about—"

"But even if he was standing still in front of her, he could have moved at any time," says Madison. "There would be no time to set up the shot."

"Point shooting," says Pete. "It's a lot different than target shooting, that's for sure. Shelby should take up practical shooting. That might be her strength."

Practical shooting simulates combat shooting and the participants shoot at facsimiles of people and objects. There are also the popular Cowboy Action events where men and women dress up in genuine western outfits and hold shoot outs. But whatever Shelby's strengths may turn out to be, I don't want to spend time talking about them so I cut the discussion short by saying it's time to get in the range to hone our own skills. I'd finally got around to calling Deb Johnson, the organizer of the competitive league and leader of the Pink Packers, and she'd immediately welcomed the Pistol Belles into the league, saying we could start next week when the Pink Packers and a couple of other teams meet at the Sure Shot Range over in the next county. I have no idea what to expect, but know we need to do well at our first competition. Practice is the only thing that will help us.

As we get our guns and ammo out, I look over at Jim. He has been unusually quiet this evening and I wonder if it's because he's upset about Christine's absence or if he is offended that I didn't speak to him ahead of time about competitive league. Or perhaps he is preoccupied because his wife's condition has worsened. Jean had briefly whispered to me that the end for Shirley Mackenzie was just a matter of days. But if that's true, would Jim be here this evening? I doubt his loyalty as range officer would take precedence over a wife who has only days to live. Perhaps Jim simply misses Christine and her desserts?

"So now we're down to the A-team," says Pete, marching up and down behind us. "Looks like there's room for a few more A-listers. I suggest you find some new shooters sooner rather than later. It will relieve pressure on the four of you."

My stomach churns and I feel anxiety welling up inside me. A new team means new people to manage. Perhaps I should bring Angelika over to the range at the weekend and let her try shooting. If she has the aptitude, I could justify giving her a slot on the team.

"I've already asked a couple of women on the rifle team," says Madison. "They turned me down saying they didn't have time, as if I didn't know that!"

"I have no-one to ask," says Caroline.

"No-one?" asks Pete, stopping behind her. "You have no-one?"

Ignoring Pete, Caroline continues to line up her 9mm ammunition. Her Beretta is out on the bench in front of her, with the action open and a yellow flag inserted.

"I'll be shooting with my 9mm when we go up against the Pink Packers next week," she says.

"There'll be a couple of other teams too," I remind her. "It's hard to know what to expect."

"I don't know Deb Johnson personally, but I've seen the Pink Packers shoot," says Pete. "They sometimes put on demonstrations. They all wear the same pink outfits."

"They have matching outfits!" I exclaim, growing more nervous. Are we going to be up against teams who are so well organized they have uniforms?

"What kind of pink outfits?" I ask.

"I don't know, but I remember they're pink. It was quite a sight."

"Mona, you don't think Pete could actually describe what a bunch of women were wearing do you?" asks Caroline, leveling a look of disdain at Pete. "It's remarkable that he not only noticed the color, but the fact that they were all wearing the same thing."

"I can assure you of one thing, Caroline," says Pete, stopping in front of her. "If you wore the same clothing as everyone else, I would see the difference. Put you in Pink Packers gear and I'd think a pink angel had come down to save me."

Can't Caroline see that Pete is crazy about her? She could rescue him with just one big smile.

"I'm a long way from being an angel, Pete," she says, looking up at him as a faint smile passes across her face.

"And that's what makes you all the more beautiful," says Pete. They hold each other's gaze and the rest of us stand and watch. I feel as if I'm back in Junior High and can barely resist the temptation to go and push their faces together.

"We wear khakis and a long-sleeved burgundy shirt on the university rifle team," says Madison, interrupting the magic.

"I think we need something a little foxier than burgundy and beige," I say. I may not be a *fashionista* but know we need to make a splash. "Caroline always wears black and looks fantastic. Why don't we make black our color?"

"I have black jeans and a black polo-necked shirt," says Madison.

"Black is fine with me, obviously," says Caroline.

"I can drag out some widow's weeds," says Jean. "But we need to focus on shooting and not what we're wearing."

"It doesn't hurt for you to show up looking like a real team," says Pete. "Black is good. It's intimidating. And Caroline has already set the standard."

I smile at him. If I was single, I would go for Pete without hesitation. He's intelligent, generous and handsome.

"Black it is," I say. "The Pistol Belles are the women in black!"

Chapter Nineteen

We have yet to find out about the shooting abilities of our competitors, but I'm guessing they're of a higher standard than the team names. I named the Pistol Belles in honor of Belle Starr, yet often worry that it creates the impression of a group of little ladies with little shooting skills to match. And, not only am I concerned about our image, but that the name of the 'Bandit Queen' is being used in a diminutive, feminine manner. Yet, even given these concerns, I didn't feel a spasm of envy when I heard about the Pink Packers, and I've now been introduced to the captains of the Gunpowder Gals and the Bullseye Babes and I wonder if women shooters enjoy flaunting their femininity, or believe their identification as shooters must include a statement on their gender. Or perhaps the women's shooting skills and self-confidence are so high that they cannot be undermined by a girly team name. Whatever the reason, the women and their team names are great material for Madison's thesis.

More worrying than our team labels, is discovering the number of shooters each team is fielding. The Pink Packers are a group of eight women dressed, just as Pete described, in pink jeans and bright pink sweatshirts emblazoned with the team name. Even their sneakers are pink with white stripes, although most are filthy, no doubt from the mountains of lead and gunpowder they've stomped in.

The six members of the Bullseye Babes are all sporting bright red pants and red long-sleeved shirts. And, yes, red sneakers. Their captain is a short, cheery woman named Alison Welles who tells me she put together her team five-years ago and their line-up still consists of the original members. In other words, these six women have been shooting together since around the time I first climbed into Jean's truck and had a gun thrust into my unskilled hands.

The Gunpowder Gals are an impressive looking group, all appearing to be over six feet tall until I notice that beneath their boot-cut denim jeans, they are wearing identical black leather boots with four inch heels. Such narrow high heels don't seem to be practical for an evening standing on the concrete floor of a range but with their matching tan leather vests, blue gingham shirts and bolo ties, these eight women look as if a gun is an every day accessory, as familiar to them as their mobile phone or purse. Though neither the boots nor their semi-automatic pistols fit the Western motif, the message is clear: these cowgirls can shoot.

I think it's time to get out of Dodge.

Jean motions to me from her seat on a plaid covered couch set alongside an enormous stone fireplace in Sure Shot's spacious clubhouse. Angelika is at her side, not having spoken a word since we arrived half an hour ago.

"These broads are thirty or forty years younger than me," Jean says. "You need to find some more shooters."

"Don't bail on me now," I tell her. "We're all nervous."

"I'm tired," says Jean. "It's close to eight o'clock and we haven't started shooting."

"Deb says they start at eight o'clock on the dot," I say, glancing up at a clock which is nestled between a rack of antlers and the head of a moose. Someone has been shooting far from home.

"I'm sure we'll start soon," I add. "And I know I'll feel a lot better when Caroline and Madison get here."

As I speak, our two finest shooters walk in the door looking every bit the competitors with their head-to-toe black clothing and their long hair drawn back tightly from their handsome faces.

"Thank goodness you're here," I say, pulling Angelika off the couch and hurrying over to them.

"It's my fault we're late," says Madison. "Rifle practice didn't end until after six and Caroline was giving me a ride so I made her late too."

"You're here now, that's all that counts. You both look fantastic, but I hope you're not already tired from rifle practice, Madison."

"On the contrary," Madison replies. "I'm in the zone. The sooner we start shooting, the better."

Caroline is studying Angelika, coolly looking her up and down with what appears to be approval.

"This is Angelika," I say. "She's our new Pistol Belle."

"Where have you been shooting, Angelika, that we didn't find you before?" asks Caroline, a look of surprise spreading across her face.

"Nowhere," Angelika replies, straightening up to her full height. "Mona take me to Skyline last weekend. Now I'm a Pistol Belle."

Madison and Caroline exchange glances.

"I see," says Caroline, turning her piercing gaze to me. "Let's hope we can all stand up to the competition."

"I'm sure Angelika will do fine," says Madison. "You look like a shooter, so glamorous and strong!"

"Thank you," says Angelika, smoothing her hands over her skin-hugging stretch turtleneck and Spandex pants.

Caroline turns away from Angelika and surveys the sea of pink, red and gingham.

"It's no fashion parade in here. If their shooting is as bad as their attire, we'll win—even with someone on the team who has barely shot before."

Angelika's face falls and I smile and stroke her arm. Her statement about her visit to the range and her spot on the Pistol Belles is accurate in both its brevity and fact. After Angelika had confirmed with the *au pair* agency that she could change host families, she'd called Shelby and told her she did not want to return to the Lombardi home. Shelby had retorted that that decision had already been made and that they would pay Angelika for the three months remaining on her placement on condition she did not speak to anyone about their family and, in particular, the shooting. Angelika had guffawed when she'd reported this conversation to Carl and me, saying she didn't know you could forbid someone from speaking.

"I think in America there is freedom of speech," she'd scoffed. "At least that's what they tell everyone else. Now this American woman says I can't talk about her family or that she killed a man? Who does she think she's kidding?"

Carl and I advised her to comply with Shelby's request in order to ensure she received her three month's pay. Thus, while Angelika was engrossed in freeing herself from Shelby's bondage, I'd been busy next door persuading Susan to not only hire Angelika as her *au pair*, but accept that I would pay her salary. Susan had been hesitant on both counts until Michaela, who'd crouched secretly on the stairs while I spoke with her mother, rushed into the living room and begged her to let Angelika move in with them. Her daughter's obvious desire to have Angelika in their home won her mother over, and I'd finally convinced Susan to let me pay for their new *au pair* by telling her that I'd already committed to hiring Angelika myself and, with no work for her to do in my house, this energetic German girl would be so much happier with them. Two days later, the agency had formally enrolled Susan as a new host family, Angelika had applied for a twelve month extension to her visa, and her few possessions were retrieved from the Lombardi home—with the help of Shelby's housekeeper—to the third bedroom in Susan's home.

In the middle of all this activity, we'd managed to sandwich in a trip to Skyline and, as luck would have it, Pete had been at the range shooting. He'd given Angelika two hours of undivided instruction, followed by two more hours the following day. At the end of the second session, Pete had pronounced Angelika a natural and told me to put her straight on the Belles line-up.

"She can take the Basic Pistol class when it runs next month," Pete had said when I'd pointed out that I'd be breaking the one rule I'd fought hard to protect. "In the meantime, she's only shooting with the Belles and will be under your control."

"What, no dinner tonight?" he now calls out across the Sure Shot clubhouse.

Angelika grins broadly at Pete and flamboyantly holds her cheek out for a kiss. Pete strides over to her and gives her a European-style peck on both cheeks.

"Angie girl," he says, handing her a bright blue case. "I brought my .22 Kimber for you to shoot tonight. It's the gun we sighted in for you on Sunday. Stick with this and you'll do great."

"Thanks, Petie," says Angelika. "You make me a shooter!"

"Let's hope that's all he makes her," says Jean, who has got up from the couch and is standing behind me. "Some feathers will soon be flying. You're getting too many hens for one rooster, Mona."

I ignore Jean and steal a glance at Caroline who is staring silently in front of her. Madison leans in to her and whispers in her ear.

"You're right," Caroline responds to her. "I'm sure we're allowed practice time."

Caroline's voice is strong and she shows no discernible sign of discomfort, but I know from the time I've spent with her in class that when she appears to be at her most composed, she is a cauldron inside. Caroline's ice queen demeanor disappears when she is relaxed and confident, as she is with our students. But the ice queen is here with us tonight.

"We should all go in to practice together," I say. "We're a team, don't forget."

The Sure Shot indoor range is several notches above Skyline's and is equipped with automated target systems, separate shooting booths and bright lights. Each of the four teams is given four stations and some of the members of the Pink Packers, Gunpowder Gals and Bullseye Babes are already in place.

"Is it alright if we fire off a few practice rounds?" I ask a member of the Bullseye Babes.

"Practice is at seven o'clock for half an hour," she replies. "The range is cold right now. We start competition in a few minutes."

"No problem," I say before any of the Belles can complain that we weren't told about seven o'clock practice. "We'll just take our positions. We're five shooters so I guess we rotate through our four spots."

"I hear Shelby Lombardi isn't with you tonight," says the Bullseye Babe. "That's a shame. I was looking forward to meeting her. It seems she put in some fine shooting when she needed to."

Deb Johnson had asked me on the phone if Shelby was one of our shooters and I'd told her she was no longer a member of the Pistol Belles.

"You should give her an honorary spot," Deb had said. "We're just playing at shooting but she used her skills in real-life."

I'd wanted to say that just hours before Shelby shot Frank Jones, she'd refused to go into the range to prove her shooting skills. But it's clear that Shelby has become our claim to fame and is the Pistol Belle everyone wants to meet.

"You can divide up your shooters how you want," the Bullseye Babe says, looking at me blankly when I fail to respond to her comment about Shelby. "If you want three to shoot first and then two, you can do that, or four can shoot and then one."

I know exactly how to get us off to a good start.

"Caroline, Madison," I call. "Take your positions now. Jean, Angelika and I will shoot second."

"Good strategy, boss," says Jean, looking slyly at the Bullseye Babe as she continues to study us. "Show these gals right off the bat that we have some great shooters."

Caroline and Madison smile at each other and take their positions. Jean, Angelika and I put our gear on a long wooden bench and sit down.

"We're both shooting 9mm's," says Madison. "My Glock and Caroline's Beretta. I forgot to ask if we were restricted to any caliber."

"No, I spoke with Deb about it. She says most of the women shoot .22's, but you can shoot higher calibers. It's good that you're both shooting together. We three have .22's."

I've brought my Ruger, of course.

"I've got my revolver, like always," says Jean. "These Gunpowder Gals should be impressed with it. They look like they just got in from the corral."

"And Angelika has Pete's silver Kimber," says Caroline, glancing at our newest member. "If Pete sighted it in for you, you should be able to hit the paper."

"She'll do more than hit the paper," I say. "Pete says she's a natural."

"Good," says Caroline, stiffly. "Then we've replaced Shelby and Christine with someone who can actually shoot."

"You can all shoot," says Pete. "I'm here tonight to bear witness to that fact."

"First shooters take your positions!" calls Deb Johnson. "Range goes hot in one minute. We follow our usual sequence. Ten shots at slow fire. That's ten shots in ten minutes, nice and slow. Then we go to timed fire. Five shots in twenty seconds and then another five shots in twenty seconds. Then my personal favorite, rapid fire! Five shots in ten seconds and another five shots in ten seconds."

"This is standard competition drill," Pete explains. "It takes about fifteen minutes and then the next set of shooters go up. Angelika, pay close attention to the shooters and watch their stance and positions."

"No coaching during competition," calls Deb Johnson. "Spectators only."

"My apologies, Deb," says Pete, sitting down on the bench. "I'll just enjoy the view."

Madison turns around and smiles at Pete. Caroline is facing forward, her curvy rear sleek and taut in her tight black pants.

"Petie," says Angelika, moving closer to him. "I think you're hot for someone, and it's not me."

Jean guffaws.

"These foreign hens are pretty sharp. I don't have to worry that the Belles will turn into a bunch of polite ninnies when I'm gone."

"You're not going anywhere," I say, firmly. "But, you're right, Angelika figures things out fast."

"Angie girl," says Pete, patting her muscular thigh. "You're a sharpshooter. If your aim is as good as your eye, you're going to be a champion."

Caroline turns around and sees Pete's hand on Angelika's leg and her head quickly swivels back.

"Sharpshooter!" cries Angelika. "That's what I want to be. Wait until I tell everyone back in Germany!"

"Quiet," calls Deb Johnson. "Range is hot. First shooters may start firing now."

Madison and Caroline are loaded and ready to fire. I want to remind them that they have ten minutes for these first ten shots and to take their time.

"No coaching during competition," Deb Johnson says again, as if reading my mind.

Madison fires two shots. Both hit the X. Let the Bullseye Babes see that! Caroline fires three shots. They're all in the first circle, just shy of the bullseye, and each worth ten points. Madison fires two more, and Caroline three. They complete their shots in less than five minutes. Madison scores a perfect one hundred points, having placed each shot in the inside circle. Caroline scores ninety. This is a fantastic start.

Most of the other shooters take the full ten minutes and earn scores ranging from forty to eight, with two exceptions. Deb Johnson has scored a solid ninety and a young woman with the Bullseye Babes has matched Madison's one hundred points.

"Good shooting, Pistol Belles," says Deb Johnson. "It's a pleasure to meet some fine shooters."

Madison and Caroline are beaming.

"Range is hot," calls Deb. "Shooters begin timed fire when I call. Five shots in twenty seconds and then another five shots in twenty seconds."

Caroline and Madison each bring up their gun from the bench and hold it steady.

"Fire!"

Madison fires five shots. They're all in the second circle and are worth nine points each for a total of forty-five. Caroline's five shots are spread between the first and second circles and are worth a total of forty-seven. This is excellent shooting.

"Get ready for your second round of five," calls Deb. "Ready, fire!"

Madison gets all five shots in the second circle. Forty-five points. Caroline's are in the third circle. Forty points.

"Great shooting, ladies," says Deb. "Now rapid fire. Five shots in ten seconds, followed by another five shots in ten seconds. Shots fired after I've called time do not count."

Madison and Caroline bring up their guns again in one graceful movement. They each fire off five fast shots, placing them in the second circle for forty-five points. They fire again and get exactly the same score. Out of a possible total of three hundred points, Madison has scored two hundred and eighty and Caroline has scored two hundred and sixty-seven. These are impressive scores and Madison's is the highest of the first group of shooters.

"Outstanding shooting," I say. "You are dynamite! But now I'm worried that the rest of us are going to let you down."

"You won't let us down, Mona," says Madison. "If it wasn't for you, we wouldn't even be here."

"Madison, it was you who told me about the competitive league," I remind her.

"I don't mean that. I mean there wouldn't be a Pistol Belles team if you didn't get us all together in the first place and have the patience to keep it going. I know we aren't always easy."

"Thank you, Madison, you are actually making me teary," I say, wiping my eyes. "I love the Belles. I just wish Christine and Shelby could be here."

"Don't get sentimental," says Caroline. "You've added Angelika and that could make us the team we were meant to be along. If Christine and Shelby want to keep up their shooting, they can."

"I'm guessing it's going to be a while before Shelby wants a gun in her hands," I say. "I don't think she ever expected to kill someone."

"Don't be too surprised," says Jean. "She might have taste for it now. She'll be all over the range."

"Well, it's early days yet," I say, not relishing the thought of Shelby becoming trigger happy. I turn to Jean and Angelika. "It's time for us to shoot.

Deb Johnson leads us all through the same three sections as the first group. Jean's shots are all in the outer circles, finishing with one hundred and ninety points. I end with a score of two hundred and thirty. The real surprise is Angelika. Shooting poorly in the slow fire shots, she barely hit the outer circles and scored only fifty points. In timed fire she earned a decent seventy points. But in rapid fire, she came into her own. Her first five shots were all in the second circle for forty-five points. Her last five were all in the first circle for an impressive fifty points. Her total score was two hundred and fifteen points, and this from a woman who until five days ago had never held a gun in her hands.

Angelika rushes over to Pete and smacks a rapid fire barrage of kisses on his cheeks. He laughs and strokes her hair. His manner is not of a lover, but of a father or older brother.

"Thank you, thank you, Petie! You make me a shooter! Now make me a sharpshooter!"

"I'm happy to help a beautiful young girl find her groove. I'll give you more lessons this weekend if you'd like."

"Like?" cries Angelika, now jumping up and down on the range floor. "Yes, I like, I like!"

"But these ladies can also teach you a lot," adds Pete. "Caroline, would you be able to come with us to Skyline on Saturday?"

Caroline looks at Pete and then at Angelika.

"Please say yes, Caroline," says Angelika. "Petie says you hottest shooter."

Pete smiles and rubs his hands over his face. Caroline's dark eyes shine in the dim light of the range.

"Sure, I can shoot with you on Saturday," she says, slowly. "I'll show you how to handle a 9mm. You're strong enough for it."

Angelika walks over to Caroline's side and, though affecting to whisper in her ear, speaks in a voice loud enough to carry around the range.

"And I'll show you how to handle Petie. You're definitely strong enough for it."

Chapter Twenty

"I guess this was bound to become an issue," I say, sitting down at the dining room table with my cleaning kit and the Ruger resting on an old towel. "I'm surprised it took two weeks."

"So am I," Carl agrees. "At first everyone thought it was a good thing that Shelby was able to protect herself and her kids, and there was general amazement that a young wife could kill a guy stone dead within minutes of him breaking into her home. But now public opinion has shifted against her."

I'd rushed in the front door eager to relate to Carl how well the Pistol Belles had done at our first competition, but my bubble had quickly burst with Carl's report of the talk on campus. It seems support for Shelby has evaporated and become a cry for stricter gun control.

"Is it because no charges have been filed against her?" I ask, pushing the wire brush through the barrel.

"People want to see her punished," says Carl, sipping his wine. "The sensational, even glamorous, idea that she could sit up in bed and fire and kill an intruder has turned into questions about her fitness as a mother."

"Two weeks have gone by and she hasn't been charged," I say, as if I have firsthand knowledge of the workings of the police and county district attorney. "It might help if she was charged with something."

"Child endangerment is what most people are talking about," says Carl, who has not only tapped into the on-campus gossip, but numerous internet sites. "Putting a loaded gun in the same bed as four small children clearly puts everyone at grave risk."

"The gun wasn't loaded! Everyone says she had a loaded gun under her pillow, but that's not true."

"It was as good as loaded," Carl says, stiffly.

"The magazine was loaded but it wasn't in the gun. Before she could fire, Shelby had to slot the magazine into the gun. I'm not defending the stupidity of putting a gun and its ammo in the same bed as the kids, but none of those children would have been able to load the magazine into the Glock, even if they knew how to do it."

"As a gun woman, Mona, you know that. But most people don't and nor do they care. A gun was used to kill someone and the killer was a mother who had the gun in the same bed as the kids. Charging Shelby with child endangerment might satisfy people's need for blood.

"That must be a serious charge. Shelby would be devastated if she was publicly paraded as the mother who knowingly put her children at serious risk."

"It's in the best interests of all gun owners if Shelby is charged with something," says Carl, coming up behind me and massaging my shoulders. "The gun control advocates have bided their time to see what the police would do. Now it looks as if Shelby may get away with manslaughter, if not murder, and they're using this opportunity to vent their outrage."

"What about Christine? She left a gun and ammo in an open safe. Frank took it, but her daughter could just as easily have got to it first."

"Another case of endangering a child," Carl agrees. "In addition to the fact that Christine's gun wasn't properly stored and used in a crime. And, you're right, the talk I'm hearing is not just about Shelby, it's also about how a man who has been charged with domestic violence got hold of his estranged wife's gun."

"You're not allowed to own a gun if you're a convicted felon," I say, pouring cleaning fluid onto a rag and rubbing it over the two magazines. Carl takes his hands off my shoulders and moves away from the table. "Does that include domestic violence charges?"

"According to one article I read, if you're under a protection order of any kind in this state, you are not allowed to possess a gun. Forget about owning one, you're not allowed to possess one. Frank had possession of Christine's gun—the very person he was barred from being in contact with."

"Frank is dead, but Christine is more alive than I've ever seen her."

Carl goes back to the couch and picks up his glass. He watches as I pick up cleaning papers, douse them with oil and push them through the barrel. I pour oil on a rag and rub it around the trigger and the muzzle.

"The national media lost interest very quickly," he says. "I'm guessing it's because neither the Lombardi's nor Christine would speak out and, surprisingly, no-one picked up the thread about the women's shooting league or that Christine and Shelby knew each other."

"There have been some widely-publicized home invasions around the country in the last couple of years and I think that's why so many people supported Shelby's actions. People were relieved that the only victim was the criminal. A guy breaks in, a woman shoots and kills him and everyone is happy."

"Yes, it makes people feel safer," Carl agrees. "One less attacker to worry about and one less horror story to read. I guess that's why the media dropped it."

"And that doesn't make gun control maniacs happy," I say, putting the Ruger in its case. "What a terrible world we live in when a woman can actually use a gun to defend herself and her children!"

"Many gun control advocates are not maniacs, Mona," Carl says, sitting up and adopting the position which usually heralds a lecture. "They genuinely believe people should not have guns in their homes, particularly not in reach of children."

"And that's why I'm happy to teach gun safety! We teach children to not touch a gun if they find one and to immediately tell an adult."

"In this case, it's the adults who need to be taught," Carl says, dryly.

"So now Christine and Shelby are going to be vilified," I say, picking up the gun case and my cleaning bag and heading toward the basement stairs.

"They must be charged with something," says Carl after I've returned from the basement. "And that would be a good thing for anyone who believes in the right to bear arms. It could be child endangerment or that a gun was used in a crime, but if they are charged and pay the penalty, then people will be satisfied."

"But they could go to prison! Even with her newfound confidence, I doubt Christine would make it through a prison sentence. Nor do I think Shelby is planning on an orange jumpsuit for her spring wardrobe."

"Hopefully they would get probation or community service," Carl laughs. "I don't want Shelby or Christine to serve time, but their laxity with guns is giving all gun owners a bad reputation, particularly women."

"Why women in particular?" I ask, defensively. "We're generally thought of as being more careful with guns."

"That belief may be true in the shooting community, but many people find it easy to portray women as unfit to own firearms. This case gives them all the ammo they need, forgive the expression. Christine is in a hurry to go to the supermarket, tosses her gun in the safe but doesn't lock the door. Shelby's husband is on a business trip and she puts her four children in her bed and a loaded gun under the pillow."

"A loaded gun is what people believe," Carl quickly adds, before I can correct him again. "Neither Shelby's nor Christine's actions demonstrate a sense of responsibility, or even simple common sense."

"I agree they both acted stupidly," I say, sitting down next to him. "And I wish Christine had locked her safe and hadn't made it so easy for Frank to get her gun. Beyond that, we don't know what might have happened."

"But I'm guessing the reason no charges have been filed against Shelby or Christine is because John Williams is working his connections," says Carl thoughtfully. "It's not just that Williams has money, he is genuinely respected in this town. And he's shrewd enough to know that if his daughter doesn't get charged, he'd better make sure Christine doesn't either."

"This will seal the fate of the land next to Skyline," I say, laying my head on Carl's shoulder. Shooting is tiring and competing even more so.

"Ah, yes, the land that Williams is apparently going to bequeath to the town. He may have to turn it over sooner rather than later. The police may not indict Shelby if the town gets its hands on the land and can put in their soccer fields."

"He should give the land to Skyline. If it wasn't for the club Shelby wouldn't even know which way to point a gun. And she sure as heck wouldn't have been firing at an intruder."

"By that reasoning, Williams should give the land to you," says Carl, with a smile. "If it wasn't for you, Shelby wouldn't know which way to point a gun and—"

"—and wouldn't have killed Frank. Thanks, Carl! I really don't want to take responsibility for Shelby's shooting."

"There goes that responsibility word—"

"Or for Christine's gun ownership!"

"Didn't you go with her to the gun dealer?"

"Don't level that at me. You know I feel implicated in all of this."

"I understand, Mona, of course you feel implicated, but you really shouldn't. Shelby and Christine got involved in guns and shooting through their own free will."

I see his mouth twitching.

"You just helped them along," he says, laughing and pulling me against him. He kisses my forehead and I push him away.

"Seriously," Carl continues. "We must hope that neither of them gets away with such negligence. The gun control advocates will make them the poster-girls for everything that's wrong with gun ownership."

"But what can we do? They're my friends and we can't join the throng who are against them. And I'm sure they've both learned a lot from this horrible incident. Christine will never be so casual about a gun again, and I doubt Shelby relishes the thought of shooting and killing another human being."

I stand up and walk around the coffee table. Carl watches me as I bend over to pick up the books, papers, pens and coasters which are strewn along the floor.

"No matter what Jean might say," I add.

"What does Jean say?"

"That Shelby will now have a taste for shooting and will trade on her achievement, if you can call it that."

"Defending yourself and your children is an achievement," says Carl. "I don't think anyone could argue that when it comes to killing Frank, Shelby is morally in the clear. But she mustn't give the impression that she thinks a gun is the answer to every threat, nor be perceived to be enjoying her notoriety."

"The latter will be difficult. Shelby loves attention and won't be shy about strutting her stuff. But I'm sure her father and Carmine will keep her in line."

"How sexist, Mona! Do women still need their fathers and husbands to control their feminine excesses?"

"In this case, yes," I admit. "John Williams will be working hard to prevent his family from being turned into a public spectacle. And Carmine is shrewd enough to know that publicity may be good for business in the short term, but over the long term it's best to be far removed from controversy."

"Well put, Mona, perhaps you should go over to the Lombardi's and offer your services as their advisor."

"I'm already more involved than is good for me. A long time ago I responded to Carmine's plea to teach his wife to shoot and for years I've tolerated Shelby's trouble-making. I'm one of the few people who know that John Williams is dying and I've taught gun safety to two of their children. And now I've taken an unwanted *au pair* off their hands. I think I would do well to stay away from that house."

"But you won't."

"Actually, I will," I say firmly, plopping myself down next to him again. "Next time they'll probably send me away with one of the kids."

"Talking of other people's kids," says Carl. "Have we heard anything further from Susan?"

"Only that she will be forever grateful to me for making her hire Angelika, and that she will let me know when she has told Michaela about her condition."

"And that Michaela will be moving to California?"

"I guess. Poor Angelika will be out of work again."

"Maybe she'll go to California too. Angelika is the kind of person who lands on her feet. She'll find the US citizen of her dreams playing beach volleyball."

"That will be a happy ending."

"Will it, Mona? Or are you hoping we become Michaela's guardians and Angelika stays right here?"

Carl's face is so close to mine it's as if his breath is blowing words onto my lips.

"I don't know, Carl. I don't know."

"Thank you for being honest. I don't know either."

I take hold of his hand and am about to suggest we go to bed when my cell phone beeps. It's a text message from Christine.

"Mona please call me," I read aloud.

"Her diffidence hasn't completely gone. Why didn't she just call if she wants to talk to you?"

"Christine is a considerate woman," I say, scrolling down for her number. "It is possible to be bold without being a bulldozer."

"Mona, thank you, thank you," Christine says breathlessly, answering on the first ring. "The police just called and I have to report to the station at nine o'clock tomorrow morning! Oh, Mona, what am I going to do?"

Christine is now whimpering into the phone and I picture her pacing up and down the small living room. Carl is right, as always. Her newfound confidence seems to have vanished.

"Please come with me. I can't do this alone."

"I'll come with you," I say without hesitation, simultaneously remembering we have a program in the morning. I pick up a pen and scribble a note to myself to call Caroline. I'll ask her to run both sessions alone.

"I'll come with you, Christine," I repeat. "But you need a lawyer."

"I don't know any lawyers. You have a lawyer don't you?"

"I know only two lawyers. The woman who settled my parent's estate and the guy we used when we bought this house."

Carl is shaking his head in obvious dismay that Christine thinks the same lawyers who handle wills and real estate could defend her against possible criminal charges.

"I'll come over at eight o'clock," I continue. "I'll try to get the names of some lawyers who will be able to help you. Then you and I will call them before we go to the police station."

"Alright, at least you know what I should do."

"Does Sophie know about this?"

"Yes, I'm afraid so. I wish she didn't have to know, but she hears every word in this place. And, anyway, if I'm going to get sent to prison, she'd have to know."

"I don't think you are going to be incarcerated," I say confidently, though I have no idea whether this statement is true.

"I'd better not be!" she suddenly shouts into the phone. Christine's neighbors must think a new tenant has moved in, as more noise will have emanated from her unit in the last two weeks than in all the years she's lived there.

"And Shelby better also be under arrest! If she's not in bigger trouble than me, I will take back everything I said about not suing her. She killed my husband!"

"Christine, everything—"

"I take it back right now! I bet your lawyers know how to sue a rich bitch for all she's worth—and she's worth a lot!"

I'm fairly confident John Williams and Carmine Lombardi could soon arrange for Shelby to be worth very little, at least until a lawsuit is settled. I know for sure that neither of my pleasant polite lawyers would be adept at handling such a case.

"We need to find you the right lawyer," I say, calmly. "And then you can ask him, or her, about your chances of successfully suing Shelby."

"I'm supposed to be at work at eight thirty," she says, suddenly calming down and switching to her old air of resignation. Christine is smart enough to know that staying employed may be worth more to her than a risky lawsuit. "I'll leave a message that I'll be late—and that I might never be there again."

She starts to cry.

"Plan, don't project, Christine. We don't know why the police want to see you. Maybe they just want to return your gun to you?"

Carl stares at me with an expression on his face which suggests it would take too much energy to shake his head. I assure Christine that I will be at her apartment first thing in the morning and I toss my phone on the couch.

"Were you born with such remarkable prescience?" I ask him. "You come home from campus saying it's time Shelby and Christine were indicted and now it seems that at the very moment you were speaking to me, the police were on the phone with Christine."

"And Shelby, we hope. But this doesn't make me a seer. It was inevitable and now the gun control advocates will see that the law—inadequate as they believe it to be—is dealing with two negligent gun slingers."

"Gun slingers," I snuggle close to him, feeling the need of the comfort of his solid chest. "And I thought the Pistol Belles were going to be such a great group."

"Well, Christine and Shelby aren't Belles anymore," he says, stroking my hair. "No matter what I say, they're not yours or your responsibility."

"They'll always be mine. That's the way it is with us shooting gals."

Chapter Twenty-One

"Jeez, Mona, you scared me," says Jean when I call to ask for her granddaughter's phone number. "Phone calls at six o'clock in the morning usually bring bad news."

"It is bad news," I say. "But I'm sorry if you thought it was about your family. It's Christine. She needs our help."

"We've known that all along," says Jean, dryly. "But you've called the right place. If she needs a good lawyer, my Maggie will get her set up."

Jean gives me Maggie's office, home and cell phone numbers and I am about to thank her and hang up when she tells me that she has something to say.

"One favor deserves another, Mona. Now I'm going to ask you for something."

"Go ahead," I say, slowly.

"I need your understanding."

I know what's coming.

"I'm going to retire from the Pistol Belles," Jean continues, her voice full. "I can't keep up with those gals we were with last night."

"You did fine—"

"I did fine, Mona, but you need more than that. You need some real good shooters. You need another Madison or Caroline, not an old lady who fumbles her ammo and doesn't have the strength to handle anything bigger than a low caliber revolver."

"I don't want to lose you," I say, my own voice quavering.

"You need to lose me, Mona. The Pistol Belles could be a real team one day, but not with me."

"How can you say that? We all—"

"Keep that German gal. She has the makings of a fine shooter. If Madison and Caroline accept her, they'll be a powerful trio."

"But this will leave only—"

"Like I said last night, you need to find some new girls. Maybe that's something I can help you with, but I'm off the Pistol Belles as of now.

"Oh, Jean, it's you who taught me to shoot and inspired me to take on the women's league," I wail.

"Then my job is done. You and me can go and shoot at Skyline whenever you have time. It will be like old times, no pressure, no personalities."

"That's a deal," I say, knowing Jean is right to bow out now. Driving to a new range each week to shoot in competition will be too much for her. She's had a lifetime of shooting and is wise enough to know that except for some friendly firing at a familiar range, its time to give it up. "But please start scouting for shooters. You know practically every family in town."

"I have a niece who might be interested. She's my brother Hank's daughter. She hunts and is a master with a 12 gauge shotgun. She's filled my freezer on more than one hunting season. I could transfer my pistol to her and that might get her interested."

"Bring her up to Skyline as soon as you can. Any Muirhouse woman is good enough for the Pistol Belles.

"I'll call Deandra today. Her husband may have a couple of pistols she could use but, as I say, hunting is their big thing. Their house is full of heads and skins and antlers. I think she'd enjoy being a Belle. She's obviously competitive otherwise she wouldn't stick all those trophies up on the wall."

"I'd like to meet her even if she isn't interested in joining the Belles."

I say goodbye to Jean, tell her I will call her later and punch in the numbers for Maggie's cell phone.

"Margaret Delaney," she answers crisply.

I remind Maggie that we met recently at her grandmother's house and blurt out the details of Christine's legal problems. Maggie immediately names a lawyer she recommends.

"Does your friend have money?" she asks.

"No, but I'm willing to pay for her lawyer."

My willingness to cover Christine's legal costs is an impulsive offer and one that will be questioned by Carl. He is aware that I paid for the gun safety materials and for Frank's funeral and that I'm now paying Angelika. From the moment I received my inheritance, Carl has insisted that the money is mine to spend as I wish. But he remained adamant last night that both Christine and Shelby should be punished, and I know he will question the wisdom of my paying Christine's legal fees.

"That's nice of you," says Maggie. "Check his hourly fee and make sure he has handled child endangerment cases. That will be your friend's biggest problem."

I go upstairs, take a shower and pull on slacks, a black shirt and jacket. Carl is still sleeping so I write him a note, place it in the frying pan and leave it on the kitchen counter. He will take one look at the note and drive over to campus to eat breakfast in the cafeteria.

I arrive at Christine's apartment to find her in the kitchen slicing bagels.

"I've been up half the night," she says. "I just went out to the bakery and bought fresh bagels. I need to eat if I'm going to hold up today."

The shower is running and I guess Sophie is in the bathroom. I step into the living room and see that it is not only tidy, but positively shining.

"I scrubbed the entire apartment," Christine says coming up behind me, a bread knife in her hand. "I want to leave everything neat and clean if I'm going to get locked away."

"You're not going to get locked away," I say, unconvincingly. "You'll be back here this afternoon."

Christine looks at me and shakes her head.

"I've already made arrangements for Sophie. I called her friend's parents and told them I may have to leave at short notice for a family emergency. They said Sophie could stay with them for as long as we needed."

"It's good to make plans, but let's hope you don't need them."

"I'm sorry for screaming at you last night, Mona," Christine says, coming up close to me, the knife dangling down the side of her thigh.

"Christine, you don't need a problem with another weapon," I say, reaching down and carefully taking the knife away from her.

"Sorry, Mona, I'm so careless. I just want to say I'm sorry for shouting at you. I'm not going to sue Shelby whatever happens. My gun was used to threaten her and it is best if I accept that and take my punishment. Whatever I think about Shelby doesn't change the fact that it was my husband and my gun in her bedroom that night. I really am thankful she killed him and that he didn't harm her, or those children."

She starts to cry.

"Imagine if Frank had fired at her in her bed and hit those babies—"

"He didn't," I say, firmly, softening my harshness by putting my arms around her. "Those kids are probably jumping up and down on that bed right now driving Shelby and Carmine crazy. They're very much alive."

"Can we go early to the station?" asks Christine, pulling away from me and drying her eyes. "We could drop Sophie at school in half-an-hour and be at the station before nine."

"Yes, I got the name of a lawyer from Jean's granddaughter. I'll call him while we eat."

"Alright, but I think I qualify for a public defender. I'm just going to be straightforward about everything. I don't want my gun back. I'm done with shooting, Mona, it's not for me."

The Pistol Belles—past and present—are dropping like cans off a prairie fence.

"I think it will help if I say I don't want my gun back. I bought it for my own protection and the person I was afraid of is now dead. But I'm also afraid of the gun. I've learned the hard way, but I've learned. It could have been much worse. What if Sophie had got it and loaded it and…?"

She starts to cry again and I know I must divert her from these imagined tragedies to the very real problems she faces. I ignore Christine's suggestion that she could use a public defender and take out my cell phone and call Jeffrey Jarvis, Esq. His phone rings several times and a recording says he is out of the office but to call his cell phone if it is an emergency. I call it.

"Jeff Jarvis," he announces in a high-pitched, reedy voice. This doesn't sound like the gritty, courtroom brawler I imagined.

I introduce myself and explain that I am calling on behalf of Christine Jones and that we will soon be heading down to the police station where she may face charges relating to the theft of her gun by her estranged husband and its subsequent use in a robbery attempt.

"Where is the husband?" asks Jeff. He sounds like a boy whose voice has not yet broken.

"We buried him two weeks ago."

"Was he killed in the robbery?" he asks and, without waiting for me to answer. "Or did your friend kill him?"

"He was killed during the robbery. It was another friend of mine who killed him."

Jarvis must think I'm running a street gang.

"So the husband stole the gun from the wife and used it in a robbery and got himself killed?"

"Yes."

"How did the husband get the gun? Wasn't it under lock and key?"

I tell him about the open safe.

"Does a child live with your friend?"

"Yes, she has a teenage daughter, but she was out."

"It's still child endangerment. The girl could have got the gun if her daddy hadn't gotten to it first."

"Right," I say, glad that I'm the only one privy to this conversation. Christine would think Jeff Jarvis was working for the prosecution.

"Mrs. Jones's biggest problem is a child endangerment charge which is very serious. It's a felony and carries up to ten years imprisonment."

"I see."

"The fact that her gun was stolen and used in a crime is less of an issue, particularly if the only person who was hurt is the guy who stole it."

There is silence for a few seconds before he continues.

"I'm guessing this is the case where the Williams' girl killed an intruder a couple of weeks ago?"

"Yes, everyone knows about it."

"Not only that, I was in high school with Shelby. Her old man pulled her out of some fancy prep school and sent her to the local school with the rest of us slobs for her junior and senior year. She was cute, but not too smart. I was surprised when I heard she'd shot and killed a guy."

"Shelby is a surprising young woman," I say. If Jarvis was in high school with Shelby, he's not yet thirty-years old.

"Is this the kind of case you handle? We're due at the station and Christine needs representation."

"Yes," he says, firmly. "I represented a mother on child endangerment charges recently and it came out better than anyone expected."

"You mean she got less than ten years?"

"She got two years probation and was very happy she didn't go to prison."

I breathe hard into the phone.

"Is there a possibility…?"

"I'm guessing Mrs. Jones is otherwise a responsible mother, in which case we will present the fact of the unlocked safe and the easy access to a handgun, and presumably ammunition, as a foolish and dangerous mistake, but not one that will be repeated."

"That describes Christine perfectly! And she doesn't even want her gun back."

"She'll have to forfeit the gun and any chance of obtaining a handgun permit in the future. We'll aim for probation and hope for a fast hearing."

"She doesn't have any money," I say, quickly. "But I will pay your fees."

Jarvis tells me that it's not unusual for the defendant's legal bills to be paid by another party and advises me of his hourly rate. My mother would be aghast that a portion of her retirement money will be used to pay the fees of a criminal lawyer young enough to be her grandson. But I think she would also admire this young man's enterprise. Jarvis sounds like the kind of guy who paid his own law school tuition and chose to specialize in a grubby, and perhaps not particularly lucrative, area of the law. He says he will meet us inside the police station and, as his office is around the corner, he asks me to call him when we get there.

While I have been on the phone, Christine has been scurrying between the kitchen and bedroom urging Sophie to eat and to check that she has everything she needs for school. She is repeating to Sophie the arrangements which have been made with her friend's family. Sophie is silent and sleepy and appears to be doing her best not to overreact to her mother's nervous ministrations. Now Christine walks quickly into the living room and, without asking about my conversation with the lawyer, puts on her coat, picks up her bag, entreats Sophie once again to check she has everything and heads towards the door.

"We'll talk about what Jeff Jarvis told me after we've dropped Sophie off," I say quietly.

"Nothing to discuss, Mona, I accept whatever is going to happen to me."

I preferred the fighting Christine I was speaking to last night. I'm not sure blithe acceptance of one's fate is appropriate when you're a good mother who faces imprisonment for endangering her own child. But I remember I'm here to help Christine find a lawyer, deal with the police and be of practical assistance. It's not my place to exhort her to fight against something she is willing to accept as her due.

As I pull up outside the high school, Sophie is already out of her seat belt and is opening the rear door. If she falls out of my car while it's moving, I'll be up on charges myself. Christine turns to her and smiles and we both wait until Sophie joins the throng of youth outside the school. In a flash, a young girl runs over to her and takes her arm and they walk together, linked as one, toward the school entrance.

"Thank goodness Sophie has such good friends," says Christine. "She's much more sociable than me. She's like Frank in that respect.

I'm not sure sociable people break into houses and threaten the occupants and, judging from the few people at his funeral, Frank doesn't seem to have amassed many friends. But Christine's daughter clearly has an easy way of connecting with people.

In a few minutes we pull into the parking lot across from the municipal building where the police station is on the main floor. I take out my cell phone and call Jeff Jarvis's office number and he answers immediately, saying he'll be with us in a couple of minutes.

"I don't know if I'll ever be able to repay the money, Mona," says Christine. "These bills will be huge. It may be impossible for me to ever pay you back no matter how much I want to."

"Don't even think about that right now. We can talk about money in the future when your troubles are over."

"I may have to sue Shelby after all. Even Frank paid child support occasionally. Now I've got nothing."

Jeff Jarvis is walking briskly towards us. He is of a slight, scrappy build and makes me think of how Carl would have looked at his age. I like him already. He introduces himself and has no trouble identifying each of us, looking at me and speaking my name the instant he grabs my hand. His eyes linger on Christine, taking in the drab coat and worn face.

"We have a few hurdles to get over this morning, Mrs. Jones," he says. "Let's see how it goes and then we'll examine all our options."

Christine slowly raises her downcast eyes to look at him.

"Your husband was gunned down by a member of a rich and prominent family," says Jeff, taking Christine's arm and guiding her towards the building's main entrance as I follow behind. Jeff stops at the door, releases Christine's arm, and opens the door and motions for us both to step in before him.

"The scales of justice," he continues, as he closes the door behind him, "are usually put back into balance with money."

Chapter Twenty-Two

I pull into the lot of the Chester County Fish and Game Association and park in front of a dilapidated clubhouse. The facility is home to the Gunpowder Gals, and the weather-beaten building looks as if it was built when cowboys first roamed the plains. I push the gear into park, click open my seat belt and let out a big sigh.

"What's wrong, Mona?" asks Angelika, jumping out of the passenger seat and opening the rear door of the car. She pulls out her sports bag, containing a new set of ear muffs and protective glasses, and taps me on the shoulder. Without turning around, I pop open the trunk.

"You're not happy, Mona," she says, leaning into me from behind my seat. "Tell me what you feel."

"What I feel, Angelika, is exhausted," I say, hoisting myself out of the car onto the rough gravel.

The past week has flown by in a whirlwind of activity involving Christine, Jeff Jarvis, Angelika, Michaela and several elementary schools. And just today I've been called into the principal's office to be asked if Caroline and I were connected with the shooting at the Lombardi home. I explained to Sandersen that Shelby and Christine were former members of our women's league and that Caroline and I know them both well, but our association does not extend to any entanglement in the shooting. Sandersen responded by pushing a copy of this morning's *Sentinel* across his desk. The charges brought against the two women were splashed across the front page of our region's leading newspaper, along with a photograph of Christine and me arriving at court. I assured Sandersen that I was supporting a friend during a difficult time and, presumably, could not be considered guilty because of this association. I also pointed out that he too, as principal of Lincoln Elementary, was connected with the Lombardi family as two of the children are students at his school. This had soon brought the interrogation to a close and Sandersen seemed satisfied that the instructors of his gun safety program were not about to be indicted for a crime involving firearms.

"Get the gun out," I say to Angelika who has hurried to the back of the car and is rummaging in the trunk. She shot for several hours with Pete and Caroline this past weekend and has been impatient to get here this evening. She is going to shoot with my Ruger as Pete, regrettably, won't be at tonight's competition.

"I carry it," says Angelika, pulling my gun case close to her as I reach out to take it from her. "You go in and sit down. I find everyone."

"That won't be hard. Look for the two women in black. The rest of the room will be red and pink with a smattering of denim."

The Chester County Fish and Game Association range is located just a few miles from Madison's campus and Caroline had offered to give her a ride. She'd also asked Madison to bring a couple of her rifle team members along, either still believing that one of them might join our team or with the unlikely objective of building a fan base.

As we approach the front entrance, I see two women in Gunpowder Gals' outfits standing on the clubhouse's ramshackle porch, each with one arm folded across their waist and a cigarette cocked outwards in the other hand. I don't recognize either of them from last week.

"I hear you ladies are decent shots," says one of the women, studying us as she takes a long drag on her cigarette.

"Thank you," I say, heading toward the door. "But we're short of shooters I'm afraid."

If I'm going to lead a team of winners, I must stop revealing my innermost concerns to our competitors.

"You need to bring that Lombardi girl back," says the other woman, a tall blonde who, with big hands and leathery skin, looks as if she just got in from a day wrangling steers. "Deb Johnson says she used to be one of yours shooters."

"I hear you dropped her because she wasn't a good enough shot," says the other, blowing smoke out into the evening air.

The two women cackle and the sound echoes around the hollow porch.

"She sure knew how to shoot when that punk got into her bedroom," says Big Blonde, turning to her friend and shaking her head as if dropping Shelby from the team is a decision no sane person could fathom. "We should recruit her for the Gunpowder Gals."

I don't want Shelby back on the Pistol Belles and, in spite of Carl's doubts of my ability to stay out of other people's business, I really do want to put some distance between myself and the Lombardi clan. But the prospect of Shelby joining one of the other teams makes my stomach churn with an intense possessiveness. Are my years of labor with Shelby to be rewarded by her taking her newfound celebrity to the Gunpowder Gals?

"She's a free agent," I say, yanking open the door to the clubhouse and turning to Angelika who has stopped dead in front of the two women, her eyes running slowly up and down their bulky bodies.

"Smoking is bad for your skin," she says, looking directly at Big Blonde. Angelika's English may not be perfect but it is sufficient for her to have picked up on the women's hostility.

"Angelika," I say, holding the door open with my back. "Let's go."

Big Blonde flicks her still smoldering cigarette into the parking lot and gently places a closed fist on Angelika's arm.

"I think it's a little late for that," she says, softly. "But it's real nice of you to remind me."

Her friend turns to look at her and they cackle again. A flock of starlings flies out of the dense trees surrounding the range.

"Hold the door," says Big Blonde to Angelika who is now following me into the clubhouse. Angelika grabs the door handle and, with an exaggerated flourish, flings the door wide open. Without another word, the two women brush past her, their high-heeled boots clomping on the rough wooden boards, and Angelika is left holding the door like their personal concierge.

"You're welcome," she says, sticking out her tongue at their departing backs.

"Angelika, please don't make enemies of the other shooters. We're new and they'll kick our butts in the range."

"Nice guys finish last," says Angelika. "I'm going to learn to shoot better than those two. And if Shelby joins their team, I'm going to get even better. I'll get better, I'll get even.

And I'll get stuck in a weekly conflict between Shelby and Angelika. Fortunately, this thought is quickly dispelled by the sight of Madison and Caroline hurrying across the clubhouse toward us.

"Quickly," says Caroline. "We've bagged two slots for practice. We have five minutes."

"It will take me five minutes to set-up," I say. "I don't want to rush. Take Angelika with you and I'll see you out here when you're done."

"Are you OK, Mona?" asks Madison. Young women seem to be getting more perceptive than I generally give them credit for, but I ignore her solicitous inquiry.

"Did you bring any prospective shooters with you?" I ask instead.

"No," says Madison. "Like I've said before, everyone on the rifle team is too busy."

"What about someone else? Isn't there a woman on campus who might have done some hunting?"

"It's tough to find out who that might be, even if such a person exists. We don't discuss hunting season at school."

"Maybe it's time you did. I'm sure everyone likes to eat."

Madison looks at me and her dark brows knit together. I know I am being short with her, but it is time someone else brought a new shooter onto the Belles.

"I'm sorry, Madison," I mumble in a half-hearted apology. "I'm tired. Please go and practice with Caroline and Angelika before our time is up."

Madison disappears into the throng of the clubhouse and as I look around I see Deb Johnson surrounded by several Pink Packers, along with women from the Bullseye Babes and Gunpowder Gals.

"Over here, Mona," Deb calls, waving at me.

I head over to the group and smile at everyone. Alison Welles is in the middle of the group, a notepad and pen in her hand.

"Bullseye Babes are our usual six shooters tonight," says Alison. "And Deb's Pink Packers are eight. The Gunpowder Gals are short and will be five shooters."

"I was just talking to two of your shooters outside," I say to Janet May, captain of the Gunpowder Gals. "I don't recall seeing them last week."

"That'll be Barbara and Missy," says Janet. "They couldn't make it last week. I have ten shooters to draw from so we're not always the same women every week."

This is not good news. It will be tough for the four Pistol Belles to compete with teams with such deep rosters.

"We're only four," I say. "We were five last week, but Jean Muirhouse has now retired."

There are murmurings that Jean seemed like a nice lady, knew her way around a gun and it's a pity she couldn't continue.

"So, what we're thinking," says Deb, speaking loudly over the group, "is that each team should have the same number of shooting slots as the team which fields the biggest group. The Pink Packers are always eight, so we'll use that as the standard number of shooters."

"What that means, Mona," says Alison, jumping in as if I won't be able to figure it out for myself. "Is that with four shooters, you'll each get to shoot twice in each round."

"This way," continues Deb. "we'll keep team scores, as well as our personal scores."

"And that will add to the competitive spirit," says Alison, brightly. "It will foster some friendly rivalry between us."

Angelika has just fostered enough unfriendly rivalry to cancel out whatever goodwill these team captains are striving to develop, but I nod to Alison and Deb and try to appear enthusiastic. I'm so tired I'm not sure I can shoot one round, let alone two. The group disperses amidst excited chatter about the differing strengths of the shooters and which team is likely to place first. The Pistol Belles aren't mentioned.

Ten minutes later we are all in the range, jockeying for position. Deb shouts for the first shooters to take their spots and Madison and Caroline immediately move up to the bench.

"Angelika," I say, loudly. "You shoot first with Caroline. Madison will shoot with me."

Madison and Caroline turn around, surprise registered on their faces.

"But, we—" says Madison.

"We are not going to shoot in the same pairs each week," I say, firmly. "And as Angelika is using my gun, she and I can't shoot at the same time."

Madison quickly comes and joins me on the bench, her Glock case resting on her lap.

"We mustn't become too predictable," I say, taking hold of her solid, muscular arm. "And tonight I need your cool professionalism alongside me."

Madison smiles at me.

"I'll help you any way I can, Mona. You know that."

"Let's put some good numbers on the board tonight. If they want to score the teams, then let's show them what we can do with four shooters."

"We need to find more girls like Angelika. She's fierce, and she's going to be a great shooter."

"Thanks for making her feel welcome tonight. I can't deal with any more personality clashes."

"I know it must get tiring. If only people would just get along and accept everyone for what they are."

Madison looks down at the floor and from the pensive expression on her young face, its clear she's encountered some rejection in her life. I tell her about Jean's niece, Deandra, and what a great addition she could be to our group.

"How about bringing Shelby back?" she asks suddenly, and then giggles nervously as I throw my arms up in the air.

"I can't believe I'm hearing this from you! You had no patience for Shelby, or for her shooting, or for what she represents."

"Maybe I was wrong," says Madison, quietly. "Caroline and I have talked about this a lot the last couple of weeks. Shooting isn't just about putting perfect holes in paper targets in predictable, controlled circumstances. It's about survival and self-defense."

"I agree and, by that definition, Shelby is a darn good shooter. She reacted to what she believed was a threat to her own life and those of her children."

"It was survival in its purest form," Madison adds. "We all have a new respect for Shelby. I'd be willing to spend some time with her and help her develop better range skills."

"We've all tried to help her, but she doesn't have the patience which is needed to be a truly skilled shooter. You know that better than any of us."

"Maybe I do," she acknowledges. "But now everyone knows that Shelby can shoot under pressure."

"Yes, everyone knows that and everyone also knows that, as of yesterday, Shelby and Christine have both been charged with child endangerment. Depending on the judge's decision, one or both of them could go to prison."

"That would be outrageous! They are really good mothers!"

"Good mothers make mistakes, and when those mistakes are made in a blaze of publicity, it's that by which they are judged."

"I know, I've read all the stuff in the media. Shelby and Christine have plenty of detractors. I've had to defend them on campus."

"Let's hope they both get probation and are able to work through it without any further problems."

"Christine will never shoot again," says Madison. "But she's right to relinquish her gun. She was too timid around it. We all need to be cautious, but if you're not confident with the gun in your hand, don't use it. You're in charge of your weapon and mustn't be scared of it. Christine was afraid of her gun."

I've been watching Caroline and Angelika shoot and it's obvious neither is scared of their guns. At the end of the slow fire portion, Caroline has scored ninety out of a possible one hundred points and Angelika, who has little experience with my Ruger, has put a cluster of ten bullets in the seven and eight point rings for a total score of seventy-five. These are great scores.

I stand up and motion to Caroline, that although we are each shooting twice, we will keep alternating so that we get a break. This is primarily for my benefit as though the others have the stamina to keep firing I have to pace myself tonight. I am fighting the picture in my head of Carl on the couch, the house still and peaceful, his body warm and his smile welcoming. But, instead of being curled up with the man I adore, I am in a cold range with gun shots ringing around me, under pressure to place a series of bullets in small circles on a distant target.

Deb Johnson calls for the shooters to be ready for the next round. Madison has her gun and ammo out and is standing still, her hands resting lightly on the bench. She is the only Pistol Belle with experience in competition and it shows. Madison has none of the jumpiness I feel and is so obvious in Angelika. Even Caroline looks a little rattled when she first takes position. But Madison is serious and calm, as if generations of struggles have found peace in this young woman's bones. I must learn more about her. I have known her for two years and know so little of her life.

Madison scores a perfect one hundred points in the slow fire section, matching last week's stellar performance. Taking my time and breathing slowly between each shot, I score eighty. The competition progresses and my weariness and frustration are replaced with a new surge of energy coming from deep inside me. Big Blonde and her friend strut around, each shooting twice, but fail to match Madison and Caroline's results. Angelika, incredibly, is not far behind her new foes and it is clear that her goal to beat them at the game of shooting is within her reach. What a blessing that Shelby and Carmine don't want her in their home. They wouldn't have brought her to the range and I would never have found this promising and likeable young shooter.

The shooting ends and as we push ear muffs, sports glasses, binoculars and ammo into our bags, Deb Johnson and Alison Welles come out of their huddle to announce the results. Madison has already calculated that the Pink Packers and Bullseye Babes are in the lead, and that the Gunpowder Gals and Pistol Belles are close.

"Please don't let us be last," I say. "Let us start by beating the Gunpowder Gals and then we'll aim to keep moving up."

"That's right, coach," says Madison, grinning broadly.

"Starting from the bottom," calls Deb. "The Gunpowder Gals have nineteen hundred and fifty points."

Madison, Caroline and Angelika exchange high fives as Big Blonde turns to glare at them.

"She'll be waiting for us next week," I say.

"The Pistol Belles have two thousand points," calls Deb. "Congratulations, Pistol Belles! You're new to competition and you're doing real well."

More high fives are exchanged and Big Blonde scowls at Deb. If they wanted rivalry between the teams, they've got it.

Deb announces that the Bullseye Babes have scored two thousand and fifty points and the Pink Packers finished with twenty-one hundred, making them this week's winners. We all applaud the Pink Packers and they each pump their fists in the air; eight pairs of bright pink arms wave around like a flock of flamingoes.

"That will be us soon," says Caroline.

"Yes," says Madison. "We're close.

"What is soon?" asks Angelika. "I say next week."

Caroline and Madison laugh.

"Then we have to put in some serious practice in the meantime," says Caroline.

"Good," says Angelika. "I call Petie to meet us at Skyline."

"You go ahead," says Caroline, suddenly madly rummaging for something in the bottom of her bag. "I don't need to be there."

Angelika walks up to her and puts her nose so close to Caroline's they are practically touching.

"You need to be there," she says. "Don't hand your man over to me."

"He's not my man. He's not mine to hand over to anyone."

Caroline's voice is cold but her eyes are bright.

"He will be your man," says Angelika. "Like I say, you teach me guns, I teach you men."

Chapter Twenty-Three

Carl's peaceful evening at home turned out, like much of what we covet, to be not what I'd imagined. Angelika and I had returned home exhilarated by the evening's shooting and our solid scores, to find not a soul around.

I'd pushed on the handle of our front door and been surprised to find it locked. Not wanting to force Carl up from the couch, I'd put down my gun case, retrieved my keys from the bottom of my ammo bag, unlocked the door and slammed it behind me, eager to leap upon my sedentary husband. But the couch had been empty. I'd called upstairs, looked in the kitchen and noticed that the bottle of wine on the coffee table was almost full. More surprisingly still, the glass beside it was also half full. Where was Carl and why had he barely touched his wine?

Fear lurched in my stomach and I'd thrown myself upstairs, imagining Carl on the floor or sick and helpless in bed. But the bed was made up and as neat as I'd left it early this morning, nor was he in either bathroom or the other bedrooms. I'd run downstairs, yanked open the basement door and called down the empty stairs. There was no sound in the black hollow beyond them and I'd switched on the lights and run down the stairs. Carl could have fallen! But the basement was empty and, walking slowly back into the living room, I'd stared at the couch as if the force of my gaze might make him materialize out of its overstuffed cushions.

The open bottle of wine was evidence that Carl had been home since I'd left for Chester County Fish and Game. But the few moments which passed as I'd sat on the couch staring at the unfinished wine confirmed what I'd known for a long time: I could not live without him.

Suddenly the front door had burst open and, in a flash, my mind formed a picture of Carl in the entrance. But it was Angelika who stood there.

"Susan and Michaela are gone."

"Carl is gone. They must all be together."

Angelika had looked at me quizzically, her eyes widening as if everything she'd learned about Carl and me these past few weeks had now been called into question.

"There is a logical explanation for this," I'd said. "Right now it's a mystery, but all will soon become clear."

As I'd spoken, my words turned into prophesy. The door opened and this time my heart proved right.

"I was so worried about you," I'd said, rushing up to Carl and flinging my arms around his neck. He'd pulled me close to him and we'd hugged. I'd felt Angelika watching us, her original feelings about the strength of our marriage returning.

"Angelika," Carl had said, pulling away from me. "Go home to Michaela. She is very upset. Her mother is in the hospital and will be there for a few days. Mona and I will speak to you first thing in the morning. Michaela will have to miss school tomorrow."

Without a word, Angelika rushed out of the house and across the driveway to her charge. Carl sat down on the couch, picked up his abandoned glass and beckoned me to sit down next to him. He'd begun to tell me what had happened and how his evening had been interrupted within a few minutes of him taking the cork out of a bottle of his best Merlot.

"You haven't eaten?" I'd cried, scrambling up from the couch.

"In a minute," he'd said, pulling me back down beside him. "I've waited hours. I can wait a bit longer."

It turned out, just as Carl had been about to settle into the draft of a novel written by one of his students, Michaela had burst into the living room, crying and shouting that her mother was dying. Carl, thinking Susan must have told her daughter about the brain tumor, had put an arm around Michaela and steered her to her favorite spot on the opposite couch. But Michaela had pulled away from him and run to the door.

"My Mom is dying," she'd cried. "Please help us!"

Carl quickly realized that, whether or not Susan had told Michaela about her brain tumor, she must have been taken ill. He'd hurriedly followed Michaela next door where they'd taken the stairs two at a time to Susan's bedroom. Susan was on her bed, her hands on her head, rocking back and forth, a low moan coming from between her tightly clenched lips, obviously in extreme pain. Without hesitation, Carl had picked her up, carried her carefully down the steep stairs and instructed Michaela to go next door to get his car keys from the kitchen counter and to lock the front door. By the time Michaela returned, he'd lowered Susan onto the couch in the front sitting room. Telling Michaela to stay with her mother, he'd unlocked his car, opened all the doors and gone back into the house where, once again, he'd picked Susan up and carried her to the front door. Michaela held the screen door open for them and then helped Carl lay her mother on the back seat of his small sedan. They'd jumped into the front seats and driven to the local hospital.

Ten minutes later they'd pulled up to the front entrance of the emergency room and Carl and Michaela had carried Susan into the lobby, where hospital staff had put her into a wheelchair. Carl gave the admissions staff the name of Susan's doctor which he'd managed to extract from her on the drive to the hospital and, as her mother was wheeled away, he'd led Michaela to seats in the lobby where they'd sat down together in stunned silence.

"Had Susan already told her?" I'd asked him.

"Not according to Michaela. She said her Mom had been complaining about being tired and had been working shorter hours which Michaela thought was weird since they now had Angelika. She said Susan also spent more time alone in her bedroom and Michaela didn't understand why. She says she knew something was wrong and she was certain Angelika knew what it was, but neither of them would tell her."

"All of which is true," I'd said. "Poor Michaela! It's better to know than to have to imagine and worry."

"Well, as we know, Susan was putting off telling her. I guess she was waiting for the right time."

"There is no right time, but now Michaela will have to know the truth."

Carl went on to tell me that the doctor had said that there was no reason for them to wait and they should come back to the hospital in the morning. Susan was expected to be in the hospital for several days.

"So what did you tell Michaela?"

"Mona, it's not my place to tell her anything. She heard what the doctor said. I had to leave it at that."

"You're right," I'd said, getting up from the couch and going into the kitchen. "I think we should take Michaela to the hospital in the morning. Perhaps Susan's pain will be under control and she'll be able to speak with her."

"I'm teaching early tomorrow and I thought you had a gun program?"

"I do," I'd said, putting two hamburger patties in the iron skillet. "And, you're right, we're not needed. Angelika will take Michaela, that's part of her job."

"It's tough when a job includes driving an adolescent to the hospital so she can be told her mother will be dead within a few months—or less than that, if what I saw is an indicator. Susan was in agony. I've never seen anything like it before. It was terrible."

Carl had rubbed his hands across his face and taken a long sip of wine. I'd turned up the heat on the hamburgers and took taken two rolls out of the bread basket.

"It's going to be a very difficult time," I'd said, sitting next to Carl while the hamburgers sizzled in the pan. "Michaela will have to witness her mother dying before her very eyes. Fortunately, she has us, and now she has Angelika."

"However distant Susan may have been as a mother, I doubt we three will make up for her loss. And we still don't know if Susan has made us guardians or if Michaela will go to California."

Carl had eaten the two hamburgers, cooked down to two strips of leather exactly as he likes them, slugged down two more glasses of wine and we'd gone to bed. The time for bragging about the Pistol Belles had passed. What did shooting scores matter when a young girl was soon to lose her mother?

Twenty-four hours later we had the answers to our questions of the night before. Angelika had driven Michaela to the hospital at nine o'clock that morning and by ten o'clock Susan had told her daughter she was dying. A nurse had sat with them and Susan had asked Angelika to stay in the room. Michaela had at first taken the news calmly, so calmly in fact that Susan had turned from her and wept into her already sweat-sodden pillow. But Angelika and the nurse had been ready for the explosion of disbelief and grief they knew would come and, as Michaela began to cry and scream, Angelika rocked her in her arms. A few hours later, Susan had asked Michaela if she would like us to be her guardians or if she'd prefer to live with her cousins in California. According to Angelika, there had been no hesitation on Michaela's part.

"If you don't make Mona and Carl my guardians, I'll run away!" she'd cried. "I'm not going to California. Mona and Carl will take care of me. They have two empty bedrooms and one of them is practically mine already! I'm not going to live with my cousins!"

She'd also added that now Mona and Angelika would have no choice but to take her shooting. When Susan had asked her daughter to repeat what she'd said because she didn't think she'd heard properly, Angelika had jumped in.

"Michaela says Mona and me will have no choice but to take her shopping," she'd said, patting Michaela's knee. A grim little smile had crossed Michaela's face and Angelika said she knew in that moment that the girl would be alright.

"She has steel inside," Angelika told me. "Like me."

The following day, I'd arranged for my parent's estate attorney to meet with Susan at her hospital bedside. Guardianship documents and a will were prepared, along with a healthcare proxy and living will directive. She stopped at our house on her way back to her office and presented us with numerous documents to sign. And thus, Carl and Mona Milton became legal guardians of Michaela LaVecca. I was also given power of attorney to make decisions, if required, surrounding her end of life care. Michaela is the sole beneficiary of her mother's assets, including the house, which she may sell or live in, the latter made conditional upon her retaining a full-time live-in caregiver until she is twenty-one years old. I'd already started researching immigration law and the obstacles that would have to be overcome if Angelika wanted to stay with Michaela for several years.

But, I'd forgotten that Angelika's plan is to find a good American to marry and from what I've seen of her determination so far, she will succeed in her quest. One lucky young American is walking around not knowing that a fine future with a robust German girl awaits him. So I imagine one day Michaela will move into our home and we will rent out her house in order to create income for her. She will need money for college, as Susan's estate will be badly depleted by medical bills.

Now, a few days later, Susan has returned home and is on extended sick leave from work. Carl and I have surprised ourselves, and each other, with the joy and excitement we feel about being appointed Michaela's guardians. A childless man and woman fall in love and marry at an age when the possibility of having children of their own has passed, and then are blessed with the chance to love a young girl and guide her to adulthood. Michaela will never be our true daughter, but she is a gift far beyond our expectations. We are honored that we were chosen and will make sure Michaela never forgets her mother. In the days that have passed since the guardianship decision was made, we have seen Michaela numerous times and have assured her that we have plenty of room for her in our home, and our hearts.

"Don't start feeling guilty, Mona," Carl said to me after the attorney left and we were sitting dazed on the couch. "We are not getting Michaela at someone else's expense."

As I'd started to protest that it was clearly at Susan's expense, not to mention her family in California, he'd put his fingers on my lips to silence me.

"Susan is dying no matter what," he'd said, his face close to mine. "She has been dealt a raw deal but you weren't lurking in the shadows waiting to snatch her daughter away. Susan is grateful to us, and we must be grateful to her. And that's all."

Chapter Twenty-Four

"You've heard, I'm sure," says Caroline, standing outside Bloomhill Elementary with her leather folder tucked neatly under her arm. "It's all over the news."

"Christine called me the minute she got out of court yesterday and Shelby called me last night," I say.

The judge has made his decision on the child endangerment charges and put both Christine and Shelby on probation.

"At least they aren't going to prison," says Caroline. "I guess probation means they'll have to stay out of trouble and do some sort of community service."

"Yes, like this sort of community service, although I don't recall committing a crime!"

"I don't think Christine or Shelby could teach gun safety," says Caroline, laughing. "Can you imagine Dr. Sandersen's reaction?" "I don't have to, I already know. Your dear friend Sandersen called me into his office a few days ago and asked me to swear neither of us was connected with the Lombardi shooting or the charges against Christine and Shelby."

"I'm surprised he didn't call me," Caroline says, frowning.

"He's sweet on you and didn't want to put you in a difficult position. He reserves that for me."

"Why didn't you tell me you'd been to his office?" she asks, her frown deepening as if realizing she's been excluded from an important meeting. Her expression takes me straight back to Abaco and its petty rivalries.

"I was too irritated to talk about it. I was annoyed he'd called me when he clearly prefers to deal with you."

"Mona, I thought you were relieved that he and I get along."

"I am but—"

"We don't need to talk about Sandersen," Caroline says, hurriedly. "Talk to me about Christine and Shelby."

"Christine was pretty stoical," I say, happy to get off the topic of our principal. "I'm impressed with how well she's held up throughout all this. It must be terrible to be charged with putting your own child at serious risk. But she seems to accept that she made a stupid mistake and has to pay for it."

During our phone conversation, Christine told me that other than the very real threat of a prison sentence, her two biggest concerns had been Sophie and her job. She said Sophie's friends are rallying around her and she doesn't think her daughter will run into problems at school. Her boss said he knows her to be a reliable, responsible employee and that as long as she performs at her usual level of efficiency her one year probation won't affect her employment. Assured that both her daughter and her job are secure, Christine seemed relaxed and relieved and said she's made it clear to Jeff Jarvis that she has no intention of suing Shelby no matter how much he may encourage her to do so. She also said she isn't concerned about the fact that some people will never believe it was pure coincidence that her husband got into her apartment the only time her safe was left unlocked. Her resolve and confidence are back. I remind myself that the thing Christine most feared is gone. Frank Jones is buried, and his widow has been born again.

"How is Shelby taking it?" asks Caroline, with a flicker of malice in her dark eyes.

"She's enormously relieved that she hasn't been charged with manslaughter. Even with her family's influence, Shelby had to realize that she could have been in serious trouble for killing Frank. Fortunately, she quickly dropped the absurd idea that Christine could have put Frank up to it, and her father and Carmine have convinced her that it would be foolish to sue Christine over Frank's use of the gun. Overall, I think she feels lucky and wants to put it all behind her."

"Did she say anything about coming back to the Pistol Belles?"

"No, her biggest concern is that her father is not doing well."

Shelby had at first sounded brisk and efficient when she'd called.

"Mona, I want you to be the first to know, outside the family, that I got three years probation. It will be all over the media, but I want you to hear it from me. You've always been a big help to me at the range and I've never really thanked you for teaching me to shoot."

Before I could interrupt her and say she had no need to thank me, she'd burst into tears and said she was frantic about her father as the cancer is progressing much faster than anticipated.

"I feel as if the break-in has as good as killed him," she'd sniffled into the phone. "And with all these legal problems, he's had to think about me instead of concentrating on his health. I can't stop crying when I see him. Karen says I need to buck up and make the most of the time we have with him."

I'd murmured that Karen was right and had asked Shelby if there was anything I could do to help.

"Well," she'd said, her sniffling suddenly gone. "I hear Angelika is doing great with you and your neighbor."

"She's terrific! Like your father, my neighbor is very sick and Angelika is helping her and taking care of her daughter."

"If I'd known she was good with sick people, I would have kept her," she'd said, stiffly.

A close brush with imprisonment obviously hasn't lessened Shelby's selfishness and I'd wondered if the purpose of her phone call wasn't to thank me but to get Angelika back in her service.

"You and Karen have access to the very best healthcare professionals. You have numerous resources. Angelika is where she is truly needed."

Before Shelby could respond, I'd thanked her for taking the time to call me and apologized for not being in court yesterday, explaining that Caroline and I had presented our program in three different schools. In fact, we'd rushed around with barely a thought for Christine and Shelby and their respective fates. There is nothing like absorption in a task to stop your mind dwelling on other concerns. Whether paid or unpaid, work is powerful therapy.

"I predict we'll be hearing a lot more from Shelby," says Caroline. "I think we have to give serious consideration to taking her back."

"Madison has already told me how you both feel."

"Shelby has real life experience! We can't deny that she knows how to shoot, and her notoriety will get us some attention and help attract new shooters."

"So self interest is at the core of your new and generous attitude toward Shelby?"

I smile at Caroline and she smiles back, but then her face turns serious.

"We have to go inside in a few minutes, Mona," she says, checking the time on her cell phone. "But I have two pieces of news which I need to give you first."

"I don't think I can take much more news. It's been quite a week. Carl and I became guardians of Michaela a few days ago. Her mother is dying of a brain tumor."

"Oh, my goodness, that's terrible! Michaela is such a lovely girl. What a good thing you got Angelika involved."

"Yes, Shelby's cast-off *au pair* is an absolute gold mine. She's fantastic with Michaela and she helps Susan with all her personal care."

"Angelika is also very good for me," says Caroline, looking down and stroking her heavy silver belt buckle. "We have a great time practicing with Pete."

A slight flush appears on her tawny skin.

"And that leads to the news I have," she says.

"Are you going to tell me that you and Pete are finally dating?"

"No, no," she says, hurriedly. "But Pete called me at seven o'clock this morning to tell me that Jim's wife died last night."

"Shirley Mackenzie died? Jean said that it wouldn't be long, but when I called Jim last week to tell him how we made out at the competition, he didn't say a word."

"Apparently she suddenly went downhill. Pete's calling me later with the arrangements."

"We must go to the wake, but it will most likely be tomorrow evening and we're due at the Bullseye Babes range at seven."

"If the wake is also held in the afternoon, we could stop on our way to the range."

"That would mean leaving our guns in our cars at the funeral home which is illegal, but I'm sure we'll get away with it. Jim will want his shooting girls to come out and say farewell to his wife, even though we barely knew her."

"Pete says he's coming to the competition tomorrow night," says Caroline, smiling.

"I'm happy to hear that," I say. "I always feel better when Pete is in our corner."

"Yes, so do I. But there is something else I have to tell you, Mona."

I look at her and my heart sinks. The only Pistol Belle I haven't spoken to in the last few days is Madison. I pray Caroline is not about to give me some unwelcome news about our young star.

"Smith Pharma has called me back. They've offered me a job and a promotion!"

"Caroline, that's wonderful!" I say, hoping the new wave of panic surging through me isn't written across my face. I truly don't want to have to finish the gun program alone.

"My old boss has given notice and there is no-one in the department to take the job as everyone is too new. That's because they got rid of those of us who'd been there longest," she says, wryly. "I've been offered my boss's position and I accepted right away. This is no time to play hard-to-get."

Maybe she could apply this seize-the-day philosophy to Pete.

"At the risk of being completely selfish—"

"Not selfish at all, Mona. I'm not going to abandon you before we're done with these kids. I told Smith Pharma I'd start at the end of June. That's only a few weeks from now. They'll wait."

Caroline obviously let Smith Pharma know she wasn't entirely at their beck and call.

"And anyway," she continues. "I handle Sandersen more effectively than you. I don't want this wonderful program to fall apart because I didn't stay to finish it."

If being downsized put a dent in Caroline's self-confidence, then being called back with a promotion has soon restored it.

A car pulls into one of the parking spaces beside Bloomhill's front entrance and a large figure struggles out of the driver's side door. The man starts to walk towards us, a broad smile spreading across his face. I recognize the wobble immediately.

"Dr. Sandersen," calls Caroline, a brilliant smile flashing across her face. "To what do we owe this unexpected pleasure?"

"Dr. Jensen, Bloomhill's principal, cannot be here this morning so I thought it best to come over and introduce you to the students," he says. "Good morning, Ms. Cargill, and Mrs. Milton, how are you?"

"I'm very well, Dr. Sandersen," I answer. "We're looking forward to meeting more kids."

"I must confess," he says, reaching for the front door and holding it open. "This program has gone better than I could ever have thought possible."

Caroline and I briskly step through the door and he ambles behind us.

"In fact, at the statewide principal's meeting last week, I found myself bragging about our innovative—and highly topical as it has turned out—extra-curricular program. I was besieged at the coffee break by my colleagues wanting to know how I pulled it all together."

I doubt he told them that I pulled it all together.

"So my question to you, dear ladies, is whether you would be able to provide this program in a couple of neighboring counties in the next school year?"

"No!" I say, loudly and impolitely. "Caroline is going back to work in a few weeks and won't be available, and I—"

"Wonderful, Ms. Cargill, I'm disappointed to lose you, but I'm not surprised to learn you're in demand."

"I got my job back at Smith Pharma. In fact, it's a better position than the one I had prior to leaving."

"Well, that gives me confidence that Smith Pharma's products are of a high standard after all," he says. "I couldn't understand why they would eliminate the position of such an accomplished woman."

I hadn't been aware that Caroline had confided in Sandersen about losing her job. Obviously, they've become quite friendly.

"And I won't be able to take on any more safety programs," I say, bringing Sandersen back to his original question. "But I know two people who would be terrific and I'll be seeing them tomorrow evening."

Caroline looks at me quizzically.

"They also run women's shooting leagues," I continue. "And they are extremely knowledgeable about guns and the rules and regulations."

Deb Johnson and Alison Welles would do a tremendous job. As far as I know, neither of them works outside the home and their children are grown. They may have the time to take it on.

"But I'm curious, Dr. Sandersen," I say, as we lay out our materials on a table in the school's gymnasium. "A couple of months ago you were positively reluctant for anyone to talk about guns in your school. Why are you now recommending the program?"

"Well, it's clear from the shooting in the Lombardi home and that idiotic woman who gave her estranged husband access to her weapon that guns are not something we can choose to ignore. I accept now that it's better if children are made aware of their existence, and the attendant dangers, and know what to do if they find a gun or gain access to one."

"Amen!" says Caroline.

"Stop, don't touch! Tell an adult!" I shout, repeating the safety program's mantra.

"Precisely," says Sandersen, smiling not at me but at Caroline. "I'm even going so far as to recommend the Hunter Education course for our middle school and high school students. My two daughters are begging me to let them take the course and go out hunting with their older cousin, a cousin on their mother's side, of course."

I recall those two hefty girls in the photograph in Sandersen's office. They'll make fine hunters.

"Tell them my husband and I love venison," I say, and he and Caroline laugh.

"I will, Mrs. Milton, I think this program is opening some of our eyes to a tradition that made this country great, or when it was great…"

His voice trails off. Caroline pats him on his shoulder and he turns to smile at her.

"Maybe we can get back some of that rugged self-reliance?" he adds.

The children file in and rush to sit on the floor, crossing their ankles in front of them. I think of Carl's passion for teaching and his belief that every day someone in his classroom learns something that may change their life.

"They don't learn it from me, Mona," Carl will say, always modest about his influence on his students. "They learn it from a book, or a theory, or another student, or from an idea of their own. It may help them find their passion, their future, or something or someone to love. It may just be that they decide to continue with life."

Tonight I will tell Carl that now I understand what he means. For the past few weeks, I've known our students were learning about guns and how to be safe around them. But what I discovered today is that an educated man is able to confront his prejudices and change his mind.

Chapter Twenty-Five

Slowly moving along the line of mourners at the Clinton Funeral Home, I finally reach Jim. Throwing my arms around him, I hold him tight and tell him how sorry I am about Shirley's passing. I then say that the Pistol Belles need him more than ever, especially as we are hosting a competition at Skyline next week. Jim hugs me and says he won't let us down because Shirley would be mad as hell if he fell short on his range officer duties. I hug him again and move along to shake hands with his three grown children and with Shirley's sister and brother-in-law. Shirley's sister looks at me with a sour expression, but Jim's son smiles and mouths a silent thank you. I step away and scan the room for Angelika who had declared upon entering the funeral home that, having so recently watched a dead body being hauled down the Lombardi's grand staircase, she could not look upon the deceased Mrs. Mackenzie in the open casket.

"In my country, coffins are closed. I come here for Jim but won't view his dead wife."

I'd suggested she take a seat at the back of the room, but the reality of sitting alone for half an hour or more while I waited in line had not suited her and I now see her standing with Madison at the back of the line. Presumably she is keeping Madison company and is not about to change her mind about getting close to the body. I push my way through the throng surrounding the Mackenzie family and then stops dead in my tracks.

"You must have guessed Shelby would come," says Jean, suddenly appearing beside me. She grabs my arm and steers me towards a row of empty chairs. "This is her coming out ball. The whole shooting community is here to support Jim, but Shelby is providing a nice little side show."

"I'm not surprised to see Shelby," I say, continuing to stare in her direction as I sit beside Jean. "She's fond of Jim and I knew she would come tonight. It's who she's with that is throwing me for a loop."

"That's Barbara Janowitz," says Jean, pointing straight at Big Blonde. "She cornered Shelby about five minutes ago."

"Do you know everybody?" I ask, turning to stare at her.

"Barbara was married for a short while to my cousin over in Barlow. He was all but worthless so it didn't surprise me when Barbara hauled his ass out. She's a driver for one of the big delivery services and had no time for a man who didn't like to work."

I have no difficulty picturing Big Blonde hauling one hundred pound boxes on her shoulders, nor of her tossing out a husband who didn't pull his weight.

"Do you know that Barbara Janowitz is one of the Gunpowder Gals?"

"No, but it doesn't surprise me that she shoots," says Jean, rubbing her chin. "But how come she wasn't there when we were over at the Pink Packers range?"

"The Gunpowder Gals are in the privileged position of having over ten shooters on their roster which gives them a cushion if they can't all make it every week. Big Blonde showed up last week when we competed at their home range."

"Big Blonde you call her? That about describes Barbara," says Jean, laughing.

"She also told me she'd like to get Shelby on her team."

"I knew these gals were serious competitors, and that's why you've got to get more shooters. Now you've got your competition out recruiting your former players."

"Shelby's a player alright," I say, watching her preen in front of Big Blonde who, in turn, nods and smiles as if in complete agreement with every word she says. Shelby is no doubt telling her about the stupidity of the Pistol Belle's leader cutting her from their team.

I don't feel like dealing with Shelby this evening and realize now would be a good time to slip out and get over to the Bullseye Babe's range for some early practice. If Angelika sees her former employer and her new enemy deep in discussion she will think, accurately, that Big Blonde is recruiting Shelby for the Gunpowder Gals. She'll then storm over to them and tell them that she's going to learn to be a better shot than both of them. I have no intention of playing referee at a wake. I look around and see Angelika is now talking to Caroline and Pete in the far corner of the room, her back towards us.

"What is Big Blonde doing here anyway?" I ask Jean, standing up and buttoning up my jacket. "Do the Gunpowder Gals go to the wakes of shooting families so they can steal players?"

"Barbara played softball for years with Shirley. They were both great players."

"Really?" I ask, fighting an image of Big Blonde firing balls at my head.

"Why are you in such a hurry to leave, Mona? Stay and learn a bit more about Shirley. You only knew her as Jim's wife and these past couple of years we all thought of her as an invalid. But Shirley was a very good athlete in her day. She was a pitcher on the Hurricane's when Barbara was catcher."

"So that's what happened to her face," I say.

Jean laughs and grabs my hand.

"Mona, go over and interrupt their little discussion. Bring Shelby here and we'll both talk to her. If she's going to shoot in competition she may as well be back on the Belles."

"The one person everyone wanted out of our group is now apparently our number one recruit," I say in exasperation. "And no, Jean, I'm not going to go over there and join Shelby's little fan club!"

"Don't be so stubborn, Mona," says Jean, her raspy voice low. "It doesn't become you."

I sigh and sit down again.

"But it looks like you're off the hook," she continues. "I see Caroline and Pete heading Shelby's way. Maybe they'll talk her back onto the Belles."

"Is this a wake or a draft?"

"Oh, Shirley would love this," says Jean, laughing and slapping my knee. "She took her sports very seriously and pushed Jim to go to shoots all over the country. He always says Shirley made him the gun expert he is today."

I look over at Jim graciously greeting the steady stream of mourners. Christine and Sophie have arrived without us noticing and are next in line. Christine is looking nervously around, her eyes darting from side-to-side no doubt afraid people will recognize her and point her out as the town's notorious bad mother. Jim sees

Christine and smiles and leans toward her, saying something which causes her to dab at her eyes. I imagine Jim is telling her that he knows she's a great mother.

"She best get over to his house pretty darn fast with her brownies," says Jean, nodding in Christine's direction. "The ladies are already circling."

"So now we're at speed dating? Isn't there such a thing anymore as coming together to honor the dead?"

"Was there ever?" Jean asks, with a look of genuine surprise on her lined face. "Death means change, Mona, and change means opportunity."

"So this is an opportunity for Christine?"

"Yes and I hope she realizes it. She's bucked up nicely since her hubby took three bullets too many, but she isn't confident enough to realize how much Jim likes her. Jim Mackenzie is a very decent guy and I'm betting he has more than a few dollars stuffed in his mattress. I'd like to see Christine and Sophie get out of that rabbit hutch they live in and into the protective arms of a good man."

"Me too," I say, looking over at them. In spite of the long line of people waiting, Jim isn't letting Christine get away and is now talking to her daughter. "Is Sophie still working for you?"

"Yes, I pick her up two or three days a week after school. She's working out real well."

"But Jim was widowed only two days ago. I doubt he'll want to get married again anytime soon."

"He's a man, Mona! He was married practically out of high school and it's the only life he knows. He'll want a wife sooner than you would imagine."

"But will he want such a young step-daughter? His children are all grown."

"Jim is a very generous man and he'll find room in his heart, and his wallet, for Sophie. His kids may have something to say about it, but that's their problem."

I watch the three of them for a while and picture a future for the new widower, the widow and her daughter. Jean nudges me and I turn and see Caroline and Pete are heading towards us.

"He's getting closer to slipping his gun in that holster," says Jean.

"Yes," I say, laughing. "After years spent sniping at each other, all it took was getting together to teach Angelika to shoot to turn them into a pair."

"It's about time. Lovers sometimes die before they find each other."

"Yes, even when that person is stuck right under their nose."

I suddenly wish Carl was with me but, although he wanted to pay his respects to the Mackenzie family, he's had an evening committee meeting which he couldn't miss. I'm looking forward to getting home, but first I must put some lead in the targets at the Bullseye Babes range.

"Time to go, Mona," says Caroline, after greeting Jean and giving her a quick hug.

"Your former Pistol Belle said she'd like to come and watch the competition," says Pete, smiling slyly. Pete may be an evolved, modern kind of guy but he isn't above stirring up a cat fight.

"That's not a good idea," I say, jumping up and grabbing my pocket book off the floor.

"Don't worry," says Caroline, turning to Pete and smiling up at him. "Shelby said she had to get back to the kids. She has a new nanny she's training."

"A nanny!" Jean exclaims, jumping up from her chair. "There's no end to that girl's high-handedness."

"Well, I'm glad she has a new nanny," I say. "A couple of days ago she was hinting about getting Angelika back."

"She said Angelika would have been a big help with her father," says Caroline.

"Angelika would never go back to their house! And I'm glad Shelby can't join us this evening."

"Next week you're shooting at Skyline and you'll have home field advantage," says Pete. "If you really want to make a splash, bring Shelby back into the line-up."

"You too, Pete!" I cry. My voice is too loud for a wake, no matter how crowded. Pete and Caroline grin at each other conspiratorially.

"Now you are pushing me to bring Shelby back," I continue, lowering my voice.

"It will spice things up," says Pete. "And it will unnerve the competition."

"I think things are getting spicy enough," I say, looking from Pete to Caroline and then back to Pete. "Do you want to lead the Pistol Belles, Pete? Do you want to keep Angelika off Shelby's throat every week? Do you want to deal with Shelby's showing-off and all the new resentments she will breed? Do you want to devote months of practice to her so she can actually score some points? Do you want to teach Shelby how to really shoot so she doesn't have to rely on pure dumb luck next time she's faced with an attacker?"

"No," says Pete firmly, looking directly into my eyes.

The four of us stand silently, our manner finally befitting the occasion.

"Jean Muirhouse! I thought it was you! How the hell are you?"

Our moment of silence has passed. Barbara Janowitz has discovered her long-lost cousin by marriage and is ready to pounce. Jean may be in her eighties but in a flash she grabs Big Blonde's arm and pulls her down with her into the two empty chairs. I take this opportunity to leave and, without saying a word, walk away.

I am relieved to see Angelika standing by the front door. She tells me Madison has already left for the range.

"She asked me to go with her, but I tell her I wait for you."

"Thank you, that's nice of you. I'm feeling pretty upset right now. Everyone is pushing me to let Shelby come back."

"So, let her," says Angelika, as we walk toward the car. "Who cares?"

"I thought you would care," I say, somewhat surprised. "I thought you didn't want to have any more dealings with Shelby?"

"If Shelby wants to be known as a famous shooter she is going to have to prove she can shoot. Right now she is a star because she killed a bad man. But she'll look like an idiot when she can't hit a target in the range! Then she'll get tired of being a famous shooter because it will be too much pressure."

"Then why don't we let her join the Gunpowder Gals? She'll shoot badly and then quit."

"I saw Big Blonde in there," says Angelika, snorting. "She was sniffing around Shelby like a horse dealer. But Shelby doesn't want to be a Gunpowder Gal. She wants to be back with you."

"How do you know that?"

"Because you got rid of her and she wants to beat you at your game by coming back to the Pistol Belles. Shooting with the Gunpowder Gals would be proof that you didn't want her, not even after she killed a man and became famous!"

I slide into the driver's seat and pop the lock on the passenger side door.

"So in order to get rid of Shelby for good, I have to bring her back so that she fails and then quits?" I ask, turning to Angelika as she deftly snaps her seat belt.

"Right, Mona. Shelby fired at Frank and she got lucky, everyone says that. If she wants to learn properly, like me, that's good. But if she doesn't learn and shoots badly at the competitions, then she'll make an excuse and give it up. But she'll always be able to say that she quit."

In the past couple of weeks Angelika has spent time with Carl talking late in the evening when everyone else has gone to bed. Angelika brings her chilled German Riesling and, with the bottle side-by-side with Carl's Merlot on the coffee table, they keep each other company. Angelika's shrewd suggestion of how to manage Shelby so closely matches Carl's clever, reasoned analyses that I am starting to wonder if wine drinkers are possessed of magical powers. Perhaps the act of sitting down and sipping a beverage which has been long in the making, promotes a mature, calm approach to life.

"And we'll be done with Shelby without her becoming a big problem," I say.

"Yes, Carmine will be happy and her daddy will be happy because you gave her a second chance."

"And she'll still be a local legend," I add. "And no-one will remember that she couldn't hit a target."

I pull out of the parking lot and head east toward the Bullseye range.

Chapter Twenty-Six

Madison holds a 9mm semi-automatic in her hand as if it's no heavier than a number two pencil. Maybe all the time she spends with a high-powered Garand butting up against her shoulder makes a pistol seem like a featherweight. She fires five shots, each one in the inner circle, and then lays the Glock on the bench and props a yellow plastic flag in the open action. I am in the spot next to her and she turns to me and, with a toss of her head, motions me to follow her out of the range. We step into a dark corridor and take off our eye and ear protectors.

"I have the first draft of my thesis on women shooters," she says. "I'll be giving it to my professor to review over the summer. I'm planning to finish it in the fall."

"Great, I'd love to know what you say about us!"

"That's why I want to talk to you. I have a copy in my car and I wondered if you would ask your husband to look at it."

"I'm sure he'd be happy to," I say. "But I should warn you that Carl doesn't need a 9mm in order to inflict some serious damage."

Madison laughs. "You've always said he's a brilliant writing critic and it would be such a favor to me if he would read it and give me some feedback."

"Asking Carl to read something and not give you elaborate, painstaking feedback is like pulling the trigger of a loaded gun and expecting it not to fire."

Madison laughs again.

"So if you are willing to set yourself up as a target, then by all means give me the draft when we leave tonight."

"Thank you so much! It's not finished yet and Carl's critique will be so valuable."

"It will, of that I have no doubt."

We put our protective gear back on and open the door to the range.

"Am I allowed to read it?" I ask. "Or is it for Carl's eyes only?"

"You're in it, but I'm not worried about you reading it. You're a model recreational shooter, Mona."

"Then I'd better get in some practice before you have to rewrite everything you say about me!"

As we walk through the door, Deb announces that practice is over and the range is cold. It's time for the first shooters to take their positions and Madison, Angelika and Caroline all turn to me for direction. They have clearly listened to what I said last week; it's good to be the queen.

"Madison and Angelika shoot first," I say, sitting down on a small wooden bench which sits against the back wall. Pete hands his Kimber case to Angelika and sits beside me. I've taken the middle of the bench, leaving Caroline no choice but to sit on the other side of me. The three of us begin chatting about the Bullseye Babes range and it's location behind a gun store in the middle of a strip mall. With a nail salon on one side and a pizza parlor on the other, the Bullseye is in an odd mixture of businesses, particularly in a state which is not known to be gun-friendly. Pete tells us that the strip mall was built a decade ago and the Bullseye is the only one of the original occupants to be in business ten years later. Stores, restaurants and beauty parlors have come and gone, but the Bullseye is still going strong. We'd walked through the middle of the store in order to get into the range, and the number of customers on this Wednesday evening suggests that the Bullseye is indeed a profitable concern.

Deb announces that the range is hot and everyone puts on ear and eye protectors. Madison and Angelika start to take their first shots in the slow fire section and I settle into my perch between Caroline and Pete. I feel Caroline's warm thigh on my right and Pete's long solid leg stretched out beside me on my left. I feel like an overgrown child lodged safely between her protective parents. The feeling takes me back to some ancient time when my legs didn't touch the floor and the only gunfire was from the cap guns fired by my brother and me and our neighborhood clan. Pete and Caroline's muffled voices float above me as I lose myself in an old pleasant memory. But then, in a flash, I see my parents trapped in the wreckage of the car accident and I jump up, suddenly feeling as if the bench is on fire.

"What's the matter, Mona?" asks Pete, quickly taking the opportunity to move over to sit beside Caroline. "Did we crowd you out?"

My eyes have filled with tears.

"Are you alright, Mona?" asks Caroline, looking intently at me.

"This may seem odd from an old broad like me," I say, my voice trembling. "But Shirley's wake has made me sad about my Mom and Dad."

As I say it, I realize it is true. In the years since my parents died, I haven't attended a wake or a funeral without reliving the days following the accident. First the news of the crash, then the fruitless dash to the hospital, then the visit to the crash site, the funeral arrangements, the crowded wake, the burial—and then nothing.

Pete stands up, gently lowers me back down onto the bench and goes back to his place on my left. Once again I am sandwiched between Pete and Caroline, safe in their custody. At moments like this I need Carl, but the affectionate friendship of my shooting friends is a comforting substitute.

"Nice shooting, ladies," says Pete, as Angelika and Madison complete their slow fire. Madison has scored a perfect one hundred points and Angelika seventy.

"It's too slow for me," she says. "I like to shoot fast."

"Life isn't always a shoot-out, Angie," says Pete. "It's important to be able to slow down and shoot methodically."

They complete the timed fire section of two five-shot strings each in twenty seconds. Madison scores ninety points and Angelika sixty. She marches towards the three of us.

"I blew it!" she pronounces, promptly turning her back and striding away.

"But now watch me," she calls behind her as Deb announces the start of the rapid fire section.

Big Blonde and her friend are shooting for the Gunpowder Gals and are in the spots closest to Angelika. This is the first time I've seen Big Blonde this evening and I've yet to discover if her acquaintance with Jean will soften her attitude towards the Belles. These two Gunpowder Gals have each scored ninety and one hundred points in the slow and timed fire sections and are proving to be their team's most talented shooters.

Ten seconds is followed by another very loud ten seconds as two shooters from each team fire two strings of five shots. The shooting is over almost as quickly as it began and the targets are brought up for scoring. Big Blonde and her friend look at their results and give a loud whoop, slapping each other's hands in a high five. They have each scored one hundred points, with every shot hitting the bullseye or the first circle.

"Ninety," Madison mouths her score to me from the bench.

Ear protectors are designed to reduce sound, although noise is by no means eliminated and gunfire can be heard. Conversation is difficult but is not impossible and a common language and a little lip-reading make for understandable verbal exchanges. Although the sound now emanating from Angelika's mouth is a string of foreign words, there is no mistaking their meaning. Whether she is speaking German or English, or some mixture of the two, her message is loud and clear: Angelika's rapid fire score is an amazing one hundred points.

She rushes over to Pete and plants a rapid fire series of kisses on his cheeks, and then pulls Caroline and me off the bench, leading us in a jig which must have first been performed on the banks of the Rhine. Madison cheers and claps and Deb Johnson and Alison Welles smile broadly. If they were hoping for enthusiastic competitors, they've got them.

After five or six spins, Angelika releases us from her grasp and we go back to our bench. Deb announces the range is cold and, as Caroline and I are shooting next, we start to pick up our gun cases and ammo bags off the floor.

Suddenly Big Blonde's voice bellows across the range.

"The Gunpowder Gals are only five shooters tonight and I'll be filling all three empty slots!"

"The Pistol Belles are each shooting twice," I shout, and Deb nods her head in acknowledgement and makes notes on the score cards.

"That's a lot of shooting, Barbara," I call over to Big Blonde. She turns and walks towards me.

"The other four don't want to shoot more than once," she says. "I don't understand why not. The whole point is to shoot."

"Maybe they find it tiring," I say.

"That why I'm looking for new talent," Big Blonde says, her eyes sweeping Caroline, Madison and Angelika.

Is Big Blonde going to try to steal all my shooters? Fortunately, my three Pistol Belles respond to this blatant cattle call by turning their backs on her. Caroline goes up to the shooting bench and takes her position, and Madison and Angelika take a seat on either side of Pete. He is sandwiched between them, looking relaxed and happy.

"Barbara," I say, looking into her pale, narrow eyes. "Now that we've discovered we have a friend in common, I'd like to keep things nice between us."

She stares down at me, her elbows out and her thumbs hooked into her cowhide belt. I avoid her eyes by looking around at my team. Caroline is carefully taking out her ammo and scope, but I know from the tilt of her head that she is listening to every word. Pete and Madison have their heads together and are most likely discussing the differences between .22 caliber and high-powered rifles. Angelika, whose enthusiasm for firearms so far is limited to handguns, will have no interest in listening to a conversation about long guns and is staring pointedly at me and Big Blonde.

"That foreign babe is a bitch," says Big Blonde, flicking her eyes at Angelika as if I have more than one foreigner on my team. "But she's going to be a mighty fine shooter and that makes her of real interest to me."

"It's just one of the reasons she's of interest to me," I say, deciding not to waste my time defending Angelika against name-calling. She is more than capable of doing that herself. "That's why she's on my team."

Big Blonde doesn't respond and I decide it's time to let her know that I won't tolerate my shooters being poached.

"So far this evening," I say, staring up at her in the most threatening manner I can adopt with a woman who is a head taller than me. "So far you've cornered Shelby over at the wake and now you've let all three of my Pistol Belles know that you're looking for new shooters."

"That includes you," she says. "You shoot nice and consistent."

I'm tired of being nice and consistent.

"The Pistol Belles have been together for a long time and it is our intention to stay together," I say, haughtily.

"Then you need to learn how to hold onto them! From what I've heard, you kicked Shelby off the team and Jean told me she quit a couple of weeks ago and that the woman whose ex- broke into Shelby's house used to be a Pistol Belle."

I guess Jean couldn't resist bringing Barbara up-to-date on the Belle's history.

"You had women on your team who people would pay to see shoot," she continues. "But you got rid of them!"

"Shelby and Christine were off the Pistol Belles before they became famous," I say, knowing as soon as the words are out of my mouth that I have fallen into Big Blonde's trap. She has succeeded in getting me to talk. Fortunately, it's time for me to take my position and I walk away from her, looking behind me to make sure she doesn't buttonhole Madison. I'm pretty confident she won't go near Angelika.

Caroline and I both score ninety points in the slow fire section, and Caroline gets a perfect one hundred in the timed fire. I score seventy points in the rapid fire, which seems to be turning into my weakest area. At least Angelika's stellar score will make up for it. The competition moves along and we switch back and forth shooting. Big Blonde puts on a great performance for the Gunpowder Gals and, though our total team scores are going to be close, it's looking like Big Blonde will be tonight's victor.

Madison and Angelika have completed their second rounds in the slow and timed fire sections and are now ready to shoot rapid fire. Angelika looks noticeably nervous and is no doubt regretting her earlier display of triumph as all eyes are now on her to see if she can repeat it. Debs calls for the shooters to start shooting and we are bombarded with the sound of eight handguns firing. The shooting ends, the targets are brought forward and a heavy silence hangs in the air. Standing close together at the shooting line, Madison and Angelika suddenly start to jump up and down and hug each other. The guttural words which earlier poured from Angelika now spew forth again. Pete is showered with kisses and Caroline and I dance again on the banks of the Rhine.

Angelika has scored one hundred points.

Deb reads out the final scores, confirming that the Pink Packers are in last place with two thousand points, and the Pistol Belles and Bullseye Babes are tied at twenty-one hundred.

"Barbara," Deb calls out across the range. "Your sharp shooting has made the Gunpowder Gals tonight's winners at two thousand, two hundred points!"

Big Blonde grins and looks around, her eyes brimming as we all applaud. She is just another soul looking for approval.

"Same time next week," calls Deb. "The Pistol Belles are hosting us at Skyline!"

"And we'll kick your butts," says Angelika loudly.

"Fighting words," says Pete. "You'd better get in some practice. Saturday and Sunday, two o'clock at Skyline."

"I'll be there," says Caroline.

"Madison too," says Angelika, putting her arm around the Belle's true competitor. Madison is shorter than Angelika and her face is buried in the bigger girl's arm pit.

"I can't," she says, her voice muffled. "It's the Regional Collegiate Rifle finals in Pennsylvania this weekend."

"How do you do it?" I ask. Madison shrugs her shoulders in response.

"I'll walk with you to the parking lot," she says, releasing herself from Angelika's headlock. "I'll give you my paper."

"Mona! You come shoot this weekend?"

"No thanks, Angelika," I say, although I could benefit from the practice. "I'm going to spend the weekend holed up with my husband."

"Ahh, Mona and Carl are little love birds. That's what I want."

"That's what we all want," says Caroline, quietly. "But not everyone is lucky enough to find it."

"I'll find it," says Angelika. "If you want it, you get it."

"I hope you're right," says Pete, gently taking Caroline's arm and easing the Beretta case out of her hands. She reflexively moves to hold on to her gun but then releases it and smiles at him. Independence is a hard habit to break.

We walk back through the Bullseye store where customers are still lined up at the counter, and Angelika asks if we can take a few minutes to look at the guns. As she is in this country on a temporary visa, she will not be able to obtain a permit to own a handgun, at least not in our state, but it's always good to look at a nice spread of pistols.

Madison, Caroline and Pete say goodnight, and I slowly follow Angelika around the display cases.

"That one for my pocket book," she says, pointing to a Charter Arms Lavender Lady .38 special.

"And that one for competition," she adds, neatly identifying the Beretta 9mm owned by Caroline.

"Forget about one for your pocket book," I say. "You'll have to move to another state for that."

Suddenly a shadow spreads across the glass and the light is blocked from the display.

"I'd like to talk to you, Mona," says Big Blonde. "Soon, and preferably alone."

Chapter Twenty-Seven

"Aren't you curious to know what she wants?" Carl asks for the fiftieth time in three days.

"Not really," I say, tossing a pillow to him across the bed. "It's you who's so curious to know what Big Blonde wants. You love all the intrigue between us gun women."

"I do," says Carl, deftly catching the pillow. He lunges at me, wraps the pillow around my waist and pulls me towards him. It is noon on Saturday and we've spent the past four hours wide awake in bed enjoying ourselves. The telephone rang several times and we ignored it; our cell phones are turned off.

But now the noonday sun is shining fiercely in the bedroom window and our stomachs are growling. Carl heads downstairs to make breakfast and I straighten the sheets and pick up the thin comforter off the floor. After fussing for a minute, I toss the sheets and quilt in a heap on the bed. If the weekend goes as I've planned, we'll be back up here before the afternoon is out. Why waste energy making the bed?

The phone rings again and, now up and dressed, I reflexively pick up the handset on the bedside table.

"I hear the end is close," says a deep voice.

I don't know what kind of end our caller is referring to, but I have an instant foreboding that it's my sexy weekend that is coming to a close.

"This is Bob Finch, Mona," says Skyline's current president. "I don't know if you've been in contact."

I want to tell him that the only contact I've had today has been of a conjugal nature, and that it's the only kind I intend to have all weekend.

"Bob, I have no idea what you are talking about."

"Williams!" Bob exclaims, as if only an idiot couldn't understand his verbal shorthand. "I hear John Williams is at death's door."

Then in hurried and, inexplicably, hushed tones, Bob tells me that a guy he knows who does business with Carmine told him that Carmine said his father-in-law is going downhill fast and may not make it through the weekend. Bob is more worried than ever about the land that Williams' owns next to the club.

"So we don't care if the man is dying, we just don't want his property to get into the wrong hands," I say, curtly.

"Mona, the future of Skyline is at risk if Williams leaves the land to the town and little kids are kicking balls around there every weekend."

"I understand, Bob," I say, more gently. "But we have no control over the land and will have to wait and see what happens."

"Shelby is one of your girls! If her father is dying, you'll surely be going over there with a dish."

The delicious aroma of bacon is wafting up the stairs, but now it seems like a tray of lemon chicken is going to have to be squeezed into my love nest schedule.

"And what if I do take a dish over there?" I ask, putting the phone in my ear and straightening the sheets across the bed. It's looking as if the next time we're laying across it, we'll be sleeping. "Am I supposed to elicit a death bed promise from Shelby's father to bequeath the land to Skyline? I doubt I'll even see him."

"I realize there's nothing you can do where Williams himself is concerned," says Bob, in a more reasonable tone. "But if he doesn't leave those fields to the town, they'll go to his daughter."

"Or his wife."

"I hear there was a pre-nuptial agreement and that when he dies the daughter gets everything," says Bob.

Do people seriously expect us to believe what they say about other people's money? Is there the faintest chance that Bob Finch and his pals would have intimate knowledge of the financial arrangements which might exist between John Williams and his second wife?

"I've met Karen Williams," I say, "She didn't strike me as the gold digger type, but neither does she seem like someone who would sign herself out of her husband's estate."

Now it's me who's speaking with a presumed authority about someone else's money.

"Bob," I continue. "We have no idea about Mr. Williams' plans for his estate, and we have no idea what Shelby, or Karen, might do if the land is left to them."

"If it wasn't for Skyline, that young lady may not be alive today! In fact, Mona, if it wasn't for you taking her under your wing, she wouldn't have been able to fire at that creep, let alone kill him."

This is the second time I've been credited with Shelby's ability to shoot and kill.

"I hope just as much as you do that Williams does not give the land to the town," I say, resisting the impulse to hang up on Bob and ask Carl to bring us our breakfast in bed. "If one day the property goes to Shelby, I could perhaps speak with her about the possibility of her donating it to the club."

"That's all I need to hear," says Bob, suddenly brightening. "I'm heading up to Skyline right now to shoot trap. Quite a few board members will be there and I'll let them know."

"Let them know what!" I exclaim. Carl is calling up the stairs to say breakfast is ready. "I said *if* Shelby gets the land, Bob!"

"But you said—"

"And don't forget that Carmine is a real estate developer. If his wife inherits a piece of prime land, I'm betting he'll put that inheritance to work and turn it into a significant profit. He'll build on the land, Bob, that's what he'll do!"

"Yeah, Carmine sure knows how to make money, but he loves the club and—"

"Carmine might turn it into low-income housing and then there'd be lots of young families living up there," I say, determined to make Bob squirm. I tuned out the world at six o'clock yesterday evening and he's brought me crashing back to reality.

"Carmine wouldn't put Skyline's future at risk," says Bob, sounding mournful again.

"You have an impressive faith in human nature," I say, barreling down the stairs. "An ambitious young man is unlikely to put his fondness for a hobby ahead of making some serious money."

I know that this conversation must be brought to a swift close as I need food and Bob will feel better after firing at a couple of hundred clay targets.

"I have to go, Bob. I'll let you know if I hear anything."

Bob says goodbye, apologizing for seeming callous and assuring me his only concern is Skyline. I sit down at the counter and see Carl has taken out my mother's plates and yellow cloth napkins.

"At first I thought it was Big Blonde on the phone," he says. "But from your last statement, I'm guessing it's about John Williams and the land next to Skyline."

I take a bite of perfectly scrambled eggs.

"You're so smart," I say, my mouth full. "Yes, that was Bob Finch. Apparently Williams is at death's door and may not make it through the weekend."

Carl jumps off his stool and opens up the cabinet containing dishes and platters. He pulls out the large glass dish I use for lemon chicken and places it on the counter.

"Now you're getting even smarter," I say, laughing as he slides back onto his stool and jabs his fork into a thick slice of bacon.

"I guess you're cooking this afternoon, and then we'll take a drive over to the Lombardi house."

"You'll come with me?" I ask, pleasantly surprised.

"Ordinarily, no, as you know," he says, pausing to take a long guzzle of orange juice. "But this weekend I'm not leaving your side."

I lean across the counter and kiss him. Carl is a sloppy eater and there is bacon grease on his chin. I pull away and wipe my mouth.

"There's more if you want it," he says, snorting and rubbing his lips on my cheek. I laugh and push him away.

"Carl! I just washed my face!"

"A minute ago you were clean, but now you're dirty. That means you're living, Mona."

"That means I'm living with you," I say, leaning across the counter again. The granite is warm from the sun pouring into the kitchen through the skylights.

"And you wouldn't have it any other way."

"Don't even say that. I couldn't bear life without you."

"You could and, if necessary, you will," he says, coming up behind me and putting his arms around my waist. "But now we have to cook. You get everything out and I'll run to the store for chicken and lemons. I'll help you cook and we'll still have some of the day left."

"And night—at least until the next interruption."

"Let me count the ways," says Carl, checking off his fingers one by one. "Angelika, Michaela, maybe even Susan. Jean, Caroline, and perhaps Pete. Christine and Jim. Bob Finch and any Skyline member who wants to know the contents of the last will and testament of John Williams. Or Carmine begging you to take Shelby back on the Belles."

"I don't think Carmine begs twice."

"Dr. Sanderson, wanting to take his gun safety program national."

"Please, no!"

"Big Blonde!"

I grimace at the prospect of Big Blonde being the next person to arrive on our doorstep.

"It's interesting how all this has played out," Carl continues. "One serendipitous day, you meet Jean and she takes you shooting. It turns out that you're a natural and you join Skyline and start the Pistol Belles. Carmine begs you to take Shelby and you take Christine under your protective wing. Christine's husband steals her gun and breaks into Shelby's house. Shelby kills him."

Carl is now in full professorial mode, striding up and down the kitchen as I, his only student, sit in rapt attention.

"Shelby doesn't try out for the competitive team but, that very same night, shoots and kills a man defending her family. She becomes a notorious *femme fatale* and everyone wants her on their team. Shelby's father dies and leaves her a piece of land which is crucial to the future of Skyline."

I put up my hand.

"Professor Milton?" I ask, in a girly questioning tone. "What happens next, sir?"

"You sell Shelby a spot on the team. The price is the land. You're the hero of the story."

"I don't want to be a hero. I couldn't handle such power."

"You have power whether you want it or not! And all because you locked yourself out of your car one day and Jean came to your rescue."

"And all because I went out to buy ingredients for a Valentine's Day dinner, which means I have this unwanted power because of you."

"Correction, you have it because of us."

I reach over and take Carl's hand, feeling that surely I can postpone my lemon chicken contribution for one more day. The Williams-Lombardi clan isn't exactly a charity case. If the patriarch is dying, the family's considerable resources will have been deployed, including ordering an abundance of food. I'm about to tell Carl not to go out to the store when there is a knock at the door.

"Any bets?" asks Carl.

"Too easy," I say, not moving from my stool. "Michaela or Angelika—or both."

Carl goes to the front door and, with the exaggerated flourish he reserves for our young neighbors, flings it wide open. Standing on the stoop on the other side of the screen door is not Michaela, nor Angelika, but Barbara Janowitz. I stare at her, not knowing whether to jump up and slam the door or slither down off my stool and hide under the counter.

Fortunately, Carl can be counted upon to be gracious even when taken by complete surprise.

"You must be looking for Mona," he says, smiling and opening the screen door.

"Barbara," I say, starting to walk towards her. "I wasn't expecting…"

As Carl struggles to control the broad smile spreading across his face—the smile which always shows his intense pleasure at being proved right—Big Blonde steps across our threshold.

"I'm sorry to butt in," she says, with no semblance of apology in her voice. "I got your address from the team roster. I tried calling you but no-one picked up the home phone or your cell phone."

"I wasn't expecting—"

"We've had a busy morning," says Carl, motioning Big Blonde to follow him into the kitchen. "In fact, we just finished a late breakfast. Can I get you coffee or something to eat?"

Big Blonde marches behind him and takes my seat at the counter, obviously used to settling in with strangers.

"I can always eat," she says, patting her belly. Her bulk seems even greater in the confines of our small kitchen. Without missing a beat, Carl reaches into the refrigerator and takes out eggs, ham and cheese.

"How about a nice breakfast sandwich?"

"How about that!" she says, smiling and nodding her head vigorously. "Mona, you've got one helluva fellow here!"

"My husband is a remarkable man," I say, wondering if Big Blonde stopped by because she was feeling a little peckish, or if she actually wants to speak with me. I decide to make myself useful and fill the coffee pot with cold water and spoon ground coffee into the filter.

"Coffee?"

"You bet," says Big Blonde. "I drink it all day and all night."

"Really? It keeps me awake if I drink it late in the day."

I look at the kitchen clock and, seeing it is already one o'clock, wonder how much of this precious day is going to fall into Big Blonde's grasp.

"When you're my size, nothing has much of an impact," she says, slapping her thigh.

Carl and I both look at her; neither of us can think of anything we can say out loud.

"But I don't want you good people to think I came over just to eat," she continues, cackling so loudly the dirty breakfast dishes vibrate in the stainless steel sink. I'll have to install sound absorbers if she's going to visit on a regular basis.

"I mentioned the other night that I needed to speak with you about a matter of some urgency," she adds, her laughter gone.

I don't remember her saying it was urgent, but she did say she wanted to speak with me alone and I'd repeated her words to Carl.

"I'm almost done with this," he says, flipping the egg and placing a slice of ham and a wedge of cheddar cheese on top. "If you need to speak privately—"

"I'm sure we don't," I say.

"Your husband seems like a professional kind of guy," says Big Blonde, as if Carl isn't standing in front of her fixing her a sizeable snack. "I'm betting he'll be interested in the opportunity I'm about to present."

So whatever she needs to talk about is now both urgent and an opportunity. Is she here to formally poach Shelby? I'm starting to feel I'm in the major leagues.

"If it concerns Shelby," I say, before she can continue her preamble. "You should know that her father is dying and may not make it through the weekend."

Carl looks at me and frowns, clearly surprised that I am repeating personal information about Shelby's family.

"That's a damn shame," says Big Blonde, looking crestfallen. "It's not good timing."

"Well, I guess it never is—"

"I mean from our point of view," she adds, quickly. "We need Shelby to be available and not dealing with a dying father…"

Is there anyone who doesn't see John Williams' impending demise as an inconvenience?

"…or in mourning. Although you girls do at least wear black."

Carl puts the egg, ham and cheese on a huge white roll and slides it in front of Big Blonde. She grabs it with both hands and with one bite a third of the sandwich is gone.

"From your comment about our team color," I say, taking advantage of her stuffed mouth. "It seems you acknowledge that if Shelby Lombardi returns to shooting, it will be as a Pistol Belle."

"Oh, yes," she mumbles through her food. "It's doesn't matter which team she's on. The most important thing is that she shows up and shoots."

This is a significant change from three days ago. I am becoming increasingly curious about what Big Blonde wants to talk about and, feeling in need of a physical task, I start to load the breakfast dishes into the dishwasher. Carl pours coffee for the three of us, Big Blonde, predictably, takes it black, no sugar.

"Because we need her, Mona," she continues through her second bite of the sandwich. "The guy at the TV station says Shelby's a deal-breaker. If—and only if—she's one of the shooters, they'll give us Wednesday nights at eight."

She swallows what is left of her sandwich and wipes both hands on Carl's unused napkin. I have a large plate in my hands but seem to have forgotten how it fits in the bottom rack of the dishwasher.

"Every week," Big Blonde adds, tossing the yellow napkin onto the plate which is all but licked clean. "Wednesday's at eight. Live from Skyline."

Chapter Twenty-Eight

Shelby's enormous vehicle is parked in front of her home, but there are none of the dozens of vehicles which jammed the Lombardi driveway the day after the shooting. Perhaps everyone is gathered at John and Karen Williams' home, although Shelby's house is usually the center of activity. Carl offers to take the dish out of my hands but I suggest he goes ahead of me to ring the front door bell. Even in the absence of a parking lot of cars, I imagine Carmine's brother or an old high school friend of Shelby's will be here to relieve us of our offering. Carl pushes on the doorbell, its elegant chimes peal and, in an instant, we hear high-pitched squeals and the sound of bare feet thumping on the entrance hall's marble floor. The door is flung open.

"How nice to see you, Mona," says John Williams, balancing Paolo on one arm and stroking Izzy's hair as she barrels up behind him and grabs his leg. "Professor Milton, I believe?"

Williams shuffles Paolo onto his left arm and reaches out to shake Carl's hand.

"I'm afraid my daughter is out, but do come in."

Carl and I both start to speak at once, apologizing for intruding and mumbling that we were just driving by and will call Shelby some other time.

"Not at all," says John, solicitously taking my arm and leading me through the door. The dish of lemon chicken is still warm in my hands. "Please come in and have some refreshments. It's a relief to have adult company."

John Williams is not only very much alive, but looks markedly better than when I saw him last.

Karen rushes into the expansive entrance hall from between a series of columns which I know from past visits lead to the kitchen. She greets us warmly and, with a little burst of laughter, takes my dish out of my hands and heads off back in the direction from which she came. John asks us to follow him into the living room and, as Carl and I exchange desperate glances, we dutifully go along. We have delivered food to the family of a dying man, but it seems the man is not on his death bed and is not only very much alive, but upright and mobile. If John Williams has difficulty getting into the living room right now, it is because three grandchildren are vying with each other to hitch a ride on his feet. He stops and wrestles them off and turns to us and laughs.

"Carmine and Shelby are out furniture shopping. My daughter has decreed that the children should all sleep in one room so they're busy buying bunk beds. Shelby says it's easier to secure one room rather than four and, given the circumstances, Carmine agrees with her. So the children are going to sleep dorm style which, frankly, will be good for them."

We are now in the immense living room with numerous sofas and chairs spaced so far apart from each other I wonder if we are going to be able to hear each other speak. Karen has returned and taken Paolo out of her husband's arms, while ordering Izzy, Tony and Lulu to let Grandpa be and go with her to the kitchen for ice cream. The mention of ice cream brings a loud and excited response and Karen leaves the room with Paolo and the three other children scampering behind her.

John plops down into an oversized chair and waves his arm to indicate that Carl and I should take a seat on the sofa opposite him. I briefly consider making a run for it so that I can drive up to Skyline to shoot Bob Finch with his own 12-gauge shotgun. Bob will be spending a pleasant afternoon shooting trap, having nothing else to do now that he's dispatched me on this embarrassing errand. Why did I trust information from such an unreliable source? Not only I, but Carl, took Bob's words as fact and rushed around making lemon chicken and driving to Shelby's home without taking time to check what we'd been told. Our collective excuse can only be that this weekend's—interrupted—love shack has addled our brains.

"Professor," says John. "Please forgive me for employing an overused quote, but it seems that reports of my death…"

"…have been greatly exaggerated," adds Carl. The two men laugh and our host wrestles himself out of the depths of his chair and ambles over to a large sideboard on the far wall. He picks up a small dark bottle and waves it at us.

"I ordered a couple of cases of sherry when Karen and I were in Jerez last year."

"Excellent," says Carl.

"Mona?" asks John.

"No, thank you," I say, getting up from the sofa. "I'll go and help Karen and get a glass of water."

"Please sit down, Mona," says John, in a pleasant, but distinctly authoritarian, tone. "Our guests don't serve themselves. Shelby's housekeeper is here, although she's probably working her way through the extensive to-do list my daughter will have left for her."

He walks to the ornate fireplace, which is so clean no flame could possibly have ever burned in it, and rings a bell on the side of the heavy mantel. I don't know if this is a cleverly designed new security system or is an idea borrowed from a couple of centuries ago as the most efficient method of summoning the household help.

"You're the third today," he says, handing a small glass to Carl and holding another close to his chest as he carefully lowers himself back into the chair.

Karen walks back into the room, followed by an older woman dressed in a bright turquoise velour track suit. I wonder if this is Shelby's idea of a staff uniform.

"Yes, the third delivery of food today," adds Karen, with another burst of laughter. "But, as luck would have it, it's Alba's church fundraiser tomorrow and, if it's alright with you, she'll take the food as a donation."

"That's fine," I say, still wondering how long Bob Finch will be at Skyline telling his good old boys about his longstanding intimacy with the Williams' family. "I'm glad it can be put to such good use."

Alba smiles at me, her head nodding vigorously, and in halting English asks me if I would like something to drink. She acknowledges my request for a glass of water and hurries off, probably calculating how much extra money her congregation will make as a result of people showing up with free food at the home of her rich employers. We will be the laughing stock.

"Alba will bring your water and she'll then take the children upstairs to watch a movie," says Karen. "It's so nice to be able to spend some time with you. Shelby talks so much about you and the Pistol Belles."

"Which is why I would like to talk to you," says John. "Your unexpected visit is remarkably fortuitous."

"Mr. Williams," I say. "I am truly sorry for coming here today in such a clumsy fashion. Unfortunately, I took gossip as fact and—"

"You were told that my husband would not make it through the weekend," says Karen, bluntly.

"Not only told, we were positively assured you wouldn't make it," says Carl, as our hosts laugh.

Alba returns and places a large glass of water on the table in front of me. Karen and John look at her and, in unison, point at the ceiling. For a moment I think they're going to break into an old dance routine, but Alba smiles and hurries out, presumably to corral the four children into an upstairs room. From her worn face and red hands, I imagine she's dealt with greater challenges than the Lombardi household and I'm already glad we've donated to her church a good dinner in my favorite glass dish.

"It seems my son-in-law told an overly aggressive business associate that he would not be able to finalize a real estate deal this weekend because he had important family obligations. He must have thrown in a comment about his father-in-law being very sick, and somehow this got translated into the sorry tale that I wouldn't see the weekend out."

"At the risk of being impertinent," I say, carefully. "You look very well."

"I am! I've rallied over the last couple of weeks. The doctors pump my body full of drugs and my wife fills my head with visualization therapy. Between them, they've got me covered. And Karen and Shelby pamper me so much I'm probably going to live forever."

John strokes his wife's slender leg and she smiles at him.

"I've led a blessed life," he adds, more solemnly. "Everything a man could wish for and more."

Carl looks at me and nods his head, as if in agreement with John's words. With the room's floor-to-ceiling drapes and plush carpeting, the silence which descends seems so much heavier than the quiet which sometimes falls in our own home.

"Professor, your glass is empty," says John, and before he can climb out of his chair, Karen leaps up to get the bottle of sherry. She refills both of their glasses, but doesn't take one for herself.

"However, as much as my life has been good and as well as I feel today, I am also making detailed preparations to leave it," he adds. "That's why it is fortunate you came to visit us."

I almost laugh out loud at the absurd prospect that John Williams is actually going to discuss his estate plans with us. Is it possible that I may get the opportunity to put in a pitch for Skyline? I daren't look at Carl.

"Having money makes life a great deal easier," says John, slowly sipping the pale sherry. "But it also makes it more complicated. There are expectations, and many obligations."

Karen shifts slightly in her chair, her awkwardness probably only perceptible to me. I feel an impulse to grab her and run upstairs to hang out with Alba and the children. I don't want to hear about the contents of her husband's will. But I remain seated and silent. Skyline needs the land and, with the exception of Shelby and Carmine, it is likely I am the only club member who is going to get the opportunity to ask for it.

"My daughter has always expected me to solve her problems. In the past I've frequently used money and influence to make her life easier and to get her what she wanted as soon as she wanted it. Unfortunately, such an upbringing breeds a sense of entitlement."

Now Karen reaches over and strokes his leg. He takes her hand in one of his own, holding his sherry glass in the other.

"I am deeply thankful that Shelby met Carmine and that she had the good sense to marry him. Carmine is successful, but he doesn't believe it is his unassailable right to be possessed of more money than the next fellow. He is a bright, hardworking young man who has proved to be one of my greatest blessings. Along with the children, of course," he adds, looking up and smiling as four pairs of feet march across the ceiling.

"Shelby knows I love her dearly and that, other than my concern about her storing a gun and its ammunition in the same bed as the children, I heartily endorse her actions on the night of the shooting," says John, pausing for a moment as a slight shudder passes over him. Suddenly, he doesn't look as healthy as when we arrived.

"Like all of us, she has the right to defend herself and her children. But, like everyone else in town, Shelby knows that my connections with people in authority have helped her avoid a manslaughter charge. She has been charged with child endangerment and that's serious enough, particularly when you have four very young children, but we managed to get a possible prison sentence down to three years probation. I did insist, however, and this is not to assume a moral position I don't deserve, that whatever punishment was meted out to Shelby, Christine Jones should receive not the same, but less."

"She got one-year probation to Shelby's three," I say.

"How is Christine Jones?" asks Karen.

"She's doing remarkably well," I answer. "She'd been separated from Frank Jones for a long time and apparently he was a real menace. She intends to dutifully fulfill the terms of her probation."

"I made it clear to Shelby that I would not stand idly by if she chose to sue Mrs. Jones because Frank Jones was in possession of his wife's gun when he threatened my daughter," says John. "Not only is there is no point in suing someone who has no assets and minimal earnings, but it prolongs an incident which everyone wants to forget. And, not least of all, it gives the family a bad name."

Karen reaches across to take the empty sherry glass out of her husband's hands. Carl is nursing his half full glass.

"Fortunately, Carmine shares my opinion and we have avoided the very real possibility of this family being turned into a spectacle. But there is still something Shelby wants and, in keeping with Shelby's adorable but demanding nature, she wants it very badly. And this is something that I can't give her."

I no longer feel we are about to discuss the relatively simple matter of a piece of land being bequeathed to the club.

"But you can, Mona," says John, staring directly at me.

I look him in the eye and hold his gaze. Karen stands up and goes to the sideboard where she picks up the sherry bottle, fills her husband's glass and then crosses the room to give Carl a refill which he cheerfully accepts.

"Mona," continues John, not breaking eye contact with me. Like his daughter, this man is used to getting his way. "Shelby desperately wants to be back with the Pistol Belles. She understands that she wasn't able to demonstrate the required skills to be a competitive shooter, but she now feels that her real-world experience qualifies her for your new league. I don't necessarily agree with her assessment, but I can tell you she wants this more than anything else."

More than anything else right now, I could add.

"She can join one of the other teams," I say, determined not to acquiesce simply because a man of power and influence expects me to. "The Gunpowder Gals have already approached her and would be delighted to have her."

I can feel Carl's eyes burning into me. Am I really going to be too stubborn to welcome Shelby back? Do I want Shelby to become the star of the Gunpowder Gals and stand by while they benefit from her notoriety? Don't I want the Pistol Belles to be the team everyone wants to watch?

"Shelby doesn't want to join another team," says Karen. "She wants to be back with her old pals."

Her old pals were not even friendly to her, although it seems they're now all eager to get her back.

"John," I say, sitting forward in my chair. "A couple of minutes ago you used the word spectacle."

He nods and leans in towards me.

"You should know that the Pistol Belles—and the Gunpowder Gals—have the opportunity to be the resident teams on a new television show about women's handgun shooting. If Shelby comes back, she will be on television."

I pause for moment to let this information sink in.

"We'll be broadcast live every Wednesday evening at eight o'clock."

A heavy silence returns.

"Shelby's celebrity, and her considerable appeal, will get her a lot of air time," I add.

Her father starts to smile.

"It could create quite a spectacle," I say.

Williams throws back his head and guffaws, the sound reverberating around the cavernous room. Karen, Carl and I glance at each other and, with the vision of Shelby as the shooting star dancing in our minds, join him in his mirth.

Chapter Twenty-Nine

Not everyone thought the prospect of a television show about women shooters was cause for joy. Though a couple of weeks ago Bob Finch and the Skyline board had enthusiastically agreed that we could host the women's competitive teams at the club once a month, it was the prospect of all those women shooters strutting their stuff up at Skyline that had been too good to pass up. But the idea of a film crew camping out at the facility for several weeks in order to shoot a complete television season brought a wary and distrusting response.

Big Blonde's unexpected arrival at our home on Saturday and her startling proposal had launched a frenzy of conversation and ideas. By the time she'd left an hour later, Barbara, Carl and I had outlined the format of the show and selected the cast. Carl and I had also agreed with Barbara that Skyline would make a better location than the run-down range at the Chester County Fish and Game Association. The brainstorming had continued with John and Karen Lombardi, and numerous questions and concerns had been flushed out and answered. Dozens of phone calls and emails over the next forty-eight hours resulted in us needing only the final contract with the television station, and the official approval from Skyline to film at the facility.

So when I call Bob Finch on Monday afternoon I am armed and ready to counter his objections.

"This will put recreational handgun shooting on the map, Bob," I say, confident that the prospect of increasing the shooting population will be the only argument I need to make. Hadn't my mandate with the Pistol Belles been to create new women shooters?

"We don't want Skyline on the map, Mona," says Bob. "We're quite happy tucked away down our winding lane. This will be the equivalent of putting a neon sign at the entrance, and we'll have scores of anti-gun protestors camping out there."

Giving Skyline a bigger part of the map is exactly what Bob wants as I was quick to remind him.

"Shelby is back on the Pistol Belles," I say. "John Williams made it clear I should take her back and, as always, timing is everything. A couple of hours before I saw him, I learned about the TV opportunity. Even I had to accept that we needed Shelby back."

"Did you get him to give us the land?"

"No, I didn't get him to give us the land! Do you think it's as simple as asking him just once? Not to mention I'm sent over there because he's supposed to be at death's door but turns out to be very much alive!"

"I'm sorry, Mona, I told you I was only repeating what I'd been told myself."

Bob was genuinely embarrassed that he'd relayed information about Williams which turned out to be unsubstantiated rumor.

"Having Shelby back on the team is, however, the first step in securing the land you so badly want," I say, more calmly.

"I understand that even if we're successful in getting that land, it will take time," says Bob. "And, you're right, a weekly program about women shooters and their skills and personalities will help promote the sport."

"Yes," I say before he can repeat that his main concern is the anti-gun lobby. "The reason so many people are against guns is because they don't understand them. Many people are, understandably, afraid of them. Guns are weapons and they can be used to kill. That's why our show won't just show us shooting, but will be educational and will include lots of safety information. Don't forget, Bob, I run the school gun safety program and I'll include all that material as public service announcements."

"Yes, but folks will really watch to see the women."

"Maybe, but I hope they'll also learn about guns and shooting and become interested."

Big Blonde believes people will watch because of the dynamics between the shooters. When I'd told her that if the Pistol Belles and Gunpowder Gals are going to be the lead teams on a weekly show she would have to make peace with Angelika, she'd heartily disagreed.

"Nobody wants to watch a love fest!" she'd exclaimed, as Carl had nodded in agreement. "But they'll stop to watch a fight. A few spats between me and that German broad will have the viewers coming back for more. We all slow down when we see an accident."

"There won't be any accidents," I'd said. "The show will promote safe, responsible, skilled shooting."

"Right," said Barbara. "The crashes will be between the personalities only."

"A common path to peace is a shared venture," Carl had interjected. "A story depends upon conflict in order to be interesting but, over time, you'll all become compatriots in a lucrative enterprise."

In the hour she'd spent in our home, I'd learned that Barbara Janowitz is more than the sum of her oversized parts. She'd explained that the proposal she was presenting to us had come as a result of her daily deliveries to the television station's studios. The station's main source of revenue is apparently a successful shopping channel and, as a delivery driver, the bulk of Barbara's days were spent picking up shipments from the studio.

"It isn't always worth my time to leave and then go back, so my supervisor gave me permission to spend part of my time doing the station's paperwork. They're our best customer and everyone agreed it made sense. The station even set up a table for me where I could work and now I'm almost one of their employees. I often have to wait around for the final shipment, and we all get talking."

She'd rolled her eyes at this last comment and I'd imagined this big woman marching up and down impatiently waiting to get back to her depot.

"I'd told a bunch of the staff about how much I loved shooting pistols and made no bones about the fact that I'm a good shot! Last week the station manager comes to me and says he needs a new program for one of their other channels. They have all those boring home improvement and gardening shows just like everyone else. He asked me if I could organize a couple of women's teams to shoot against each other and that he'd come up with a catchy title and market the heck out of it."

"Shop and shoot?" Carl had asked.

"I don't think so," Barbara had laughed. "I doubt he wants to dirty up his money-making shopping channel. But he's willing to take a chance on something new and believes people will watch shooting if we can help them understand it."

"Most people watch sports they've played themselves, like football, baseball, soccer and basketball," Carl had said. "It may be years since they've played, but they know the rules and know it's hard to do well. Or they watch something they play now, maybe golf or tennis, and they admire the skill and talent of the players. Those players become heroes and everyone knows who they are and wants to watch them play."

"Right, but there's a lot more shooters around than most people realize," Barbara added. "There are about three hundred and fifty million guns in this country, which works out to one gun per person. However, it's estimated that those guns are owned by about a quarter of the population."

"That means close to ninety million men and women are familiar with shooting," Carl had said. "That's a lot of prospective viewers."

"And add to that people who will watch because they're interested in learning something," I'd said. "We'll teach people that shooting is a respectable pursuit and when women see how well Caroline and Madison shoot, they'll want to be like them."

Big Blonde had looked crestfallen.

"And you too, Barbara," I'd added quickly.

"I don't know if people will want to be like me, but I bet I can get people to understand the depth of knowledge and skill involved in firing a gun. Then they'll start imagining that they can become good shooters."

Early this morning Barbara and I had met with the station head and had come away with a provisional contract which is now being reviewed by lawyers. I'm starting to develop more than a passing acquaintance with the practitioners of law. But I know the next piece of information I'm going to give Bob Finch will result in his approval of our new venture.

"Skyline will be paid a hefty location fee for the use of the facilities."

"That helps," he says, pausing. "But we'll need a contract and we don't have expertise in television deals or such matters. We'll get taken."

"We won't get taken, Bob, because Carmine Lombardi is to be executive producer of the show. He'll do all the negotiating and deal making. His lawyer is reviewing the contract right now."

Bob, like most of us at Skyline, could only dream of having Carmine in his corner on a business deal. When Carmine and Shelby returned from their Saturday afternoon furniture shopping trip—and after Shelby had unleashed on us all a flurry of hugs and kisses upon learning she was officially back on the Pistol Belles—the prospect of the TV show had been discussed. Carmine immediately decreed that the show's producers must be Pistol Belles' insiders. He volunteered his services as executive producer and said there'd be room for one more. I already knew who that was going to be. This isn't going to turn into a Lombardi show.

"Carmine makes a difference, Mona. Like I said the other day, he has the club's best interests at heart."

"To be frank with you, Bob," I say, ignoring his dig. "This is another piece of security that the Williams' land won't end up being used for soccer matches or low-income housing. If Carmine is executive producer of a successful television show, he'll be less likely to jeopardize Skyline's existence."

"I'm glad you now agree with me," Bob says, smugly. "I'll tell the board that we stand to make some money out of this and I'm betting they'll give the go-ahead. The coffers are running low, as you know. But the club's reputation is on the line, Mona. You gals are good shooters, but we can't have it turn into a big joke."

"There'll be no joking," I say, ready with my next load. "I've asked Jim Mackenzie to be range officer and he'll be prominently featured. He's a pro and a stickler for the rules. The show will present the reality of safe shooting and not dumb us down to a bunch of airhead women shooting at cans."

Firing at cans is a fine pastime, but no-one is going to think our shooting is just another girl's night out.

"Jim's only been widowed a week or so," says Bob. "Things seem to be happening fast with him. Now he's going to be a TV star."

Bob is referring to the gossip which is already circulating about Jim spending time with Christine. I decide not to tell him that I plan to ask Christine to serve as production assistant. She needs the extra money and an administrative role will keep her involved with the Pistol Belles without her having to pick up a gun again. She and Shelby will have to learn to get along or ignore each other. Either way, as Big Blonde pointed out, their presence will help attract an audience.

"But you can't ask Jim without including Pete. He's very committed to you ladies."

I'd like to tell Bob that Pete is becoming very committed to one particular lady, but that is another piece of information which can wait.

"We have an important role for Pete. He's going to be a commentator. He knows guns and shooting and has a great voice. He's also not hard to look at and will be fantastic on screen."

"I guess there's going to be lots of ladies tuning in just to get a piece of Pete," says Bob, laughing.

And that will ensure Caroline doesn't wait too long to seal their relationship.

"And I've already secured the services of another commentator," I say.

"You have this all figured out, don't you Mona? It sounds like the board doesn't have any choice in the matter."

"Of course you do!" I shout, attempting to hide my insincerity.

"Are you bringing your husband in as a commentator?" asks Bob.

"Carl doesn't know enough about the finer points of shooting. But Jean Muirhouse sure does, and she's already agreed to do it."

It had taken Jean a full five minutes to stop laughing at the picture of Carl and me delivering food to the family of a dying man only to have him sweep us into his house and, as she put it, get one over on me. I'd protested to no avail.

"He got one over on you, Mona!" she'd exclaimed. "Shelby was driving him crazy, crying about the Belles not wanting her, and then you show up with your little potluck dish like his very own angel of mercy. Only he didn't need your food, he needed you to do what he wanted. And you did it."

She too had been amazed that Carl and I had not checked the facts before rushing to the Lombardi home.

"I can't believe you didn't call me."

"I can't believe I didn't call you, either," I'd said. "But I'm calling you now and I need you to agree to be a commentator on our show. You'll be outstanding."

"Yes," she'd said, quietly. "I'll do it. I can't shoot much anymore, but I sure as heck can talk about it."

Chapter Thirty

"Are you ready for prime time, Mona?" asks Carl, smiling and swirling his glass. It is Tuesday evening and Carl is sitting on the couch while I pace around the living room.

"I don't know," I say, bouncing down beside him. "I'm excited and scared at the same time."

I've spent the past few days climbing a precipitous learning curve made up of television contracts and dozens of decisions about the format of the show. In the last two hours I've fielded several calls from Carmine concerning details of the contract, along with two separate phone calls from Shelby. Her first call was to say she wanted to talk to me about her ideas for a uniform.

"The Pistol Belles already have one," I'd said. "Pants and turtleneck in any color…"

"Oh," said Shelby, her shrill voice rising. "It would be better if we all wore the same—"

"…as long as it's black."

There had been a brief silence on the other end of the line.

"Black really isn't my color," she'd said sourly, reminding me that the old Shelby is not only back, she never left.

"Shelby, we chose black as our color when we started competing. We'll be happy to change it if someone wants to sponsor our clothing."

I'd thought of this last comment only as I was saying it and immediately recognized it as a good idea. I must get back on the phone with Carmine.

"Alright," she'd agreed, although I could hear the reluctance in her voice. "I guess everyone has plenty of black clothing. Caroline never wears anything else."

"It's a much better choice than pink, red or blue gingham. We look like professionals compared to the other teams."

Her second call had been to check the start time for tomorrow evening's competition at Skyline. This is Shelby trying hard to appear to be a team player.

"Seven o'clock mandatory practice," I'd said, certain I'd given her this information on Saturday. "Competition begins at eight."

She'd then gone on to tell me that she'll be shooting with her Ruger as the Baby Glock—even if it hadn't been confiscated by the police and not yet returned to her—is no good for target shooting. This brings me right back to the Baby Glock incident and to where my recent problems with Shelby began. I hope the Ruger really is registered to her as if she is now stopped driving around in possession of a handgun which does not belong to her, I doubt even her father's influence will be able to save her.

I take Carl's hand and rub it against my leg. I'm twitching and want to stride around the living room but force myself to stay seated.

"I'm excited and nervous because I will have to manage the Pistol Belles under the added pressure of cameras, live filming and an audience. People behave differently on camera and I'm afraid some of the shooters will act up simply because they're being filmed."

"The chance of posturing is high," Carl agrees. "But if everyone plays to the camera it will seem false. The viewers need to be able to identify with you all as normal women who like to shoot."

I laugh out loud. "I don't know how normal we are!"

"You've got a lot of people you can depend on," says Carl, reassuringly. "You've got Jim as range officer, Pete and Jean as announcers, and you say Caroline and Madison are on board."

"I was amazed at how quickly they took it in stride," I say. "It was as if they got calls all the time about appearing on television."

"They're savvy women and they'll be naturals on screen."

I'd spoken with Pete over the weekend to offer him the role of announcer and had sworn him to secrecy where Caroline was concerned. I'd wanted to put more pieces in place before speaking to my leading ladies. The notable exception had been Shelby, but I'd made it clear on Saturday afternoon that if she spoke to anyone about the television show, I would cut her from the Belles faster than a speeding bullet. Her eyes had filled with tears.

"I won't, Mona," she'd said, as John, Karen and Carmine nodded their heads in agreement with me. "I promise I won't."

This morning I'd known it was time to call Caroline and Madison. Although not given to displays of enthusiasm, Caroline had practically whooped down the phone, saying she'd known something was going on because Pete was excited about some news he'd received but said he could not yet share it with her. He'd reassured her she would soon receive a similar piece of good news and Caroline had obviously patiently waited.

"I know you're about to go back to work," I'd said to her. "And we still have a couple of weeks to go on the safety program. I hope this doesn't turn into a problem for you."

"Where's the problem?" she'd asked. "We'll shoot the show, so to speak, in the evenings so it won't overlap with work. And if we become famous shooters, then I'll quit my job and make a living doing something I love."

"What about Sandersen? He's come around amazingly, but do you think we should give him the heads-up that his gun safety instructors are going to be shooting live on television?"

"I'll deal with Sandersen," she'd said. "We can give him a cameo on the safety segments."

Madison had also been full of enthusiasm, her only concern being scheduling.

"The semester is almost over and I won't be so stretched. I'll have to let my rifle coach know in case it's considered a conflict, but I'm sure it will be fine. And it's fantastic material for my thesis."

Jean had dropped in earlier in the day and volunteered her grandson's services.

"Matthew can help haul equipment. The station will be happy for a free pair of strong hands, and he's still mooching over Madison so he's gonna jump when I tell him."

"So what else are you nervous about?" asks Carl, knowing there is more behind my huffing and puffing this evening. "Do you think being on television could cause a problem with our guardianship of Michaela?"

"Not according to what Michaela told me this afternoon. I couldn't put off telling Angelika about the show any longer so when they came over after school today I told them both. Michaela literally squealed with delight at the prospect of us being on TV. She also told us that last week she'd asked her mom if Angelika and I could teach her to shoot and her mom told her that it would be up to you and me to make that decision after she's gone."

"Really?"

"Yes, can you imagine having these conversations with your child? It's heartbreaking. Susan is so courageous, and Michaela, too."

"They're both handling it well. Susan is preparing to die and is helping her daughter in the process. There's no point in arguing about something when you know you're going to be dead in a few months. I'm happy Susan trusts us enough to let Michaela know that there are some decisions that will be made by us."

"I have to spend time with Susan in the next few weeks. It may be all she has left. Then we'll be guardians of a young teenager. I don't think we realize how much it will impact our lives."

Carl puts his arm around me and we sit in silence for a moment.

"Tell me about Angelika's reaction to being on television," he says.

"She is wild with excitement as you can imagine! She rushed out of here saying she was going to let all her family and friends know right away. I cautioned her to wait until we have a signed contract before she broadcasts it to the world."

"Wasted words, Mona. Angelika is living the immigrant's dream. She's making it in America. She'll be fabulous."

"And there is no doubt she will act-up for the camera," I say, shaking my head. I need to let go right now of what I won't be able to control.

"Did you tell her that Shelby was back on the Pistol Belles?"

"Yes, and she reminded me that she advised me to let Shelby come back. Shelby will fail miserably in competition, then she'll quit and we'll be done with her."

"How wise," Carl says.

"And she said she'll shoot better than Shelby and attract more fans."

"There'll be no shortage of rivalries for the viewers to enjoy. And this is just one team. What do the women on the other teams know about the show?"

"I'll talk to Deb and Allison when we compete tomorrow evening. The competitive league still stands, although all the matches will have to take place at Skyline. The Pink Packers and Bullseye Babes will be part of the show, but the Belles and the Gunpowder Gals will be the stars."

"What if the Pink Packers or the Bullseye Babes don't want to be televised?"

"Then they can take their competitive league back to their own clubs! Barbara and I will find shooters to make up some new teams."

"You're getting ruthless, Mona," says Carl, stroking my leg. "You *are* ready for prime time."

We laugh and I seize the chance to wriggle away from him. I jump up and sit on the couch opposite. I need to see his face.

"Carl, we need to talk."

He looks at me and I see confusion in his eyes. Slowly putting down his glass on the coffee table, he leans forward, his fingers locked together.

"Shoot," he says, then grimaces. "Not a good word choice."

"No, professor, not a good word choice."

Carl is still, his face solemn, and he looks fearful of what I'm about to say.

"I'm not going to shoot you," I say, smiling.

"Mona, don't worry that you're going to be too busy for me," he says, hurriedly. "I'll be fine here."

"I know you'll be fine here," I say, not taking my eyes off him. "That's why I need to talk to you now."

I pause for a moment and take a deep breath. Why am I so nervous talking to my own husband?

"You are going to get your butt off that couch every Wednesday and be up at Skyline sweating it out with the rest of us. You are going to be with me every night we film."

Carl's shoulders stiffen. I've issued an order and put him on alert.

"Are you telling me what to do, Mona?"

We stare at each other across the coffee table. For the first time I realize that it takes up too much space. Now I know why I'm always crashing into it.

"Because if you are," Carl says. "It's been a long time coming."

He smiles and I'm tempted to pour his precious glass of wine over his head. Is my avowedly independent husband saying he's been waiting for me to make some demands? Carl reaches across the table and takes my hand in his.

"You're the show's executive producer," I say.

"But Carmine—"

I bring my finger to my lips. Carl stares at me intently.

"Carmine is executive producer responsible for contracts and money. These are things for which he has a great talent."

Carl nods his head slowly.

"You're in the contract as executive producer responsible for the content and creative aspects of the show. These are things for which you have a great talent."

Carl is silent, but on his face is an expression I know well. His head is already bursting with ideas and he is struggling not to blurt them out. But my husband knows how to be cool and I stay silent for a moment.

"Are you ready for prime time, Carl?" I ask.

"I'm with you for all time, Mona," he says, standing and walking around the coffee table. If it wasn't so bulky he would already be next to me. He pulls me up from the couch and we stand and lean against each other, our heads together.

"We lost most of last weekend," I say, looking into his eyes.

"That's alright," says Carl, spinning me around and guiding me towards the stairs. "We are about to get it back."

THE END

About the Author

Veronica Paulina is the author of *Siege at Sorrel Rift: A Story in Sonnets*. *Potluck and Pistols* is her first novel. The author enjoys hearing from her readers. Email: veronica@veronicapaulina.com

Lightning Source UK Ltd.
Milton Keynes UK
UKOW04f0612140817
307260UK00001B/58/P